A
Deadly Dagger

Janey Clarke

First Published in 2021 by Blossom Spring Publishing
Daisy and the Deadly Dagger
Copyright © 2021 Janey Clarke
ISBN 978-1-7399126-3-5
E: admin@blossomspringpublishing.com
W: www.blossomspringpublishing.com
Published in the United Kingdom.

AUGUST 4th DAISY

CHAPTER ONE

I stepped out of my van just after midnight. Large letters on its side shouted BURT'S BEEFY BANGERS, with the large smiling face of a man holding aloft a giant sausage on a fork. I'd been in that van exactly five hours, and thirty-two minutes and thirteen seconds. I wore my bright lurex purple top, glittery pink and purple sweatshirt, jazzy trainers, and my dark denim jeans. I'd been wearing that outfit since early morning. My hair with the purple streaks now drooped over my ears, limp and listless in the wet Cornish drizzle. I clutched a meowing cat in her basket in one hand, and crumpled journey printouts in the other. I stretched my stiff limbs, trying to ease out the knots between my shoulders.

What had I done? I shivered. A sinking feeling gripped me. What was a sixty-nine-year-old woman doing in a 'Bonkers' van after midnight on Bodmin Moor? Should I just turn round and go back? I was tempted. A gust of cold wind laden with January's sleety rain whipped at me. Still, I stood, immobile. My husband of forty years had left me. "Gone off with the Floozy," said my son Jake. He was gold prospecting in Australia. Not that I wanted Jake as constant support, but it was hard knowing he was out of reach. Unable to face the pitying glances of so-called friends who'd left me in ignorance of Nigel's affair, I decided to start a new life. Nervous, shy Daisy, I was the typical mousy librarian and took a momentous decision. I was going to change. Back to the confident fun-loving girl I'd been, before marriage to Nigel had sapped my energy and personality. Now, I stood in the shadows of a dark looming mediaeval building wondering if that decision had been utter madness!

I'd parked in the middle of the cobbled courtyard. Ahead of me was that large stone building. A single porch light hanging above a door gave off a feeble light. On one side of the courtyard, were boarded-up buildings, obviously old stables. New cottages were on the other side of the courtyard, with a couple of lights hanging over freshly painted stable doors.

Tossing the printouts onto the passenger seat I slammed the van door. I patted BURT'S face for luck. The light extinguished from my headlights had left me in darkness. I walked towards the faint glow that came from that wrought iron porch light. Creaking in the gusts of wind, it swung in a chain beside a heavy oaken door. Another light shone across the wet cobbles from above a cottage door. My footsteps echoed around the courtyard. It was a splashy squelchy noise as I walked through the many puddles. That walk across the dark gloomy courtyard in the drizzly rain felt endless. I shivered again, not from the cold, but from nerves and exhaustion. Jaffa cakes, crisps, and cheese portions were not a sustaining diet.

A brass bell hung beside the door. I pulled it, startled at the loud noise that reverberated into the silence. Cleo shifted again in her basket. She didn't like the noise. Her eyes glittered through her basket in the porch light. The door handle rattled and the door creaked open slowly. Was I living in a third-rate horror movie? What was behind that door?

"Daisy! You must be exhausted. What a horrid long journey you've had in this terrible weather. I'm Maggie."

"Sorry you had to wait up for me, the roadworks and traffic accident after Exeter caused a huge hold up." I apologised.

"Not a problem. I'm a regular night owl anyway." Closing the door behind her, she stepped out and reached for Cleo's basket. Maggie was in her late forties, plump, with bouncy black hair in a mop of curls. "Hello pussycat, let's get you settled in your new home. We'll get your luggage, and then I'll show you to your cottage." We walked back to my van across the cobbled yard.

I opened the boot and was conscious of her inspection of me. The boot light showed her my jazzy outfit. I heard her gasp and then she rushed into speech. "How was your journey? Apart from the problems you phoned me about?"

Grabbing my cases, Cleo's bed, and food, I answered her. "Great, the van was easy to drive, and I took it slowly and used the map. I took your advice, and ignored the satnav for the Cornish lanes. Eventually I got here safely." I'd been worried. How would she react to my hair, clothes, and my van? She was the housekeeper at my new residential complex. But laughter lines around her eyes and her widening smile put me at ease. "It really was a bargain, and I needed transport immediately to come here. I needed space to carry Cleo, all her stuff, and my painting gear." I gestured to the logo on the side of my van. "That's why it was such a bargain."

Maggie stood still and stared at the van. I saw her lips quiver, and to my utter relief she grinned at me. "I love it, and can't wait to have a ride in it. This way, just across the courtyard." Maggie led the way, smiling down at Cleo who was alert, and peering out of the wicker basket. She paused beneath the lit cottage door, and took a keyring from her pocket.

She unlocked the door with a bright new key from the ring. The light was glowing above us, shining a shimmering welcome across the wet cobblestones. She stood with her hand on the doorknob. Smiling at me, Maggie said, "welcome to your new home, welcome to the Priory." She flung open the door, and hand still on the doorknob, ushered me in. "This is your new home, and as I promised you, a bottle of wine and one of my special chocolate cakes."

I stepped in and stood on the welcome mat. The light shone on a designer country cottage interior. A glowing log burner, a welcome tray with a bottle of wine, large chocolate cake, and box of exotic teas and coffee stood on the kitchen table. A low coffee table held a bowl of golden roses echoing the colour scheme of soft green and gold. A soft green sofa looked inviting with plump squashy cushions of green and gold botanical flowers. The small Aga in the kitchen area echoed the colour scheme in warm cream. The welcome mat beneath my feet was soft, and rustled in its newness beneath my feet. I stared about me revelling in the warmth and comfort of the cottage. I felt myself relax, and I knew I could be comfortable in this wonderfully appointed cottage. My gaze went to the fireplace as I stepped off the welcome mat.

But I stopped dead in my tracks. Well, to be truthful I stopped. But it was the glamorous redhead sprawled across the fireside rug that was dead, an exotic and ornate dagger plunged into her chest.

CHAPTER TWO

It was a joke. It had to be! Surely it was staged as a scene from Midsummer murders. All to welcome me. I waited for the redhead to jump up and shout surprise! But she didn't. The eyes stared sightlessly towards the ceiling, an outstretched hand lay open palm upwards, and her legs seemed to belong to a ragdoll. She wasn't going to jump up and shout surprise ever again.

Maggie opened her mouth to scream. She stifled it with a hand over her mouth. The colour drained from her face. Her eyes widened with shock. "Is she dead?" she whispered.

"She looks dead, but I'll make certain." The voice came from behind me. I whirled round to see a slim white-haired man. He walked past me, knelt awkwardly, and felt for a pulse. Rising to his feet with obvious discomfort, he limped towards us shaking his head. "I'm Jim," he stuck out his hand towards me. "Not how I expected to meet you, Daisy."

"Not the welcome I was expecting, either" I muttered as I shook his hand. A tall man, pleasant faced, with a determined chin and piercing blue eyes. A decisive manner and air of authority hinted at a military background, despite his casual jeans and polo shirt. Exhausted, hungry, and thirsty with my brain foggy with fatigue, I could only stare in horror-stricken silence at the redhead, the man, and Maggie.

The man took the keys from the limp hands of Maggie. He ushered us out of the cottage, locking the door and put the key in his pocket.

Taking another key from Maggie's keyring he handed it to me. "I'm Jim, we'll chat later. This key is for the other empty cottage. It's all set up ready, just needs…"

Maggie pulled her eyes away from the door, and the images of the awful scene behind it. At this reminder of her duties, she briskly turned towards him, "Jim, can you contact the authorities? I'll settle Daisy and then we'll…"

Jim interrupted her, "I'll get on the phone right away. You get Daisy settled in the other cottage, and we'll all meet up in the kitchen."

Taking a deep breath, Maggie turned towards me. "This is your cottage now," and she walked towards another door. We passed the cottage from which Jim had emerged and walked on.

My new cottage, was the other side of Jim's cottage. Maggie paused for a moment and stared at me. Her fingers hovered over the doorknob. I knew what she was thinking. What lay behind this door? The cold chill struck us both as we entered. It was a complete contrast to that of the warm cosy cottage we'd just left. My eyes went to the hearth rug immediately. I was conscious that Maggie also stared at it. The hearth rug was empty. Relieved, we both gave each other a weak smile. The cottage struck me as cold and miserable after the last one. At least it had no dead body decorating this hearth rug! "I'll take your pussycat and put her on the floor in the kitchen." I looked around my new home, at least for the next three months. There was a lounge diner, the lounge at the front with a log burner and window seat overlooking the courtyard. Narrowing towards the back of the cottage, the kitchen area was bright and gleaming with new appliances, worktops, and a pretty Aga in duck egg blue. A bench upholstered in matching duck egg blue with brightly coloured cushions was beside the scrubbed pine table. My spirits lifted as I glanced around. I could see how this had been intended as a boutique holiday let. It was delightful.

Cleo was anxious to be out of the cage. I couldn't blame her. She had been so good for me after the sedation from the vet had worn off. Opening her cage, I set down a fresh bowl of water, and opened a tray of her favourite. food. I unpacked her basket of goodies placing them in a cupboard. Her basket was set down with her favourite blanket, and her toilet box. Cleo was settled, time to think about myself.

"Such a pretty little cat. Cleo isn't it? The courtyard garden is perfectly safe for her in this cottage. The high walls, the fence, and gate at the back would make it difficult for her to climb over." Maggie had followed me into the kitchen to wash her hands after lighting the log burner. She smiled down at the cat. Cleo, always anxious to make friends, was rubbing against her ankles.

Maggie switched on the light at the back door for the courtyard. The tiny garden was flooded with light. High stone walls and a tall bottom fence enclosed a patio and turfed area. The cold drizzly wind blew off the moor. However, the enclosed garden kept the worst of the January weather at bay. A sheltered spot, and already I had visions of flowering climbers, and tubs and pots covered with masses of summer flowers. Cleo pottered about, relishing in her freedom. Daintily she picked her way across the lawn, sniffing at the new fence and paved patio. Again, I thought how pretty she was with her tiny face, and dark striped fur and tail.

"Sorry about the pile of rubbish. We cleared it from the other cottage, it'll be gone soon," Maggie said. Old windowpanes, broken tiles, and decorating debris sat in a pile under the window. Cleo sniffed it, then backed away. Maggie then swung into action, muttering constantly under her breath. "Oh dear, poor Arabella, what a thing to happen. Oh dear, how could this happen here at the Priory."

Together we made the bed, and I dumped my suitcase on top of it.

"Arabella was the…" I began, hoping Maggie would tell me all about her. Maggie turned towards me, bit her lip, hesitating as if she thought it would be wrong to gossip about the newly departed. I said nothing. I just waited and looked inquiringly at her. It worked.

With a sudden resolve, Maggie began speaking. "Arabella married Hugo. His family owned the Priory and land around here for generations. Unexpectedly, he inherited a year ago. He is a sweet, lovely man, and was completely fooled by her." Pausing, Maggie thought for a moment, "to be honest, we all were," she admitted.

"Arabella wasn't what she seemed to be?" I prompted. I was eager to hear more. Not that I'm a gossip. Oh no, just a student of human nature!

"She wanted to turn this place into a smart boutique and spa hotel. The cottages were to be expensive holiday lets. She'd tried to get planning permission for glamping yurts in one of the paddocks. Hugo didn't mind the holiday cottages or turning the Priory into a small family hotel, but not an expensive Michelin star place. She'd even found a chef! Planned menus with him and was pushing Hugo into it."

"What happened? How did it turn into this residential complex?" I asked, watching Cleo as she explored, and sniffed her way round the lounge and bedroom.

"There was very little money left after death duties and bequests. Hugo inherited the land with the Priory, but very little cash. These renovations to the cottage and part of the house took all the money, and the bank refused another loan. Arabella wanted to sell the Priory and buy a large hotel in another area, a cheaper area that they could afford. But Hugo was beginning to hate the whole idea of a hotel and refused. She threatened to divorce him if he didn't agree."

"That was a bit harsh," I said.

Maggie nodded agreement. "We've finished here. Let's go back to the Priory kitchen to get the rest of your stuff. The log burner will soon warm the place up. I'm afraid there's no chocolate cake, the one I baked is still sitting in the..." her voice faded away. My immediate callous thought for which I was thoroughly ashamed, was that it isn't doing that redhead much good, and I would have loved it! I was shivering, not from cold but reaction. That poor woman, I thought, fighting back tears. Arabella had been so beautiful, so obviously full of life. Why had someone murdered her? Who had hated her so much that they had stabbed her? It took an effort to keep my emotions in check.

Leaving Cleo in the kitchen, I followed Maggie. She gave a gulp and sort of strangled sob as we passed the cottage where Arabella lay. That welcoming light still shone at the door. With our knowledge of what lay beyond that door, I felt it had a harsh new quality in the darkening night. The ancient oak door creaked as Maggie pushed it open. "The rain hits this door and makes it creak. I hate this noise, and I'm always oiling the hinges." We entered a dark stone corridor that had that musty indefinable smell of the past. The huge room we entered had a row of ancient stone arches on one side, and a vaulted ceiling. The stone flagged floor stretched the length of the room. It was an astonishing sight. On the other wall a veritable bank of appliances, glittering stainless steel gadgets and cupboards in a brilliant red lacquer were complemented by the largest red Aga I had ever seen. It should have been wrong, that juxtaposition of ancient and modern. It wasn't. Despite its vastness and antiquity, it was homely. Not cosy, its size made that impossible. But it was a comfortable cheerful room. "This room was part of the original Priory, it's even mentioned in the Domesday book," said Maggie. She started opening cupboards and filling a large wicker basket, and then a box. My gaze swept around from the ceiling to the walls and to the well-trodden floor. It was astonishingly bizarre to have a wall straight from the cloister in your kitchen. I fully expected William the Conqueror to drop in for tea. I suddenly became aware that Jim sat at the longest kitchen table I'd ever seen.

"It was a monk's refectory table. It's an antique of great value. But it's been used as a kitchen table, and always been here. Amazing sight isn't it?" Jim said. "Daisy, this is a terrible welcome for you," he added.

I nodded, and muttered something under my breath. What the hell could I say? Why did she have to get murdered in that cottage? My cottage! Why couldn't the woman get murdered in the empty cold cottage? Not that warm one with a cosy wood burner, and chocolate sponge sitting beside a bottle of wine, waiting for me! I know that was horrible of me thinking like that, but I was so very tired.

Laden with boxes full of milk, bread, toilet rolls, wash up sponges, and other things that Maggie deemed essential for my new life in the cottage, we trotted back. Maggie had been so efficient apart from that first stifled scream on seeing Arabella. I opened my new cottage door, already with a possessive feeling. Maggie put the boxes and bags on the counter top. Then she slumped in a chair and began sobbing uncontrollably. "I'm sorry Daisy, so sorry, I didn't even like Arabella." She gave a large sniff, and I reached for the box of tissues on top of the toilet rolls. Screwing it up to a tightwad in her hands, she dabbed her eyes, and then her nose with the tissue. "Arabella was horrible. She was cruel and spiteful and made Hugo's life hell. I shouldn't be speaking ill of the dead, especially as she's not even cold!" Awkwardly, I patted her shoulder. I'm no good at emotional stuff. "A cup of tea, that will make you feel better," I escaped to the kitchen. A cup of tea solved every problem, didn't it? I reached into the box Maggie had carried over. I found teabags and milk and put the kettle on. Placing the mug in her shaking hands, I said, "I need to freshen up before I see the police. What I can tell them I don't know. But I feel so scruffy after my journey."

I looked back as I went to the bedroom. Maggie had stopped crying, was sipping her tea with one hand, and stroking Cleo with the other. The tiny cat had jumped on her lap and was purring contentedly. I went to shower. What did one wear in the house of a murder victim? I doubted sequins, lurex, and bright zingy colours were suitable for a police interview!

CHAPTER THREE

I opened my case and spread an assortment of clothes on the bed. They could have been labelled my 'After' pile. My image change had been the result of my harrowing break up with Nigel. The before pile, had included my serviceable drip-dry elastic waisted trousers, blouses and cardigans mostly pale blue, navy or black, and a number of 'oldie' beige accessories. All from Marks and Sparks, now donated to the charity shop. Now I wore pink. Shocking pink of course! Add in a dash of lime green and scarlet. Purple sequined tops, orange glittery tops, and multicoloured cardigans and jackets. All trousers were black or indigo denim. My bum was too big to be seen in colour! Fat Face, Weird Fish, Sea Salt, and other unusually named brands were my new' go to' for clothes. I glanced at my watch, could it really be that late? It was nearly one o'clock and here I was showering and choosing new clothes to wear! I'd have showered anyway before I went to bed. I only wished I could wear my pyjamas across to the Priory to meet the police! Arabella was dead. I'd now to meet the grieving husband, the other residents of this mediaeval pile, and be interviewed by the police. Perhaps they are all still in bed, I thought. Doubtful though, even if they hadn't heard Maggie shouting for Hugo, police sirens would have woken them. Not the wonderful beginning I'd imagined for my new life on Bodmin Moor!

Who would have thought this would have happened? Nigel would of course! I discovered this place on the Internet only four days ago. Now I had arrived to make my home here. My long-time neighbour Elsie, had decided to move nearer to her daughter in Bournemouth, because of her increasing frailty. A builder wanted to develop the site on which our two houses stood, and offered us a good price. My seafront apartment for the over fifty fives's in Devon, was everything I'd ever dreamed of. Wonderful views of the sea and the bay, pleasant walks on the hills behind, and a charming little town to potter about.

"Daisy, you took Alfie from a previous litter of my kittens. I heard that he passed away a couple of months ago," said Pauline, who stood on my doorstep five days ago. She was the cat breeder from whom I bought my beloved Alfie two years earlier. Rushing on before I could speak, she thrust the prettiest little kitten into my arms. "Cleo's family have got a transfer to New York. They have to go next week, it's all in a terrible rush. They need a new home for Cleo, and of course I thought of you! So sad Alfie dying so young." Her words tumbled out. The cat rubbed her head against my chin, give a tiny meow, and stared up at me. I now had another cat! The seafront apartment was strictly no pets. The builder was about to demolish my house in a week's time. My frantic search on the Internet, yielded very little accommodation that was either vacant immediately, or was pet friendly. I had a choice of a city apartment in Bristol, or a half-finished residential project on Bodmin Moor.

I thought back to a month earlier when Paul from the garage had contacted me. My elderly car was due for service and was going in next day. "Hi this is Paul, your car is due for service. Jake emailed me from Australia about it. We both think that car of yours is on its last legs, and not fit for a long journey. I've got a smashing bargain here. I sent Jake all the details and he said it would suit you. It's a van, but it's ideal." Slowly I had put down the phone and stared at it. A van almost new, one careful owner, and at a ridiculously low price. Why? Jake and Paul had gone through school together. He wouldn't cheat me. Something about the 3D logo and slogan that kept putting everybody off. The price I had to pay with my part exchange meant that I actually had money back! The test drive proved that the van was a joy to drive. I was no longer bullied by other cars, who had previously noted my staid 'oldie' car. I was given a wide berth, and people even smiled when I passed. Jake's email had assured me that the van was a real bargain. Lisa, my future daughter-in-law told me it could be part of my new image. Back in the garage I'd stood beside Paul looking at it. The fat man stood smiling, holding the giant sausage, with the words BURT'S BEEFY BANGERS on the side. I was dithering. Why not I thought? I agreed to buy it before I could change my mind! My great friend and neighbour Elsie had been horrified at my new image of streaked hair, bright glittery tops, and designer jeans. I suddenly thought of what she would think when I drove the van home. Was it devilment? Was that why did it? But both Jake and Paul had said I wouldn't regret it.

"There's no way you can get rid of it or paint over it?" I had asked.

"Not without spending a huge amount of money on it." Paul replied. "When I told Jake that no one else wanted it, he bet me that his mum would have the bottle for it."

Did I have the bottle for it? Did I want to be known as the lady with the sausage van? After all, I didn't want to be one of the grey insignificant women that were ignored as they aged. "Okay, I'll buy it on one condition. If I hate it, you promise you'll sell it on for me."

"I won't be seen in that van!" Elsie had shrieked. "I'm not having you run me around Bournemouth in that... that thing." Her face had contorted with anger and fury as she turned to face me. "You don't expect me to get in that?"

"I don't. I'm not going to Bournemouth with you. I'm going to Cornwall and am going tomorrow! The builder wants to start on my house immediately. I've got a temporary let with a view to buy a cottage in Cornwall. You won't have to see me or my van ever again!" We had calmed down enough to say goodbye the next morning. We gave each other a hug, neither of us bringing up Bournemouth or my sausage van!

Here I was in Cornwall now. I shook my head. Was Elsie going to be proved right? Had this been a terrible mistake? I reached for a pair of black trousers, a navy sweatshirt, plain with no sequins. I did however wear my favourite red, white and blue trainers. The purple streaks in my hair sprayed into shape, a dash of lipstick, and I was ready. On my return to the lounge, I was surprised at how cosy it had become. The log burner had worked its magic and it was warm. Maggie had recovered, and on the kitchen counter, were an array of teas and coffees, bottle of wine, a box of chocolates and artisan sweet biscuits.

"No chocolate cake?" I asked her.

"Sorry, I only made the one," was Maggie's apologetic reply.

I glanced around, and noted that there were cushions plumped up on the sofa. In that huge box she had carried across, there had been a Christmas cactus plant in full flower.

"That's a nice touch," I gestured to it. "Thank you, the cottage looks cosier now. I like this one. This lovely blue Aga is nicer than the cream one in the …other cottage." I stumbled over the words.

"Let's get back to the Priory kitchen, Hugo will need

all our support, and you can meet the others, if they are awake."

"Not exactly how I expected to meet my fellow inmates," I muttered as I shrugged on my jacket. "You stay warm and cosy, Cleo, be a good girl." As I turned towards the door, I saw that Maggie stood there grinning at me.

"What?" I asked.

"Inmates! Don't you dare let them hear you call them that!"

We stepped out into the cold night air. I locked the front door of my new cottage with a pleasant sense of ownership.

As we walked towards the Priory, more police cars swept through the courtyard, screeching to a halt beside us.

"Go into the Priory Daisy. You'll find everyone who is awake will be in the kitchen. I'll speak to the police," said Maggie.

"Okay," I said after casting a quick glance at the men emerging from the cars. As I reached the oak door, a tall man with blond hair and a shocked gaunt expression came out. He made his way towards a police car, buttoning up his dressing gown. Jim followed him out of the door, gave me a nod and gestured for me to go into the house.

I went down the stone flagged corridor and into the kitchen. Normally, I'm nervous in a new place, nervous about meeting new people, but this was different. The extraordinary circumstances in which I found myself had chased away any nerves.

"Come in, come in. You must be Daisy. I'm Sheila King, and this is Martin Burgess. Come on over here and join us at the table. There's freshly brewed tea in the pot, or coffee if you prefer." A white-haired elderly lady sat in her wheelchair. She smiled at me. Her eyes were those of a young child, alive with excitement and interest. She gestured me to sit beside her. "Sit down do, and tell us all about what happened to Arabella."

Wondering what to say, I sat beside her. Martin rose from his seat. "Tea or coffee? Would you like something to eat? Cheese and biscuits, or some mince pies?" Tall, thin, and bespectacled, he had long flowing brown hair and a neat little beard. He was thirtyish, and I wondered what had brought him to this residential complex in the middle of Bodmin Moor.

"Tea please, I'd love some cheese and biscuits, I haven't had a proper meal since breakfast. I seem to have been eating junk food all day," I replied. Martin brought me a huge mug of tea, and a plate with some unusual, delicious biscuits and some local cheeses.

"I feel dreadful, perhaps I shouldn't eat after what I've just seen." I looked at the plate with longing, but gazed up at the two of them doubtfully. Just then my stomach gave a rumble and a gurgle. They both laughed, and Sheila pushed both plates towards me.

Sheila was sitting in a fluffy dressing gown with a Klingon patterned blanket over her knee. Star Trek spaceships flew down her pyjama legs. Jake, my son, was a Star Trek fan, and I'd enjoyed watching it with him. This lady was interesting! She didn't seem to mourn the loss of the woman at all. Martin, beside her, was obviously shocked, and his nervous fingers beat a silent tattoo upon the table.

"Where did you find Arabella?" asked Sheila.

"She was lying on the hearth rug in front of the log burner." I paused, as I remembered the dreadful scene. "There was a dagger, she'd been stabbed, and blood. I keep seeing that ornate silver dagger and ….and the…" I shuddered, as the memory threatened to overwhelm me again.

"That sounds like Hugo's dagger! It's always kept on his desk in the study. Hugo had every reason to kill Arabella," stated Sheila, with a bluntness that astonished me. "But he is the most unlikely person to ever hurt anyone."

"Yes, that could be the dagger Arabella gave Hugo for his birthday." Martin exclaimed. "Why was Arabella in the cottage? She's never bothered with any of them since the hotel idea fizzled out."

"What hotel idea?" I asked.

Martin fiddled with his coffee cup and looked at Sheila. She gestured for him to speak and sat back in her chair. "Hugo, was a lecturer who inherited this property unexpectedly. His uncle and two sons drowned in a yachting accident. Hugo had only been here a couple of months when he met Arabella."

Sheila shook her head, and took up the story. I noticed a couple of curlers at the back of her white fluffy hair. She'd missed them in her hurry to get down to the kitchen. "They went on holiday and came back married, after five weeks. She wanted to turn the Priory into a Michelin starred hotel, and have boutique holiday lets."

"So that's why the cottages are furnished in such a wonderful style." I exclaimed.

"Oh yes, Arabella had great ideas, she even appointed a Michelin Star chef to work here. Half of the cottages, this kitchen and a couple of apartments in the Priory House have all been renovated and furnished. Then the money ran out!" said Sheila.

I stared at her, the animosity against this woman who'd just been murdered was very evident in her voice. They both stared back at me, and then looked at each other.

Sheila spoke first. "Yes, we've all grown to dislike Arabella. Even Hugo has finally seen what a money grabbing witch she was. But no one here, especially Hugo could have killed her," stated Sheila.

"Sheila's right. Hugo won't even kill a wasp, and ushers spiders out of the door," muttered Martin.

We sat in a companionable silence now. Voices, car doors and the occasional shout could be heard from the courtyard outside. Martin tried to smother a yawn. Sheila just yawned openly.

"You were late arriving, what happened?" asked Sheila. I spluttered a little bit as the crumbs of the last biscuit caught my throat.

"There was roadworks all the way up to Exeter service station. Once I was clear of them, I got stuck in a traffic jam after a lorry jack knifed ahead of us," I explained.

Martin nodded his head, "doesn't take much for the traffic to seize up along that road."

"Why did you come here?" Sheila asked me, leaning forward in anticipation of my reply.

I swallowed a large gulp of tea. What should I say? Should I spin a story? Should I give them the blunt unvarnished truth? I decided to be honest. What was the use of starting my new life with a web of lies and half-truths. Well, honest up to a point. My discovery in a broken picture frame, (Cleo's work!) of a Cornish family secret was to be my own private investigation.

I took a deep breath, "nasty marriage breakup... divorce... sale of family house." I shrugged, and stared back at them. What else could I say?

Sheila nodded, and patted my hand sympathetically. Then, her eyes alight with interest she leant towards me. "How did you hear of the cottage? Why come to Bodmin Moor? Most women in your position retire to a country cottage or seafront apartment. Why didn't you?" asked

Sheila. She just wanted to know, she wanted to know now, and she wanted to know everything.

Martin shuffled about on his chair. "Sheila, you shouldn't ask such questions. Daisy has just arrived, and she's had a terrible shock."

"Yes, my husband suggested I should do those things. A nice retirement flat on a busy main road near to the shops. That was his idea. Whilst he got a sports car and a Floozy! It wasn't what I wanted. He hated Cornwall and loathed Bodmin Moor. He dislikes cats and hated my floral paintings."

I smiled at them. "I've come to Bodmin Moor. I've a cat and bought loads of painting gear. He said our marriage was boring. Nigel was right, our marriage was boring. But it was because of him that it was boring! And I just followed him and lost my own identity. This is a new start and a new me." I gestured to my clothes, and my hair. Why did I do it? I never told people things like that. I was usually a private person. I sat back in my chair waiting for their reaction.

"Good for you! You'll fit in well here. All of us have decided to change our lives, and do something different." Sheila patted my hand, then gave it a gentle squeeze. Martin gave a nod of approval, and for the first time gave me a genuine smile.

To my surprise, I realised I'd cleared the plate of cheese and biscuits. Sitting back in my chair, I looked round. Ancient stone walls, and the stone flagged floor should have made the kitchen cold, but that red Aga was blasting out heat. The archways were at regular intervals along the wall and the huge table at which we sat was in the middle of them. I felt like stretching out my hand to touch one; they were so close, and they oozed history. I was getting fanciful. It must have been fatigue. I looked at my watch, it was past two o clock. No wonder I was tired.

Silence had fallen on the other two, broken only by the slamming of car doors, heavy feet on cobblestones, snatches of loud animated talk and the incessant drumming of heavy rain outside. Raised voices reached us, and we all turned towards the window trying to hear. Car doors slammed again, and the sound of cars driving away through the archway followed. Suddenly footsteps could be heard coming down the corridor towards the kitchen.

Maggie burst in, the door crashing back against the wall. "It's Hugo! They've taken him away to help in their enquiries. He would never have killed Arabella. No way! He's innocent!"

"Hugo? They think he killed Arabella?" Martin and Sheila echoed each other in their dismay.

Sheila thumped the table in her indignation "Well, we'll just have to prove them wrong! We've got to find out who really did kill Arabella!"

The others drifted in and out of talk. I sat silent, almost half asleep.

I was called to see the police first. It must be because I've just arrived, I thought. I was interviewed in a large library. Did anyone ever read all these books? I wondered as I walked into the room. Large squashy sofas, leather chairs, and a couple of huge desks were set before full length windows. A large man sat at the desk, and the young policeman who had escorted me to the library sat in a chair behind me.

Feeling as if I was called before a headmaster, I sat down on the chair before the desk. The large man with bushy eyebrows and heavy jowls stared across the desk at me. Dark unruly hair, still wet from the rain was pushed back from his red face. He looked as if he'd been a rugby player in his youth, but was now overweight. His eyes were sharp and focused upon me, as I told of how I'd come to find Arabella with Maggie. But his interest in my statement was perfunctory, and I was soon dismissed. My answers given, and in a few minutes, I was on my way back to my cottage. Even I could see that the police were in a hurry to get this over and done with. Now, I understood why Jim and Maggie were so worried, the police were certain they had their man. They were not going to investigate any further.

CHAPTER FOUR

The doorbell woke me, ringing again and again. I sat bolt upright in the bed, and looked around. Where was I? The previous night's events rushed into my mind, the Priory, the murder, and the change of cottage. I had slept deeply from utter exhaustion. The bell was still ringing, and now knocking had begun on the front door. The small purring body beside me hurtled off the bed, and ran towards the lounge.

"Coming! I'm coming!" I yelled, as I struggled into my dressing gown and slippers.

When I opened the door, I found Sheila in her wheelchair on my doorstep. "Come on Daisy! Time to wake up! There's a meeting in half-an-hour. We're going to organise a plan. Maggie is making breakfast for us all." She clapped her hands in delight, and those childlike eyes of hers sparkled. "It's a breakfast power meeting! Just like on the TV, hurry up Daisy." Wheeling herself back across the courtyard I heard a gleeful chuckle followed by, "a breakfast power meeting, that's what it is."

Tired after yesterday's travel, and my late-night, I fed Cleo, let her out in the garden, and had my shower on automatic pilot. Again, I put on my muted clothes out of respect for Arabella, and went to the Priory kitchen for my first breakfast power meeting!

A sudden silence greeted my entrance at the kitchen door. I stopped, uneasy, and uncertain as to whether I should enter or make a run for it. I had obviously been the main topic of conversation. Jim looked at the others, and then straight at me, as I stood on the threshold. "Yes, we've been talking about you."

I stiffened, feeling a knot of tension form in my

shoulders as I looked at them.

"Yes, we were wondering if it's necessary to involve you in this project. You've only just arrived, and you don't know Hugo or Arabella. You can opt out of our plan if you want," Jim said.

"We'd love you to join us. You will, won't you?" both Maggie and Sheila said together.

They so obviously meant it, that my tension knot began to dissolve. I walked into the room and smiled. "I'd like to join, but what about all the others?" I asked.

"What others?" Sheila said. They looked at me with puzzled expressions.

"You looked at the website!" sighed Maggie. "That website was done by Arabella." Maggie turned from the Aga, where she was doing noisy, and wonderfully smelling things with pots and pans. "You're talking about the picture of the happy smiling folks in the lounge. I'm sorry, I did try and warn you on the phone. Perhaps I didn't make it clear. That new lounge, and the swimming pool, and all the other stuff haven't been built. That website needs altering again. Martin, can you see to it, please?"

I leant back in my chair at the breakfast table. What a day I'd had yesterday. I sighed, and placed my mug back down on the table. I thought back to the website on which I'd first seen Barton Priory. Enchanting Cornish countryside had been shown in spring, at its very best, with bluebells and daffodils blowing in a light breeze. A particularly harsh clatter of January hailstones beat against the kitchen window. No daffodils now. Snow was in the forecast for tomorrow. A group of cheerful people had been seated in a gracious lounge on the website. There had been mention of a proposed swimming pool, restaurant, gym, and a wellness spa. I wasn't quite sure what a wellness spa did. It sounded interesting. Maybe it's just what I needed. Where were all these promised attractions? Where was everybody else? What did Maggie mean? To be honest, I'm an introvert. I hate crowds and lots of people. Imposed games, false jollity and cheerfulness makes me feel sick! My friends love cruises, package holidays, and escorted tours. Okay, I could go on those ships. I could go on those tours, if I was alone, or had only a few close friends with me!

Sheila grabbed my hand. "The website was all Arabella's idea. That website is all wrong, we must take it off the Internet." She almost shook my hand in order to make it clearer to me. "They ran out of money and we're all that's arrived! I'm in a newly refurbished apartment in the Priory with Maggie in the other. Jim, Martin, and you are in the cottages that have been finished. Arabella was found in the last one to be finished."

Puzzled, I sat back trying to take this information in. Maggie set a fantastic breakfast down in front of me, bacon, eggs, hash browns, mushrooms, tomatoes, and beans. "I hope you'll stay Daisy, even if it's not exactly what you wanted."

I stared at the breakfast, at Maggie's face, and at the others looking at me. I knew I'd panicked, and rushed at the only place that would take Cleo and myself at short notice. "Actually, I prefer this, I'd have hated the holiday camp type of place no matter how upmarket. This breakfast, is a treat to be enjoyed with my new…" I paused, and glanced at Maggie who gave me a warning glance. Not inmates then.

"Friends, that's what we are, your new friends!" Sheila interrupted me.

"Friends," I mumbled through a mouthful of hash browns.

Jim's voice brought me out of my rambling thoughts. "I'm not happy at last night's outcome. They decided

Hugo was a murderer in a hurry. We could check on a few things ourselves. We may have avenues to explore that the police might not think of."

Martin stared at Jim in horror. "We might get into trouble with the police," he stammered.

"Nothing illegal Martin. All within the law. Anything of use to their investigation, we give immediately to the police," Jim reassured Martin.

"We need a plan!" Sheila clapped her hands in delight. "That's what we need. That's how they always start an investigation in books, and on TV."

Jim gave a weak smile at Sheila's words, and looked round. "I don't believe in amateurs messing about in police matters," he said. There was an underlying air of authority in his words which puzzled me. "But I think in this case Sheila may well be correct."

This was my first breakfast in my new home. It was a delicious breakfast, and I ate every morsel. But I never expected to be involved in investigating a murder. I never expected to be part of a group determined to clear a man I didn't know, of the murder of his wife. Everyone told me I'd be bored when I moved to the country. I wasn't bored now! And this was only the first day!

CHAPTER FIVE

Martin and I helped Maggie clear the plates, whilst she loaded the dishwasher. Fresh coffee made, and we sat down for the meeting. Jim placed a notebook and pen on the table. The constant noise of police cars, forensic teams, and various other persons in the courtyard, suddenly seemed loud and menacing. Hugo had returned in the early hours of the morning. He pushed his food around on his plate, then looked up at Jim. "I don't think you can do anything. Realistically, what can you do the police can't?" His words echoed my thoughts exactly. What could we three 'oldies,' and Maggie, Martin, and the main suspect Hugo actually do?

"I don't know, but I think it's worth a try," Jim said, smoothing down the first page in his notebook. He pushed back a lock of his white hair which fell over his forehead. Jim was a tall man with a decided limp. His deeply chiselled face, and steel grey eyes, showed a lifetime of action and experience. What had his past life been? How had he ended up here on Bodmin Moor?

"We've got to try! Hugo is not guilty. We've got to clear his name and find the real killer!" Sheila exclaimed. Earnestly, she leaned forward gazing round each one of us, her determination evident upon her face. The sparkling blue eyes normally alight with childlike mischief were flashing with indignation. Her tightly permed white curls bounced in time as she thumped the table. Nods of heads and lukewarm murmurs of assent greeted these remarks.

"What can we do? That lot out there," Martin gestured to the window and the noise outside. "Surely they've got everything they need to get the killer." His words came out jerkily, his hands twisting. Martin was obviously a nervous type. In the few short hours, I'd known him, I soon realised that. I bet he's a ditherer, I thought, and takes ages to make his mind up about anything. Curiously, I wondered what made him take the leap of faith into this place on Bodmin Moor. It seemed so uncharacteristic of him. No doubt, I'd soon find out.

"Who'd like to go for a pub lunch? A pub lunch at the Red Lion, where Daniel is the head chef?" Jim asked.

Maggie and Sheila began smiling. Sheila turned to me and said, "Daniel is the chef Arabella brought to Bodmin Moor to run her Michelin Star restaurant. Daniel and Arabella used to discuss menus, kitchen layouts and staffing needs. He was working at the pub temporarily, until Arabella got her kitchen up and running. That won't happen now."

Hugo stood up, shook his head at Jim, and walked off. We all watched him go in silence. A tall lanky figure, with unkempt blonde hair, he made a sad figure as he walked out of the kitchen. His shoulders were hunched, as if he was fearing the next blow. What had been the relationship between Hugo and Arabella I wondered? He certainly seemed heartbroken, stunned, and distressed by her death. I didn't know him though. For all I knew, he was the world's most consummate actor.

"Perhaps it's for the best he stays here," said Jim as he watched Hugo leave the room. "We'll go and see if Daniel has an alibi. He's another likely suspect for the murder."

The ancient pub huddled into the hillside in the small moorland village. Walls of granite stone echoing moorland tors, stood stolidly against the wild weather. Inside, the dismal grey and stainless-steel trendy interior, made it cold and gloomy. Lunchtime trade was obviously sparse, and we made a noisy entrance. A modern concrete fireplace, set flush into the wall, burned only a small log despite the cold. From the outside, I'd expected a roaring log fire, perhaps even old-fashioned copper, or brass pots, glinting in the firelight.

The barmaid waved across to Maggie with delight. "She's an old school friend, I'll see if she knows anything," Maggie whispered to us. She walked over to the bar, and began chatting animatedly to her friend.

"Good job we had a decent breakfast. Have you seen the menu? A cauliflower steak with cauliflower purée and gel, and a cherry tomato marinated in balsamic vinegar and herbs. I hate cauliflower!" Martin held up the giant slate menu board that lay in each diner's place. "These prices are ridiculous. The food sounds dreadful, and there's not much of it!"

There was a huge choice of tables, but we settled down at one near the kitchen, and the bar. As we sat down, angry voices erupted from behind the kitchen door. Sheila grabbed my arm, shaking it excitedly. "Come on Daisy! Help me to the ladies. It's next to the kitchen, we might hear something," she said. Sheila rose to her feet. She was clutching her stick. Today was a good day for Sheila, she was managing without her wheelchair.

We walked slowly down the corridor. Voices could be heard arguing behind the kitchen door, which was ajar. We listened to the conversation. Sheila was open mouthed, and I was as stunned as she was.

"Now that horrid Arabella is dead, we can leave this dump! You can forget all about your posh restaurant now. Hugo is in charge and he'll never let that happen." A shrill woman's voice shouted clearly above the kitchen clamour.

"Have some decency, can't you? She only died last night! We can't leave right now; it would look suspicious. I'm in no hurry to leave, I like it here." It was

29

a deep man's voice, presumably Daniel.

"I hate it here. Always raining in the winter, and the winds blow continuously on this hill. Those fancy menus and the trendy decor that you and Arabella worked out between you, are driving the punters away. Chips with everything, that's what they want. This place is always empty now. Let's go back to London."

"I'm not leaving Cornwall," came the surly reply.

"Yes, you will! I gave you an alibi last night. I still don't know where you got to. I can always go to the police and tell them…"

"Don't even think about it. If you even whisper a word, I'll make you wish you'd never been born," the man's voice had dropped. It had become menacing. Sheila gripped my arm in excitement.

Then we heard heavy footsteps approaching the door. Hurriedly, I turned around and thrust the door open into the lounge. Sheila limped at her fastest speed behind me. Turning to help her, I didn't see the waiter. He didn't see me either. We cannoned into each other. A jug of iced water, glasses, and a bowl of lemon slices flew into the air. He crashed heavily onto the carpet. There were only four other customers in the place. The table where they sat, was showered with water, ice cubes and lemon slices. Screams and shouts erupted, and they rose in unison to their feet, shaking themselves. One elderly fat man took the brunt of the lemon slices, and his comb-over was festooned with them.

I stood shocked and irresolute. Should I help them? Should I help the poor waiter? Or Sheila? I heard the heavy footsteps coming behind me. I looked back, and realised that Daniel, a thickset large man in his chef's whites was coming towards us. He knew. He knew that we'd been listening. The fury on his face and his clenched fists was frightening.

Jim took in the situation in one glance. He rose to his feet, and grabbed Sheila's arm.

"Let's get out of here. Come on Daisy, move!" he hissed at me. Maggie and Martin rose, and taking a last horrified look at the chaos, fled out of the door after us.

"Fasten your seat belts, we've got to get out of here quickly. That Daniel is following us, and looks pretty mad." Jim drove quickly out of the car park. I turned and saw Daniel standing, staring after our car. He shook a fist after us, then turned and went back into the pub. Sheila was panting, her breath coming in little gasps.

Martin was shaking visibly, but kept muttering under his breath. "Fancy charging that much for a slice of cauliflower!"

I sat thinking, my mind whirling. Should I have taken more care rushing through that door? But I'd been so worried about Sheila. She was decidedly wobbly with her stick, and we were both rushing out. We panicked, hoping Daniel and his girlfriend wouldn't realise that they'd been overhead by us. But Daniel knew that we'd heard everything. It was obvious by the way he looked at us. The way he chased us out of the pub. That waiter should have looked where he was going, I thought. After all, he knew lay the layout of the place. I looked at Maggie. Why was she laughing?

"Oh Daisy! That was so funny. Don't worry, it was only water. Not as if it was hot soup, or anything messy." Maggie grinned at me.

Jim turned and looked at me. His eyebrow went up, and he gave a little shake of his head. I knew I looked distraught and worried. Then Jim laughed. "You saved Martin from a heart attack. He'd never have survived paying for that cauliflower steak. We got out of there without having to eat anything. You did us all a favour!"

"It was certainly worth it," Sheila said excitedly.

"We've got news!"

"Yes, I've also got news, vital news that the police don't know about!" Maggie said.

That sounded promising. Maybe a mishap with iced water, lemon slices and a waiter had been worth it after all!

CHAPTER SIX

Jim drove the car to a halt in a layby. Switching the engine off, he turned to look at us. Sheila was in the front seat beside him, Maggie, Martin, and I in the back. After the chaos and mad flight from the Red Lion pub, we were all shaken.

"Where to now? We need a discussion," Jim said.

"I'm starving. I do not want cauliflower!" muttered Martin.

"We all need lunch," Sheila said. "I know what we'll do. We go to Stonebridge, pick up Cornish pasties, coffee to go, doughnuts, and some fruit. We'll have a picnic lunch on the headland!"

The day was sunny, but it was bleak and cold. A picnic in January I thought. A picnic at this time of year? The thought of stodgy comfort food sounded wonderful after the menu of horrors at the Red Lion. Yes, I was willing to go along with the picnic idea, especially if I had pasties and doughnuts!

"Good idea, then we share our news. We'll be able to talk freely without upsetting Hugo, or being overheard by any of the police that may still be around," said Jim.

Sheila clapped her hands delightedly. "We had a power breakfast, and now we're going to have... what would it be called? It must have a special name... what is it?" Her head went on one side, and she looked from one of us to the other. She reminded me of a cheeky robin.

"A business lunch?" I suggested, loving her enthusiasm.

"That's it! A power breakfast and now a business lunch." The broad smile on her wrinkled face made us all smile. Her age seemed to slip away, and all I could see was an eager child of long ago.

Martin and Maggie dashed into the shops, whilst we waited in the car park. Carrier bags, most of them with the baker's logo on them were put in the boot. The aroma of cheese and onion, and traditional Cornish pasties filled the car. My mouth was watering. Martin's stomach started rumbling, and giving urgent squeaks.

We drove to a small car park above the beach headland. We parked overlooking the bay, and the wild incoming surf. Maggie first showed us the large bag of apples, pears, and satsumas. We all nodded appreciation, but she had no takers. The baker's carrier bags took all our attention. Kitchen roll used as napkins, coffee beakers settled in the car drinks holders, and we munched and chomped. The only sound from us were appreciative grunts, and moans of delight at the delectable pasties. The wind howled, and the car was buffeted from side to side. The waves on the beach below roared in, and only the hardiest kite surfers could be seen.

"What the hell happened to you two on your way to the ladies?" Jim finally asked, putting a half-eaten pasty down on his kitchen roll napkin.

I gestured to Sheila to tell the story. My mouth was too full of the most fantastic Cornish pasty I'd ever eaten. No way was I going to stop and speak. This pasty had all my attention, and everyone would have to wait until I'd eaten the very last crumb.

"The kitchen door was ajar and we heard them shouting. Daniel has no alibi, and Sarah was blackmailing him. Sarah wants to leave Cornwall and return to London. Daniel doesn't, so Sarah's threatening to tell the police that he has no alibi," Sheila said. There was silence as everyone absorbed this new development.

"That also means Sarah herself has no alibi. She also has a motive of her own," said Jim, his gaze thoughtful as he reached for a doughnut. "Interesting. Without Arabella there is no restaurant, and no need for Daniel to stay in Cornwall. Yet, he wants to stay. An interesting bit of information."

"How could the murderer get into the cottage without anyone seeing them come through the archway?" I asked, wiping my greasy lips.

"A footpath winds up the hill from the road to the Priory," Maggie answered. "Cross country from the Red Lion there's another footpath across the moor. It's not far, because the road winds round the valley, and is a far longer journey."

"So, it's easy enough to sneak in undetected," I mused.

"Yes, it's more than likely that's the way the murderer came and left," said Jim.

"Daniel knew we'd heard them. He rushed out and glared furiously at me. He was so angry. Why didn't he glare at Sheila? Why just me?" I said. I looked at the others who had gone suspiciously quiet. "What? What is it?" I asked them, getting a bit miffed. I looked at Jim, his bottom lip was quivering. Martin had his hand up to his mouth and Maggie was trying not to laugh. Sheila was just grinning.

"You didn't want to be overlooked. You didn't want to be grey and forgettable. That's what you told us. In your purple and black glittery top, purple streaked hair, no wonder he stared at you. You are very noticeable now!" said Maggie at last.

I sniffed. There was no answer to that, so I ignored it.

"Does he know who we are? Or where we came from?" I asked.

Worried looks passed between the others, and an uneasy silence fell between them in the car.

"Oh yes, Daniel knows this car well, it's for use for anyone at the Priory. Arabella used it, and often gave him lifts in it," said Maggie.

"He knows where to find us, and where to find me." My words hung in the air. A feeling of menace now seeped into the car. A shiver of fear ran down my spine. Was I being stupid? I had nothing to fear, or did I?

"My turn," the brisk voice of Maggie broke into the silence. Putting down her half-eaten doughnut, she wiped strawberry jam from her lips. "Paula, the barmaid was at school with me. We hung out together in the same teenage crowd."

Jim's irritated drumming of his fingers on the steering wheel, made Maggie pause, then continue hurriedly. I'd seen the careful notes Jim was making. Neat headings of times, of conversations, overheard by who and where. Was this from previous professional experience?

"Paula said Daniel and Arabella had a row last week. Daniel was getting impatient. The Red Lion owners offered him a manager/chef position, with the possible view to a partnership. They also offered Daniel a percentage of the profits. It meant tying him into a contract for three years. Arabella was furious that he was even considering it." Maggie took another bite from her doughnut. She swallowed hastily when Jim sighed heavily. "But Paula says she thinks Arabella was going to France," Maggie sat back, a satisfied glance towards Jim.

Jim put the cap carefully back on his pen. He set it down neatly on top of the notebook on his lap. "Well, for a lunchtime pub meal, which we never actually had, that was very successful. Lots of hearsay of course, but a few more motives floating about, despite what the police think."

The wind dropped, the rain ceased and a watery sun came out. Transformed, the sea sparkled with glittering lights. The green headland, was bathed in that famous Cornish light which took my breath away.

"Magic, isn't it?" said Martin beside me.

I couldn't believe it! I'd only arrived yesterday. There had been a dead body in my cottage. This lunchtime, I'd been chased out of a pub by an angry chef.

It was still winter, still January, and I was having a picnic! I was eating Cornish pasties in a car overlooking the most wonderful beach scene imaginable.

"Come on, let's have a quick walk," said Jim.

"Wow! This wind is fierce." I cried out, as my scarf whipped around my face. I struggled on after the others, finally zipping up my anorak to the chin.

"Sunshine! The sun is out!" Sheila shouted over the crashing of the surf on the beach below. Yes, it was sunshine, a weak watery sun that was soon hidden by storm clouds.

"Oh no, this is awful. I'm going back to the car," said Maggie, turning around.

"It's sleet!" I said. Stinging flakes of snow with large drops of rain now drove into our faces. Gasping and laughing, we dashed back to the car. I felt so tired on the journey back after the picnic. The emotional turmoil of leaving my former home, the journey and the murder had exhausted me. Where had the courage come from, to take this leap into the unknown? I still wondered.

Lunchtime, normally was catered for by ourselves. The main evening meal was always in the Priory kitchen and cooked by Maggie. I'd eaten enough calories on the picnic lunch, to last a fortnight. I made a cup of tea on my return to the cottage. I sat down on the sofa, Cleo beside me. Cleo loved the cottage. The sofa, in front of the log burner, and the window seat overlooking the courtyard were her special places. She obviously appreciated my company and my lap. After her previous working owners, my continual presence was a treat for her. Her friendly little face, and warm purring body beside me on the sofa, or on my bed, was a comfort for me.

That evening, the main meal at the Priory passed in desultory general chatter. Hugo's gloomy presence, fatigue after last night, and the excitement of the pub and picnic lunch, had dampened our spirits.

I returned and opened the front door of my new cottage with pleasure. Only my second night, yet already the tiny cottage was home.

"An engineer will fit your telephone landline tomorrow. Until then, you can use the phone in the Priory kitchen. The Mobile phone signal is appalling here. Martin and Jim use their back bedroom, beside the windows for a signal," Maggie had told me earlier.

Would I have to resort to snail mail? I felt lost without my broadband connection. Who carried notepaper and envelopes around with them now? I didn't. As for stamps, it must have been years since I bought any, except for Christmas. "I'll go up, and write an email to Jake," I told Cleo.

I headed upstairs to the back bedroom, Cleo following me. The tiny back bedroom overlooked Bodmin Moor. This room was going to be my study. A desk beneath the window, with the wonderful light flooding in, would be ideal for my botanical painting. "I'll enjoy painting up here, and I'll get you a basket beside me," I told Cleo. I sat on the window ledge, my laptop on my knee. Cleo jumped up, and pushed me to the end of the ledge to find her own space. "This window ledge isn't wide enough for both of us, let alone a rather large lady, and her plump cat." I'd write an email to Jake, and I could keep it in the draft section until I finally got my broadband connection.

'I coped with the journey, I used the satnav, but a map was easiest along the Cornish lanes. The van was great, so easy to handle. Unfortunately, my cottage had a dead body on the hearth rug. A woman was murdered there. I had to go to another cottage, but I like it better, it's actually much nicer. Only a few people here, but all very pleasant. We went out for a pub lunch, and instead had a picnic on the headland. It was blustery and I know it was winter. But it was lovely when the sun came out, especially with Cornish pasties and doughnuts! Hope you both getting on well and...'

I never finished my draft email. The movement was surreptitious. At first, I thought I was imagining it. I concentrated hard as I peered through the gloomy twilight. But no, there was something. A dark figure was creeping along behind the cottages. Fully alert now, I saw the figure reach the cottage which should have been mine, the cottage in which Arabella was murdered. Opening the gate, the figure crept up towards the back door.

Jumping to my feet, I waved my phone around until I got Maggie. "Maggie there's someone at that cottage, he's running away now. Maggie! There's a fire, he set fire to the cottage!"

"Daisy, go and knock up Martin and Jim. I'll phone the police and fire brigade. Hurry!"

Scooping up Cleo, I dashed downstairs and put her in her basket. I knew she'd be safe there. In seconds I was banging and shouting on Martin's back door, and then went to Jim's. "Fire! Fire!"

CHAPTER SEVEN

"Fire!" I screamed. I banged my fist on Martin's door. He cautiously opened the door. Martin stood in a check dressing gown, "What... What?"

At the back door of Arabella's cottage, the smoke was billowing and the smell of burning grew stronger. I ran, leaving Martin trying to pull himself together. I banged at Jim's door. I opened my mouth to shout again, and had my hand raised when the door was flung open. Jim stood there, fully dressed. He listened to me, stepped out, and took a look at the fire. He swung into action immediately. "Martin! Into your kitchen, grab the fire extinguisher and direct it over the wall at the fire. I'll do the same." Both men turned and dashed into their cottages.

Maggie ran up to me. "The fire brigade is on its way." She pulled the belt tight around her pink dressing gown covered with purple bunnies. "Let's go into Arabella's cottage, I've got the key."

We dashed round to the other cottage, Maggie with key in hand. "No sense letting it burn down for the sake of some yellow tape," Maggie said, and pushed the yellow crime tape aside. Inside the kitchen area we could see the bottom of the back door burning. The new cottage door was of heavy green oak, and the fire had been slow to take hold. "I'll grab the fire blanket and open the door," Maggie said. "Daisy, get the fire extinguisher and direct it onto the flames when the door opens."

"No Maggie! Maggie, the fire will spread. Don't open the door!" I shrieked at her. It was too late. Heedless of my shouts, she ignored me.

Wrapping her hand in the blanket, she ran to the door. I got ready to take aim, the fire extinguisher held like a weapon.

"Now!" yelled Maggie. She grabbed the door handle. Maggie stepped back, and flung the door wide.

The force of the aerosol jet took me by surprise. I sprayed the door and the fire. The flames shrivelled under the jet of foam. The extinguisher suddenly seemed to swing around under its own volition. I held it with both hands. I couldn't control it, and was unable to switch it off. Foam shot everywhere through the open doorway. And all over the two figures standing there. Martin sneezed. Foam flew from his head and shoulders in great gobbets. Jim, held his extinguisher in one hand, raised his other hand wiping the foam from his face and just looked at me. The one eyebrow lifted. That eyebrow had done the same at my purple hair, and glittery top, and my collision with a waiter at the Red Lion. Now, bedecked with foam it rose even higher.

"That's the fire out," I mumbled.

Maggie looked at the foam drenched wall and door. "Yes, we certainly got the fire out." At the sound of the approaching sirens, she placed the singed blanket on the worktop and walked past me. Only I could see her grin. "Good shooting Daisy!" she whispered in my ear.

I looked at the two dripping men. "Sorry, I'm so sorry, this thing… It got away from me and I didn't see you both until too late…" I put down the extinguisher on the counter top. "Sorry," I said again, and fled.

"More tea?" Maggie asked me as we later sat in the Priory kitchen.

"No thanks," I cradled the hot mug of tea in my hands. "I lost control of that extinguisher, and I didn't know they'd be there. Jim said they'd be hanging over the walls."

Maggie chuckled. "Oh Daisy, I don't know which was funnier. The two of them covered in foam, or the

41

expression on your face."

"Not so funny, from where we were standing!" Jim said. He and Martin, now foam free came into the kitchen. Hugo followed. His previously white drawn face was now absolutely haggard.

A policeman poked his head around the door. "You can all go to bed. An arson investigation will start tomorrow, and we'll take your statements then."

"I am so sorry," I said to Martin and Jim as I stood up.

Martin smiled at me, "it's okay Daisy."

"It was an accident," agreed Jim. "I'll see you home and make sure all your doors and windows are secure."

"Don't worry sir, there's a guard being left here all night. The boss is worried about the fire starting up again, and what with…" The young policeman's voice tailed off.

"Our arsonist or murderer making a return visit perhaps?" was Jim's dry retort.

It was a quiet group at breakfast next morning. We were all tired and anxious. I wasn't just anxious, I was frightened. Only two nights, and already there had been a murder and an arson attack. The drama and panic of the previous hours, unfortunately had not dulled my appetite. Quite the reverse! Always, when worried or upset, I comfort ate. I shouldn't, I didn't need to. My weight was a constant problem. When things calm down, I'd say to myself. When I get my life going smoothly. Trouble was, I never seemed to reach that calm restful happy plateau in my life. Would I ever? Time, really wasn't on my side.

"Another egg and more bacon Daisy?" Maggie asked me.

I looked down at my empty plate. I was aghast. I'd eaten a huge breakfast without even realising it. I remembered reading about those strange people who chewed each mouthful for thirty something times. That would do it, I thought. I'd have to slow down then, and wouldn't eat so much. I'll start next week, I promised myself.

"Usually, I only have toast. This is a real treat. So, yes please. Next week there won't be any murders or arson attacks. Next week I'll go on a crash diet," I said.

Maggie put extra bacon and an egg on my plate, then a further sausage and egg on her plate. "You and me both, next week for certain we'll diet," said Maggie.

"Why was Arabella in the cottage in the first place?" I asked. "Didn't she live in the Priory House?"

"I've often wondered that. Could she have gone in there to meet somebody? " Sheila said.

"Why would she meet anyone there? She knew Daisy was moving in that night. And why the fire? Perhaps the fire is nothing to do with the murder," said Martin.

"None of us here have any enemies, do we? Anybody here have any dark secrets from a wild past?" Sheila chuckled at the very idea, as she buttered her toast.

Was I the only one who saw the fleeting look of dismay cross Jim's face? Was I the only one that saw the sudden clenching of his fists? The others were all grinning at each other, as if it was a huge joke. Not Jim, a weak forced smile played about his lips.

"I only wish I had an exciting dramatic past. It would have been fun to look back on in my old age, sitting with a shawl over my knee, beside the fire," Maggie laughed.

"My excitement is in the games I play on the computer," confessed Martin. "Nothing exciting ever happens to me in real life," he paused, and then stammered, "well, not much."

There was a shiftiness in his eyes, and I wondered. Did Martin also have a secret to hide?

Later that morning the police arrived. Not really formal interviews. The investigator confirmed that it had been arson. As if we hadn't realised that! Had I noticed anything significant about the intruder, I was asked. I repeated that the figure wore black, and crept stealthily along in the twilight. They sighed, and I was free to go. We had a break for morning coffee in the Priory kitchen. I think we felt the need to get together to discuss last night's happenings. Sheila stirred an extra spoonful of sugar into her coffee. She gazed thoughtfully down at the liquid as it swirled about in the mug. Then she looked up at us. "Did this fire business have anything to do with Arabella's murder? Did someone try to burn down the cottage she was murdered in? Or was there another reason?" she said.

There was a silence as we all thought about this.

"The Priory has always been a magnet for drama. The ancient stones with which it is built perhaps causes dramatic incidents to happen," Jim spoke thoughtfully. Reaching out to the ancient stone walls of the kitchen, he stroked the rough, uneven stone which had been standing since the time of the Normans. "This kitchen is mentioned in the Domesday book. I think it's obvious some of the stones are Roman. There is documentation that states part of it was rebuilt by the Knights Templars."

"Surely not! The Knights Templars! Here in this very kitchen?" Martin jumped upright in his chair, his face alight with interest. His shaking hand touched the stones with awe.

"Yes, that's why I was so delighted to get a cottage here. It's perfect for my research. I'm writing about the Templars, and the link to this area of Cornwall. There is a possible Merovingian dynasty link here. Of course, I'm also intrigued by the legend of the Black Madonna." Jim smiled at Martin's enthusiasm, and Sheila's wide-eyed wonder.

"Oh! It's the da Vinci code for real!" Sheila's breath that she been holding while Jim spoke, rushed out in a whoosh. Then she clapped her hands excitedly. "That's it, that's the reason for the fire! They meant to torch Jim's cottage and picked the wrong one. They wanted to destroy all his research papers on the Knights Templars. We are living in the middle of a murder mystery and a Da Vinci code adventure!"

CHAPTER EIGHT

"Nonsense! My research is dry boring stuff. There is
no buried treasure and no lost heirs to the holy Grail. The
Templars were in this area, notably at Temple Church.
I'm looking for more information on that period in old
books and documents," Jim said. His slightly flushed face
showed his annoyance at this sensationalism.

"I've lived in this area for many years and this is the
first I've heard of it. I've known about Temple Church
and that's all. I doubt anyone would burn down a cottage
to destroy Jim's papers on the Knights Templars," said
Maggie.

The Holy Grail, King Arthur, UFOs, and other similar
stuff always drew fanatics and weirdos to them. Wasn't it
possible that someone felt Jim's work shouldn't see the
light of day? I thought it likely. I was glad Martin's
cottage was next door to Jim's not mine. Not that I was
fearful for myself. Oh no! I was worried about my Cleo.

"My car is in the garage for a service. Is anyone going
to Stonebridge today? Could they give me a lift?" asked
Maggie, as she leant back against the sink, her mug
cradled in her hands.

"If you navigate for me and show me where to park, I
could take you. That's if you can face getting into my
van," I said.

Maggie grinned, "I'd love it." As she reached my van,
Maggie patted BURT'S cheerful face. She settled herself
with a sigh of surprise, "this is a comfy seat." We drove
out of the courtyard and set off into a wintry landscape.
The fields were bare and frost clung to the trees and
hedges. A bird of prey sat glaring on a fence post as we
drove past. The morning sunshine had a lightness and
clarity that I'd never seen before in the Home Counties. I

46

could almost taste the sharp crispness of the salty Cornish air.

"I don't understand what's going on at the Priory. Life was always dull and boring there. There's a murder one day, and an arson attack the next night. I don't understand it," Maggie said as we drove along.

"Arabella was…" Deliberately, I let my voice tail away. I found that was often the way to get someone talking. It worked.

"Arabella, was a hard selfish young lady! But she had tremendous charm and beauty. And how she worked that charm and beauty!" Maggie declared.

"She was no favourite of yours," I remarked.

"No," it was a flat vehement answer.

Her hands gripped her gloves tightly, her knuckles were white. She straightened the fingers of each glove, smoothing them out in brisk angry strokes. Her mouth was set in a hard line. Then, she gave a deep sigh, and I felt her visibly calm down and her tension ebbed away. It was obvious that she had come to some decision.

"Daisy, you should know the full story. After all, you've landed into the middle of it. Hugo, inherited Barton Priory from his grandfather. His uncle, and his two sons drowned in a yachting accident. That meant Hugo unexpectedly inherited. He never expected it, nor wanted it."

This I had already heard from Sheila. It was good to hear Maggie's point of view. I stared ahead as I drove, scared to make a move, or say anything that would halt this story. It wasn't that I was nosy. No, I felt that I should have all the facts available to me. Shouldn't I?

"Yes," I said, hoping for more.

"Arabella arrived in the area few months ago. She rented a holiday cottage. She was having a career break, or it was a broken relationship. Those were the rumours.

She ignored the locals, and ingratiated herself with the posher incomers, the wealthier hobby farmers, and of course the golf club set," said Maggie.

"That's how she met Hugo? Playing golf?" I asked.

I drove down the hill into a small town. It lay alongside a river. We crossed over a bridge then turned into a car park. Overlooking the river and fields, with hills rising up behind a Victorian terrace, I sat looking out of the window. It was at that moment I fell in love with Stonebridge. It felt like home.

Maggie continued speaking. "They met at the golf club. Neither played golf, she went to find a man, a wealthy man. Hugo was taken there by a neighbour to introduce him into the local society. Hugo was a lecturer in a boy's school before he inherited the Priory. He is a shy, intellectual guy. He never stood a chance with Arabella. His wedding ring was on her finger within five weeks!" Maggie turned in her seat and grimaced. "It was only five weeks. A holiday in the Bahamas, and she came home with his wedding ring on her finger. Then the redevelopment plans of the Priory began."

"Didn't Hugo want to modernise the Priory? Make it pay?" I asked.

We got out of the van, and I grabbed my things and locked the van. For a moment, Maggie stood still, staring over the van at me. "I was kept on because no one else would do the job in that isolated place. I'm also very good at it. I'd been working there under the old master, and helped Hugo when he first arrived. I stayed because Hugo asked me. Arabella would have loved to get rid of me. There was no love lost between us. Hugo wanted to modernise, but didn't want a glitzy boutique hotel." Maggie threw her bag over her shoulder, and gave me a watery smile. "So, I stayed at the Priory. That's the history. Let's shop!"

The High Street was a delight. I wandered along staring in the antique shops, the bakers, and greengrocers. Even the health food shop caught my eye. I'll go in another time, I promised myself. Maggie had gone to do a supermarket shop. All the time my thoughts tumbled around in my head. Arabella was obviously a money grabbing schemer. No one seemed to have liked her. But whose dislike had turned to hate? When? And why had that hatred turned to murder? Maggie hadn't told me, there had been no need. It was in her voice, and plainly visible in her face. She loved and cared for Hugo.

At the top of the High Street, I spotted the craft shop. Brightly coloured wool, materials and craft kits were arranged enticingly in the window. No! No more knitting ever! Jake had loathed the shapeless baggy jumpers I produced. That pattern of serene sailing boats, in my finished garments showed choppy seas and sinking ships. The exciting trendy patterns with unusual yarns I'd knitted for myself, hung lopsidedly, and ill-fitting on my ample form. The patchwork materials in the window were wonderfully exciting and I gazed in admiration at the sample cushions and quilts. Then I remembered my last patchwork class. The exasperated fluting voice of the teacher, an acidic woman, had instilled panic and fear in my breast. I was scared of a teacher and paying for the privilege! And I'd been the mother of a teenage son. Never, ever did my patchwork corners ever meet. My efforts had graced many a cat basket. The cats never worried about corners and how they met! Then I saw the watercolour paints. I was in arty heaven!

I was first back at the van. Satisfied with my morning shopping I sat on a bench overlooking the river. Despite the chill wind, it was pleasant in the sunshine. My bags rustled beside me, and I smiled happily as I thought of the contents.

"You've been busy shopping," Maggie walked up towards me. "Have you been waiting long? There was a mix up at the till with the woman in front of me."

Opening the back of my van, I deposited our parcels. Maggie looked at my bags inquiringly.

"I bought a new blanket for Cleo's bed, some toys for her, and her special food from a pet shop," I said.

"And?" Maggie said as she pointed to the large bag with the craft shop logo.

"Paints, brushes and watercolour paper for myself. I'm going to start my botanical painting again. It's been some years, but when I saw the paints..."

"Good for you!" Maggie said, and smiled at my enthusiasm.

The journey back seemed much shorter, as we chatted about everyday concerns. I liked Maggie, and could only hope that she liked me. Demelza was making lunch in Maggie's absence. I wondered what she'd be like. Wasn't she in 'Poldark'? I visualised a sultry Cornish beauty presiding over the pots and pans.

Maggie's phone rang. I could hear every word.

"Maggie? It's Jim here. Where are you? Are you on your way back?"

"Yes Jim, we're in the village, just turning up to the Priory now. What's the problem?"

"Come straight in here. You and Daisy must come at once to the kitchen," the phone went dead.

"What now? I've never known Jim so rattled," said Maggie.

The van swung into the courtyard, I pulled it up sharply with a screech of brakes.

"You've no perishables in here have you?" she asked me.

"No, nothing that will spoil."

"Let's bring the shopping in, and leave your stuff in the van." Shutting the van door, Maggie raced towards the kitchen door. I ran after her. What now I thought?

CHAPTER NINE

Jim sat at the table; his usually immaculate white hair was tousled. He'd obviously been running his hands through it. A worried-looking Sheila sat beside him. Martin sitting beside Sheila also looked anxious, but as he always did, I ignored it. After a quick cursory glance at them, my attention was riveted upon the figure at the Aga. All I could see was her back, as she stirred a bubbling pot. Black tresses hung down her back almost to her waist. A black dress ending with flouncy lace trim ended in black lacy tights. The final sartorial touch was a pair of white wellingtons. Demelza turned and stared at me.

"Hello," I said and smiled at her. I kept my composure and my smile on my face, although it may have slipped slightly for a second.

Out of the corner of my eye I saw Maggie's nod of approval. Maggie stepped forward. "Daisy this is Demelza, she's my wonderful helper. Demelza lives in the village. Her family have lived in this area and have known Barton Priory for generations."

"Hello Daisy," the face was middle-aged, still beautiful but marred by the zigzag scar running down her cheek. Walking over to me she took my hand, lifting it up, she bent over and peered at it. The black hair fell forward in a curtain tickling my wrist and palm. It smelt of herbs and a strange indefinable perfume. Thrusting it aside, she stared intently again at my hand. A current of electricity flashed between us, and I'm certain I saw green sparks. Demelza drew in her breath and flung my hand away. She cried out, her voice echoing round the kitchen, and bouncing off the walls. "An old soul, that's what you are! Old magic surrounds you and hides your aura from me. You are cloaked in the old magic. You belong here. You've come home!"

Stepping closer towards me, her eyes searched my face. I flinched, but did not step away. You are invading my personal space I thought. I don't like it, but I'll stay put, and see this out. I'd better not do anything suddenly. I think she's mad. Demelza's arms stretched out and I was clapped to her bosom in a huge hug. The strange perfume she wore was mixed with onions and garlic. It swept over me in a not unpleasant wave. It was a bit whiffy. "You're my cousin! You're part of our family." With a speed that rocked me back on my heels, she turned around, and began stirring the pot as if nothing had happened. Maggie shrugged, and gestured me to sit at the table. The open mouths and shocked expressions of the others said it all. I sat in a dazed and bewildered silence.

"We enjoyed the shopping trip," Maggie's loud stilted voice broke the uneasy quiet.

"Good, good," Jim said, his thoughts obviously elsewhere.

"Daisy found the library and the art shop. She's been buying paints and brushes. Daisy is taking up her botanical art again." Maggie's voice again broke into the strange uneasy quiet of the room.

"There we are Maggie," Demelza said, turning around from the Aga. Taking off her apron she waved a hand to the covered dishes. "All ready for you to dish up. See you all in the morning. That's if none of you get murdered tonight!" With a loud raucous laugh, she strode out of the kitchen. As she passed me, she patted me on the shoulder. "See you in the morning cousin, you'll be all right. Don't you worry. You're family."

The meal was delicious. On Demelza's days at the Priory she cooked a main lunchtime meal giving Maggie a break. The morning's walk round Stonebridge, my strange meeting with Demelza, and the enigmatic, "we'll discuss it after we've eaten," from Jim, did nothing to lessen my appetite. I enjoyed my roast chicken, crisp roast potatoes, fresh country veggies, and blissfully ate the apple and blackberry cobbler. I gave up counting the calories after the first thousand! Dishwasher was stacked, and the table cleared. We sat with mugs of tea or coffee, all alert and staring at Jim.

"What was so urgent Jim?" Maggie asked.

"We couldn't talk in front of Demelza. She talks to everyone in the village about everything. A great lady, but not discreet. Hugo's been taken down to the police station again. He's to help the police with their enquiries."

Maggie began to speak, as the colour drained from her face. Jim silenced her with a raised hand.

"They want to know why Arabella was in that cottage. Who was she going to meet? Where was Hugo at that crucial time? Did they have a row in the cottage and did he kill her?" Jim sat back in his chair.

"Tell them, tell them the rest!" insisted Sheila.

Jim glared at Sheila. He'd never have done that, if he hadn't been badly rattled, I thought. "I was just coming to that Sheila. Last night somebody tried to break in again at the cottage where Arabella died, and the fire was set. They didn't get in. The policeman making his rounds saw someone and shouted. The police think someone came back in the early hours to break into the cottage, when they realised the fire had been put out. Unbelievable! A fire and then an attempted burglary. It's hard to credit what's going on here."

I stirred in my chair. Should I suggest it? I wondered if it was a stupid idea. It had nagged at me for some time. No one else seemed to have thought about it. "What if

Arabella had not gone to meet anyone at the cottage? What if she'd gone to retrieve something? Perhaps she'd hidden something, and wanted to get it before I arrived. My arrival was unexpected."

Silence. Maggie pulled out a bunch of keys from her pocket and placed one on the table. "Have the police cleared the crime scene tape yet?" she asked Jim.

"No, the policeman said a guard will be placed there tonight. There was no need during the daytime as we are all moving around," Jim replied.

"What are we waiting for? Let's go solve this mystery?" Maggie said.

Martin stared at her in a mixture of horror and disbelief. "You are not Miss Marple, and we are not detectives! The police won't like us trampling over a crime scene." Martin added with a tremor in his voice, "the police won't like any of us going in there."

"If it helps clear Hugo, I'm going in there, whether I'm in trouble or not!" Maggie declared loudly, blushing slightly at her own loud vehemence.

"I'll watch from the window and text you if anyone drives into the courtyard. I've got my whistle as well," said Sheila, pulling an ancient police whistle from her blouse.

We all stared at her. I wondered what else was kept in that bra. I had thought Sheila had a plump figure. What else did she keep stashed down there in that bra?

Jim sighed, looked down at the key, then rose to his feet. "Martin, you keep watch from your bedroom window. Text us if you see anybody coming up over the fields and footpath. Thank goodness, they fixed the landlines and broadband this morning."

Martin with visible relief sped off towards his cottage.

"Shall I come and search?" I rose to my feet. I didn't want to be left out of this!

"It's Daisy's idea and she's got a fresh pair of eyes to look at things. Only if you're willing to join us Daisy? We may all get into trouble," warned Maggie.

"What are we waiting for?" I said. I jumped up, and my chair clattered onto the floor. I mumbled apologies, and followed the others.

"We're detectives!" said Sheila as she wheeled herself over to the window to keep watch. "The Priory Five, that's us."

Jim raised an eyebrow and shook his head. We were all smiling at Sheila's enthusiasm.

"You can be our Priory Hot Wheels," I added, getting into the act.

"Please, don't encourage her," Jim whispered in my ear.

The courtyard was cold, damp, and empty of all police vehicles. Only the crime scene tape stood between us and our search. The tape was slung in front of the cottage door. Swaying slightly in the breeze it barred our way.

"Perhaps we shouldn't…" Maggie said, staring down at it.

"I know…." I replied, prodding it with a finger, and watching it dip and sway back and forth. "After all it is a crime scene," I murmured.

Taking a deep breath, Jim stepped forward, lifted it, and slipped beneath it. Maggie looked at me and shrugged, and followed. Maggie unlocked the door, as I slipped under the tape and joined them. It was a sombre threesome that entered the cottage, and stood on the welcome mat.

CHAPTER TEN

"Wait," I grabbed Maggie's arm. "You finished work here at two in the afternoon. We entered well after midnight." At Maggie's nod, I continued. "Look around very carefully. Is there anything different now from that afternoon? Is there anything out of place? Arabella or the murderer may have moved something. You'd never have noticed anything when we found Arabella. You were far too shocked."

"That's a good idea," Jim said. He stepped back, and Maggie went further into the cottage. She looked round, slowly, and methodically.

We watched, and I thought Jim was holding his breath. I was!

"Yes. That stool is over beside the coffee table. The ornaments and the lamp from the table are now on the bookcase," Maggie said.

Jim and I entered, and looked at the table. I pointed. "There are scratch marks here on top of the table." I glanced up. "What's that tiny window up there?" High up in the gable wall was a small square window, with a tiny protruding stone ledge.

"An owl hole. Barns and stables had lots of vermin, and in the past farmers encouraged owls. They left a hole so that the owls could fly in. There were more in Scotland, but we still have the odd one in Cornwall. Nowadays, large boxes are placed on barn walls to encourage the owls," answered Jim.

"Arabella climbed on the table to reach the ledge." I dashed forward. I lifted the stool onto the table where the scratch marks lay. A moment later I was on the stool, reaching up to the ledge. My fingers rummaged about. There was dust and grit, and the roughness of the stones.

"There is something… I've got… I found…" I held up the things that my fingers had finally caught hold of. "Passports!" I threw them down to Maggie, and then felt around again. "Something else here!" I held it up.

"It's a dead mouse Daisy!" Maggie squealed.

Looking in horror at the dry brittle thing I held my hand, I threw it across the room. My gasp of dismay at the nasty thing I'd found quickly turned into a shriek. Anyone would have thrown that mouse away. I did the only normal thing. It's completely understandable. Anyone would have shrieked, and jumped at finding a dead mouse in their hand! Somehow, I forgot I was perched on top of the stool, which was on top of the table! The stool slid across the table. I lost my grip on the owl thingy ledge, and hurtled backwards. Visions of imminent broken hips, cracked skull, broken arms and legs flashed through my mind. I was astonished and delighted to find myself held, and caught in extremely powerful strong arms. Carefully, Jim righted me as I struggled to find my feet on the floor.

"Thanks Jim," I said. I couldn't look him in the face. I didn't need to; I knew that there would be a raised eyebrow and that slight shake of the head. "Thanks for catching me," I muttered, feeling foolish and embarrassed.

"Oh Daisy," I heard Maggie sigh from behind me.

My flailing arm had caught the display of golden roses as I fell. I turned to look at the damage. I expected flowers and water to be all over the carpet. On the floor lay not the water and damaged blooms I had expected. Artificial golden roses lay scattered. I'd thought they were actually real! Some were still stuck in a block of that green crumbly stuff. Ugh! I hated it. The oasis set my teeth on edge whenever I touched it. The wicker basket in which the flowers had been arranged, lay on its side.

Sprawled half out of the basket, beside the roses were estate agent's details.

"Well done Daisy. We'd never found these if you hadn't..." Jim picked up the papers. I felt that words had failed him, and that he didn't want to continue. Nor did he want to suggest my stupidity had actually borne fruit! "Let's get this place to rights and get the hell out of here before the police return," said Jim.

"It's evidence! The police need to have it. We need to explain to them when, and where we found it," I protested.

"No, we need to have a look at all this. Later, I'll tell them that I discovered it all in a book in the library," Jim said. He opened the door, first checking the coast was clear.

"What a clever idea, it's almost as if you've done this sort of thing before," Maggie said putting the last rose back into the basket.

It had been fleeting, but I'd caught a strange look crossing Jim's face at Maggie's words. Again! Who was this man? What had he been in his past life? And, more to the point, what was he now?

"Come on! Let's get out of here and see what Daisy's found for us," Jim said, hurrying us out of the cottage.

We joined Martin and Sheila in the kitchen. Jim placed the passports, and the details on the table.

"Two passports. One is in the name of Penny Daniels, the other is Arabella's own. Penny Daniels is definitely Arabella, but the photo shows her as a blonde." Holding it, with his fingers alone, he showed it to us all. "The estate agent details are of two properties. One is a cottage in a village near to Bodmin. The other is of a château in Normandy." He spread them out on the table, so that we could all see.

"That's a village across the A 30. What is she doing with details for that?" said Maggie.

Still worried, I asked again, "these are vital clues, how do we explain…"

"Later, I'll take notes first," said Jim.

Taking his phone, Jim took photos of all the papers laid out upon the table. Then he wrote all the details neatly into his notebook. After all that, he smiled at me. He picked up his phone and rang the police. We all listened to his explanation of finding everything in the library.

"I've to drop it all into the police station. I explained that I found it in a book in the library." He tapped the cottage details. "Let's look over this cottage. It's for sale. What excuse can we give them if they find us there? We've got away with finding the passport and details in Arabella's cottage. But traipsing over the details we discovered, that's a different matter altogether." A subdued silence fell upon us all. The excitement of the hunt for clues and our early success which had buoyed us all up, evaporated.

"Google Penny Daniels on the Internet! Let's see if I can get anything on her, I'm going to do an image search from her photo. My grandson showed me that last week," Sheila said, reaching for her iPad. Her fingers flew over the iPad, and she stuck out her tongue between her teeth as she concentrated.

"If I ring the agent, I'll pretend to be a buyer," I said.

"But the police," said Maggie, shaking her head.

"I'll do it if Daisy comes with me. My niece is recently divorced. I've raved about this place, and she is actually considering moving here. I'm the only family she has. Would that do for a story?" said Jim.

"If you only go around that place, won't it look suspicious?" said Maggie.

60

"No, we'll get a few more viewings. Then it will be only a coincidence," Jim said.

"It'll be fun. I love looking round other people's houses, but we'll have a serious purpose in mind," I said.

Sheila had been so busy on her iPad, we'd almost forgotten her, until she shrieked. "Got her! She's on Facebook as a hairdresser and manicurist in that village in the details. She loves Chihuahua's, lots of photos of her with them. No photos of her with anyone else, only her dog in the garden. But this is an old posting, almost eight months ago."

"That's two leads. The cottage viewing in the village itself. What about the actual village? Any ideas about getting more gossip about her," asked Jim.

"What if I get my hair done?" said Sheila. "You can drive me Martin, and wait for me in the pub. Surely between us we could get some information about Arabella or Penny as she is known by there."

"Well done Sheila, you're in the hairdressers, and Martin in the pub. Daisy and I can go cottage viewing and we'll all meet up back here."

"I've got a full day here, so I'll miss out on all the fun," said Maggie sadly. She dragged the vacuum out of the cupboard with a bang and a scrape on the door. I winced. Maggie was really peeved at missing out on all the action.

"Don't worry, you can help us sort out the information we get when we get back. Perhaps you could see if Demelza has any gossip this morning," said Jim.

"Our investigation continues." Sheila smiled broadly. "This is going to be great fun. I wonder what we will discover. Let's hope we can find motives for other people. Surely, someone else wanted to murder Arabella!"

CHAPTER ELEVEN.

As we drew up outside the cottage, I turned to Jim. "What's the story? The agent is already here. He's waiting at the door. We've got to…"

"A divorced niece moving into the area after a marriage breakup," said Jim.

"Who's niece? Yours or mine?" I whispered to him as we walked down the path. The agent stood smiling at the cottage door.

"Yours. I've come with you to check out the building itself. You will embroider the story far better than I ever could," Jim said with a wry smile.

I was left wondering. Should I be pleased or annoyed at that remark?

Nodding, I put out my hand to greet the young man, who was clutching the details at the front door. His overeager smile, too tight suit, and trendy haircut made me feel less guilty at deceiving him. It'll be good practice for him showing us around. He can fine tune his estate agent spiel on us both. We were on serious business. This was no laughing matter. The police had no other suspect but Hugo. We had to find out exactly what he knew about his client, Arabella cum Penny. We needed to pump Jasper, I thought, when he introduced himself to us. One look at Jim's stolid poker face, and I knew it was up to me. Okay, here goes. Ditsy pensioner in action!

"Is it a nice village? The cottage isn't haunted? Why is the lady selling? There are no bad drains are there?" I gave him my earnest worried expression. I stood back waiting for Jasper's replies. Maybe, just maybe, we'd get some nugget of information from this guy. "My niece, Amy is a shy nervous girl. I've got to be certain the cottage is just right for her." I only hoped I could carry on this stupid chatter throughout the viewing.

Jim stared at me, then his lips twitched. He gave me a slight nod of approval.

"Goodness no! There are no ghosts here. The lady who owns it had a complete refurb done. I can assure you that the drains are in full working order. The owner is keen to move to France. She's been so happy living here. She says it will be a wrench for her to leave this cottage."

The cottage was small, neat, and superbly presented. Any home style magazine would have drooled over the artfully placed wicker baskets, piles of old battered suitcases, and the mannequin wearing a military uniform glaring fixedly across the lounge. I liked the guy in uniform, the baskets were okay, but it was a biscuit tin in the kitchen that really got to me! Didn't they realise rusty bits of paint would go in their food? Those edges could be sharp? I couldn't understand why you would disinfect a kitchen in every way known to man, and have a dirty unhygienic bread bin. I fingered the bread bin and drew my finger away with a gasp at the sharp edge. I hated what Arabella had done to that poor cottage. It wasn't a cosy cottage. It was an interior design set.

"Ugh, I knew they'd be sharp, I don't know why I had to prove it! I don't like this distressed stuff," I whispered to Jim.

"I don't understand it either. Your face shows exactly what you're thinking Daisy. Remember we're here to gather information, not criticise the décor." Jim had stepped closer to me, and whispered as he pointed to the tin.

"Okay, okay," I murmured. Looking around the downstairs of the cottage, I realised that there was very little personality of Arabella. No photos, no personal books, only some on feng shui, and home decorating bibles.

We went upstairs, but I could feel Jim's impatience at Jasper's continued presence. We returned downstairs for another look round.

"We've got to have a closer look. Can you distract him while I look upstairs again?" Jim whispered to me.

Jasper had walked ahead of us to unlock the back door.

"Okay," I whispered back. I walked into the kitchen, and banged a wall. Jasper jumped, and looked bewildered at my sudden action. "Is this a stud wall? My niece may want to open up the rooms," I said.

Jasper stared at me, and gulped, "I'm not sure, I think you need a surveyors report to knock down walls."

Loud scraping and banging noises came from upstairs. Jim was busy I thought. I thumped the wall again, and another one. I only hoped I was covering Jim's noises from upstairs. Jasper stared at me, as if I'd gone mad.

"It may be possible to remodel inside the cottage, but your niece should take proper advice, especially as the cottage is listed," Jasper said.

Jim appeared on the landing and called down to us, "Jasper, can you come up here please?" As Jasper turned away from me to climb the stairs, Jim mouthed, "your turn."

Hurriedly, I began opening cupboards and rummaging behind kitchen doors. I found the fridge and freezer, and then turned my attention even to the dishwasher. I opened every drawer I could find. They both returned to join me. Jim looked questioningly at me, and I nodded my head towards a cupboard on the utility room wall. He looked and saw the small padlock on it.

"I'd like to know about the thatched roof. Could you find out when it was done? Perhaps you could ring your boss for us now?" Jim asked Jasper.

"My phone won't have a signal in here. I tried before,

and could only get one at the bottom of the garden. I won't be a minute," Jasper dashed out of the door.

Jim stared at the small cupboard on the wall. The shelves beside it, held polishes, cleaning materials and cloths. Everything in the cottage had been open to view, except for this cupboard. We had both made good use of our time when left alone. But it had been a disappointing nothing.

"It might only contain dangerous chemicals or medicine," I said.

"Or something she didn't want seen. We have got to find out what is in there." Reaching into his pocket, Jim produced a small leather case. Almost wallet like, and extremely well worn. He unzipped it, and took out a tool from amongst some other small implements. A few seconds, and the cupboard door swung open. I stared at his expertise with his wallet of tools. That, was going to be something I'd think about later.

"Medicines, cough mixtures and plasters. That's all, nothing of any interest to us," Jim closed the cupboard door, locking it.

We walked out to meet Jasper. Jim put the tools back into his pocket.

"The thatched roof has another fifteen years left in it, but the ridge might need looking at in about five years. The boss said it's nothing to worry about."

"Great news Jasper, thanks for sorting that out," said Jim.

"I'll lead the way in my car to Willow cottage," said Jasper as he locked the door behind us. That had been arranged as our decoy cottage.

At Willow cottage, we played our part. Me, looking around for my non-existent niece and Jim checking the soundness of the property.

"Thank you, I'll tell my niece about each cottage," I said to Jasper.

Standing outside Willow cottage, it had all seemed to be a complete waste of time. We had learnt nothing more about Arabella. I'll try another angle I thought, one last attempt at getting information. "I think my niece would prefer the last cottage. How soon could she move into it? Is the owner keen to sell?"

"Yes, she is very keen to sell. In fact, if your niece is really interested, I've been given instructions to drop the price for a keen buyer and quick exchange. Once this cottage has been sold, she can tie up a deal in France. She has her eye on a château there," Jasper said. His eyes widened in excitement at a possible sale.

Jim and I were both disheartened at the lack of success of our mission, as we began the drive back to the Priory.

My phone rang, it was Maggie. "Can you bring back fish and chips for us all? Hugo wants to talk to everyone."

Hot plates from the oven, and the fish and chips were dished up. Pots of tea, or a beer to drink, and we sat back to compare notes.

"Nothing! Beautifully presented cottage, but not a personal item or sign of her personality. The agent said she was very keen to sell, because she wants to tie up a deal on a château," said Jim.

"I went to the hairdresser, as you can see." Sheila declared proudly, patting the white cotton wool curls. We all paid her compliments. I only hoped she didn't spend much, as it looked no different to this morning. "They were all a bit cagey at first. One woman admitted Penny had been disliked by the staff. Some of the customers thought she gave herself airs and graces. There had obviously been a row between her and the owner, but everyone clammed up about it."

Martin took up the story. "Only visited the pub occasionally. Always with a man, very often a different one. She disappeared from the scene months ago."

"When she came here and got her claws into me!" said Hugo, coming in and hearing the last part of Martin's remarks.

"Hugo, there's a meal for you in the oven. What do you fancy to drink?" Maggie jumped to her feet, and pushed Hugo into a chair.

Slumping into the chair, Hugo gave everyone a weak smile. "I don't know that I can manage even a mouthful," he said, looking down at his plate of steaming fish and chips. Appreciatively, he nodded his thanks as Maggie thrust a double whisky into his hand. He sipped it first, then drank deeply. A chip, picked up in one finger, was nibbled, and then eaten. He gave a deep sigh. "Thanks Maggie. Thanks everyone. I think I'm actually hungry." Hugo cleared his plate, and started on a second glass of whisky. "Thanks for all you are doing to help clear me. There has been some startling news. The police contacted me earlier. I don't really know how to take it. My emotions are all over the place. It seems Arabella was not Arabella, as you'd already found out. She wasn't even Penny the hairdresser. Her real name was Sharon White. She made a living flying off with wealthy men to exotic places. She married them under false passports obtained in the USA. After a while, she demanded an expensive divorce, or she'd agree to lose herself for a large sum of money." Hugo slammed the whisky glass down on the table. "I'm only the latest fool in a long line of them!"

Silence greeted this news. We all attempted to understand the enormity of Arabella's, or rather Sharon's money-making scams." I'm not married to her, which is an enormous relief. They don't know who is. They are still searching for her first and real husband. But I'm still the prime suspect for her murder." Hugo said, twirling his whisky glass round and round. Maggie had refilled it. He sat for a moment, still turning the whisky glass, watching the lights sparkle through the glass.

I swallowed my last chip reluctantly. They had been so good. It had been some time since I'd had fish and chips. I'd forgotten how much I enjoyed them

"Daniel rang me from the Red Lion, this afternoon. He wants us all to go for lunch tomorrow. It's definite now. He is a full partner there. As it's our nearest local pub, he wants to call a truce. Obviously, he wants our custom. He says he has vital news about Arabella. Shall we go?"

CHAPTER TWELVE

We were a silent group that filed into the Red Lion next lunchtime. The door opened when Hugo pushed it, despite the closed for refurbishment sign. Sheila looked at me. I knew she was remembering Daniel's threatening behaviour towards us, when we last visited the Red Lion pub. I shrugged, and followed her in. Sarah came forward to greet us. Her welcome was friendly. She showed us to a table set for us, close to the now open inglenook fire. That smile, playing about her lips, had a strangeness about it that worried me. The whole interior had been changed. The fireplace, an inglenook, had been opened out, and glowed with logs. The grey walls, were now washed over with a honey cream. Bright oil paintings of local scenes, vivid, arresting, and exciting in their colour, were hung upon the walls.

"This is great now." Maggie enthused, as she stood and gazed around the lounge and dining room.

"Thank you," said Sarah. "I hated that grey colour. We also have a different menu now."

"No cauliflower I hope?" Martin said with a shudder at the memory.

For the first time since I'd met her, Sarah laughed. It was a genuine hearty laugh. Not the sly, sneering smile she habitually used.

"No cauliflower steaks! Just plain old-fashioned English cooking. Roast dinners, steak pies, fish and chips, and traditional puddings including crumbles, sticky toffee pudding, and apple and blackberry pies. How does that sound? Is that better?" Sarah replied.

"Fantastic," Martin said enthusiastically.

"That's one of the reasons I asked you over here. We wanted to call a truce, especially after your last visit. I'm

69

sorry I shouted at you both. We are your nearest pub, and would value your custom. If you extend your complex further, it's even better for us," said Daniel. He came from the kitchen, carrying a couple of bottles of wine. "Also, you can spread the word about the new Red Lion pub, different atmosphere and different menu," he added.

Daniel had made a steak pie and a vegetarian gratin. The dessert had been superb. Chocolate ganache on a chocolate cake base, surrounded by liqueur-soaked raspberries, with Cornish clotted cream. Daniel, was without doubt, a talented and fantastic cook. No wonder Arabella had wanted him to be head chef in her restaurant. Jim sipped his coffee. Like me, he'd barely touched the wine. I was wary of Daniel and our invitation. I could sense that Jim also had his suspicions. What was coming next? General chatter about the area, and the weather had accompanied our meal. The plates were whisked away efficiently by a smiling Sarah. I hadn't forgotten that shrewish vicious voice of hers when she'd been shouting at Daniel. I hadn't forgotten how much she hated Cornwall, and especially Bodmin Moor. Where had this urgent need to return to London gone? More to the point, why had it gone? There had been a planned agenda to this meal. I thought that the real purpose of our invitation was now coming. Jim looked across at me, we exchanged glances. He nodded. He was also waiting.

Daniel stood up. He looked round at everyone. "You know I have no alibi for that evening." Here, he paused to give me a really nasty look. "I did meet Arabella that evening. We met at the green in Blisland. It's halfway between both our places. We sat in her car, for a discussion. I told her of the Red Lion pub owners offer."

Hugo, sat motionless. Only the half-filled glass of wine in his hand twirled around and around. He stared into it. We all said nothing, waiting for what was to come.

"She had been to the bank. The lack of money in the will, the overdrafts, and loans due, had driven her into a wild state. Arabella told me that she had quarrelled with Hugo. He refused to sell the Priory, and buy another property, a hotel that she could run. Hugo had also refused to get another mortgage on the Priory, or another bank loan."

Daniel was enjoying this, as was Sarah. Daniel watched Hugo for any sign of emotion, or distress. Hugo sat, still staring into the swirling wine in his glass. I noticed that it was moving faster, and that his knuckles were now white. Jim beside me was also tense. I felt him fiddle with something under the table. Looking down, I saw in the palm of his hand, some device. Was he recording this?

"Arabella told me that she was going to leave Hugo. She would demand a lump sum from him. Everything they had left in the bank account. She still wanted me as a chef. She still had plans for that Michelin starred restaurant. I wasn't going to wait for her dream to materialise. I told her that I didn't think she'd ever get her restaurant. I was going to stay at the Red Lion pub. I'd had a great offer from the owners. She had been furious before. Now she became absolutely raging mad. She threw me out of the car and drove off."

He lifted up his phone, and showed it to Hugo. Puzzled, we all stared at him. "Sarah and I have settled down in the Red Lion pub. We are getting married. I want to start with a fresh clean slate. I've just told the police about my meeting with Arabella, and about the row she had with you. I also told the police, that she had intended to have a final showdown with Hugo. That chief copper Tenby, is on his way to the Priory to pick you up

71

Hugo. Sorry mate, I seem to have dropped you in the soup!" Daniel and Sarah both smiled triumphantly at us.

"I see," said Hugo. He rose to his feet and smiled weakly at them both. "Thank you for a fantastic meal. We'll certainly come back. We'll spread the word about the revamped Red Lion pub and its menu. Thank you for the information. Goodbye"

Hugo strode out of the pub. We followed silently. We walked out to the car, and drove back to the Priory. I sat staring out the window. The clearing of Hugo's name I had joined, partly because it gave me an entry to the group. All right, I'll admit it, it sounded just a bit of fun, and quite exciting. Now, I was determined to help clear his name. Dignified and polite, he had shown a quiet command of himself at Daniel's news. Daniel's story now gave Hugo even more of a motive to kill Arabella. In fact, Daniel was correct. He'd really dropped Hugo into the soup!

On entering the courtyard, we could see the police car was already there. Getting out of our cars we stood about awkwardly. Hugo turned, gestured to the police car, and spoke to us. "I'm going into the Priory to chat with Tenby. Please, all of you go home. There's nothing more you can do. I didn't kill her. I'll admit I was furious, and we did have an argument before she drove off to meet Daniel. That was the last time I saw her. I did not see her when she returned." With a deep breath, and with utmost sincerity he stared at us. "I did not kill Arabella. I did not see her upon her return to the Priory. I know nothing about her death." He nodded at everyone. He turned round, and walked off to meet with the police.

"What can we do?" Maggie whispered, she stared after Hugo's retreating back. The slight drizzle, had spattered her hair with tiny sparkling raindrops, that shimmered with the slightest movement. Heavy black clouds darkened the courtyard, the mist thickening and swirling around us. Our faces were drawn and worried in the otherworldly atmosphere of a cold January afternoon on Bodmin Moor.

"There's nothing we can do," said Jim. "Leave it till the morning. We will know exactly what the police have as evidence against Hugo. Then perhaps we can…"

"Evidence against him! They've got everything they need. Hugo quarrelled with her. Hugo's knife was used to kill her. Hugo has no alibi. But he's innocent! Someone must've framed him," Maggie cried out. Her voice echoed round the courtyard and made me shiver.

Sheila reached out a hand to clumsily pat Maggie's shoulder. "Jim is right. Daisy is going to the hairdresser tomorrow, and Jim is going to sound out the folk in the pub. Martin and I are house hunting. Tomorrow we'll go over every single piece of information we have. Again, and again, until we find something to clear Hugo's name. I know we will!"

I trudged into my cottage. I felt as miserable as the weather. Cleo sat on my knee. I sipped my tea, staring into the flickering flames of the log burner. The excitement and drama and horror of Arabella's death, had with its extreme busyness kept me occupied. That had fizzled out. We now found ourselves at a loss to clear Hugo's name. There was no further information on any other possible killer. No one else seemed to have a motive, only Hugo. He was still the only suspect. Daniel's story to the police had only made Hugo's position much worse. This move to Cornwall, and the murder, had filled my days and nights. Everything else had been excluded from my thoughts. I'd liked it. How I wished my thoughts could roam freely, without that persistent jump back to the real reason I'd moved here. As I had packed for this move, I'd made a startling discovery. That discovery had shed an unexpected new light upon my birth. Finding the vacancy at Barton Priory had seemed to be providential, meant to be, fate or something. I'd dashed to Cornwall in a wild search for answers with a new urgency. I knew my reasons for coming to the middle of Bodmin Moor. What of the others? Did they too have secrets? Jim was a definite puzzle. He was no retired civil servant. His skill sets, unusual knowledge, and general demeanour were not those of an ordinary pen pusher! My thoughts wandered around and around, as I gazed into the fire. The insistent meowing and pushing of Cleo's head against my hand, pulled me back into reality.

It was time for Cleo's nightly bedtime ritual. The Cornish night air was crisp with frost, and its clarity and purity took my breath away. Cleo sniffed around the lawn and fence. She ignored the pile of rubbish from the refurbishment, awaiting collection. Then she dashed in for her treat before bed.

"You shouldn't be on my bed!" I scolded her. We both knew I didn't mean it. Her loud purring followed the nightly kneading of the blanket. I drifted off to sleep with her warm body beside me.

My phone shrilled into life at two in the morning. Startled, I jumped up and grabbed the phone, still half asleep. "Hello?"

"Hi Mum, hi Daisy," Jake and Lisa's excited voices came down the line. "We've only got a minute. So bloody expensive! Just to say we're fine. Prospecting for another month. You never know, we may find gold yet! Then we'll head home. Keep your emails coming. That place sounds cool. Love you!"

Both voices chanted love you again, and it was suddenly silent. Now wide awake, I turned and hugged Cleo in my delight. Squirming away indignantly, she glared at me. Then, she licked her fur loudly and thoroughly, to cleanse it from my touch! There was no chance of falling asleep again. I was wide awake. I slipped my feet into my slippers and put on my dressing gown. A mug of tea I thought would be the answer. Perhaps the wood burner was still glowing in the lounge. I'll celebrate Jake's phone call with a mug of tea, and one of Maggie's wonderful chocolate chip cookies. Maggie had won all our hearts with her baking. Her chunky chocolate chip cookies were fantastic. One mouthful of chunky chocolate melting into deliciousness on your tongue, accompanied by the crispest biscuit crumb was utter bliss!

Smiling still after Jake's phone call, I opened the kitchen door and switched on the light. At the window a face, clad in a balaclava stared in at me!

CHAPTER THIRTEEN

Startled by the sudden glare of the light, he whirled around to escape. Boxes, old packaging, and assorted debris from the refurbishment of the cottage, lay at one side of the garden awaiting removal. He lost his footing and fell over it. My screams, his yells, the crashing of old metal windows, and splintering glass erupted into the stillness of the night. I saw him flounder about, trying to regain his footing. Suddenly, I lost my temper. Grabbing the pile of cutlery in the sink drainer, I flung open the door. "Take that! How dare you creep about my garden! Take that!" Spoons, forks, and knives, and even my heavy-duty tin opener bought especially for Cleo's cat food, flew at him. As I shouted at him, he shielded his face from my missiles, and scrambled to his feet. All the cutlery had gone. Reaching back into the kitchen, I grabbed an aerosol from the kitchen counter. Pointing it like a gun I squirted wildly at his face. "Take that, and that!" Spluttering and limping he fled out of the gate. A few minutes later, Martin and Jim, aroused by all the noise, appeared at my gate. "That way. He went that way!" I shouted at them.

Whirling around I ran to the front door. My doorbell was ringing non-stop.

Maggie rushed in, Sheila behind her. Sheila wore her Star Wars dressing gown, and her pink rollers were wildly askew. "We heard all the noise, what's happening?"

"It was a man in a balaclava at my kitchen window," I explained.

"What?" Maggie pointed to the aerosol which I still clutched tightly.

"I sprayed him with it!" I explained.

"You sprayed the burglar with furniture polish? That should help the police identify him," Maggie said. An unladylike snort accompanied her grin.

Jim and Martin came in the back door. "Got away," said Martin. "We couldn't keep up with him, he had too much of a head start." Martin collapsed in a chair at the kitchen table. His checked woollen dressing gown was tightly tied around his waist. He was gasping for breath.

Jim, was still neatly dressed, and wasn't even breathing heavily. Despite my scare, I wondered at the man. It was two in the morning! When did he ever sleep? If ever? Perhaps he was a vampire?

Maggie made a pot of tea. It took a considerable length of time to pour it out. We had to retrieve my cutlery, wash, and dry it. Some we left where it had fallen, down behind the rubbish pile.

"I hope this hit him?" Jim held up the heavy tin opener. His normally solemn face creased into a broad smile.

"It did." Triumphantly I grinned round at them. "I know he gave a yell when I threw it."

Maggie pushed me into a chair, I was shivering from the shock, not the cold.

"What the hell does he want?" Martin asked, as we drank the hot tea and munched on Maggie's chocolate cookies.

Hugo had joined us by this time. "He's looking for something. What is it? Why did he try each cottage?" he said.

Jim, rose to his feet, and inspected my back door. "He was trying to open your door when you surprised him. Not very successfully, he's obviously a novice at this."

As he sat back down, I stared at him. I thought to myself, not like you Jim. You are our resident expert on breaking and entering, thinking of the tiny leather kit he always carried.

"Should we call the police?" asked Sheila.

"He's long gone, they won't thank us for calling them out. In fact, I doubt they'll come. Let them know in the morning," Jim said.

Sheila and Maggie were escorted back to their apartments in the Priory by Hugo.

"I'll check your back garden, and secure your back door before I go," Jim said. Martin, with a wave, drifted sleepily back to his cottage.

Re-entering my kitchen, Jim locked the door, securing bolts. "What do you really think about all this?" he asked me, leaning against the kitchen counter.

"What do you mean?" I replied, wondering where this was going.

He studied my face intently. "Come on. The others just accept everything at face value. Not you, I've seen the expressions on your face!"

As I began to protest, he waved me to silence. "Can I sit down? Can we talk properly? Without Sheila and her detective scenarios, and nervous Martin listening in fear."

I stared at him. He was worried, really worried. The calm stolid exterior he habitually wore had gone. This was a puzzled man who stared at me. I felt certain that I saw a flicker of fear at the back of his eyes.

"Okay," I said and walked over to the cupboard. "Wine or whisky?" I gestured to the bottles.

"Whisky please," his eyes lit up as he watched me pour it into the glass. "That's an exceptionally good whisky," he commented, surprise in his voice.

"I keep it in for Jake, my son. He's very fussy about his whisky." Turning, I put the kettle on for my usual mug of tea.

"So, what's this all about?" I sat down opposite him in the lounge area, each of us on chairs either side of the log burner. I cradled the hot mug of tea in my hands, relishing its warmth. He had thrown another log in the log burner, and the room had grown warmer. The threatening atmosphere had gone. Was it because of his presence? Or had the danger gone?

"I'm researching the history of the Knights Templars, specifically in this area. My previous house and garden became too big for me to cope with. My wife had died some years ago, and I felt ready for a new start. Developers were moving in around me, and the traffic had grown unbearable." Here, he swirled the last of his drink around, before draining his glass with an appreciative sigh.

Without a word, I went out to the kitchen and brought the whisky bottle in. I put it down on the table in front of him. He reached for it, and almost unconsciously refilled his glass.

"I discovered that a line of Templars who settled here in secret, have continued to this day. It's a secretive group of families who guard their heritage and lineage closely. Just like in the da Vinci code!" Jim gave a dry mirthless laugh. At my gasp of astonishment, he continued. "I know it's fantastic and unbelievable. About three weeks ago, I was sent an anonymous letter warning me off my researches. I could study the general history in the area. I was not to search out particular family histories."

"That's who you think…" My voice tailed off. I put down my mug of tea and just stared at him.

"Someone is trying to find out where I live, and what information I actually have. I doubt this has got anything to do with Arabella's death."

"How can this information harm anyone? Dan Brown's sacred bloodline was a fantasy surely?" I asked.

Jim shook his head. "There's no reason for anyone to fear my research. I have links to ordinary Knights Templars, who settled in this area. No royalty, no holy links at all. What do they fear?"

Silence fell between us. A companionable silence which was very pleasant. Before I could stop myself, I blurted out the thought that had been uppermost in my mind since my arrival. "Do you think Hugo did it? Did he kill Arabella?"

Jim looked hard at me. Grey eyes searched my face, and finally he nodded.

"Good for you! I thought you were sharp under that ditzy act. You are wise not to take anything we say as truth. After all, we are complete strangers. I do think Hugo is innocent. He was besotted with her, although I think he was losing those rose-tinted glasses slowly, but surely." Jim held up his glass, he stared at the flames from the logs through its crystal edges. "I've been here nearly three months. I love it here. I've never felt such a sense of belonging in a place before. Hugo was, and still is a charming host. He's only hoping to try and make it pay for itself. Arabella was money orientated, and ambitious for status and wealth. Hugo could have killed her. He had opportunity and motive. However, I'm certain that he did not."

Nodding thoughtfully, I stared into the flames. The silence grew again. Finally stirring, Jim put down his glass. "We've all come here from our very different lives. What are our past experiences? Who knows what secrets we all have?"

As I looked at him, those words struck home. I opened my mouth. Then I shut it firmly.

Jim laughed, a deep full laugh. "Yes, I have secrets. Daisy, you have stared at me so often, with that self-same expression on your face! Yes, I'm unwilling to talk about my past."

Holding up his glass, this time, he drained the last of the whisky. "You my dear Daisy, so ditzy, so careless and open faced, are adept at hiding your secrets."

I felt my back and shoulders tense up, as I waited for his next words.

Jim rose to his feet and walked to the front door. "There is a reason you are here." He raised a hand as I began to speak. "I've seen you look around. I've seen you watch Demelza. This place has a fascination for you. Something has brought you here. I do wonder Daisy, what secret you are hiding from us all?"

I was speechless. That does not happen very often! I stood silently, trying to gather my thoughts together. Any thoughts! I had to say something!

Jim laughed, not an unpleasant sneering laugh. It was a sympathetic chuckle. He reached for the door handle. "Daisy, I like you, I reckon we can be friends. I'll keep my secrets, and you keep yours. Agreed?" he held out his hand to me.   Shaking a little, for he had jolted my usual calm, I walked towards him and put my hand into his. We shook solemnly. Somehow, I felt I was sealing a pact. Had I shaken hands with the devil?

CHAPTER FOURTEEN

"Hi Gerald," I shouted and waved at the stocky figure plodding across the field. A wave and a muffled shout were my only reply. I stood at my gate, the morning after my tussle with the balaclava man, and gazed around. Morning sunlight shone across the fields, and up across the moorland. Cleo pottered around the garden, investigating each night-time smell left behind by visiting creatures. Breathing in the fresh air, I marvelled at my good fortune to live in such a wonderful spot.

Each morning, Gerald passed me at this time along the lane, behind the cottages. I usually got a word. Actually, a lot of words from him. He explained to me, in-depth, his latest research into the history of the tin miners, and the ancient and prehistoric inhabitants of Bodmin Moor. "Temple Moor, that's what it used to be called. Called after the Knights Templars, they owned all the land roundabout here at one time. I'm investigating the stones around the spring and stream, down across the fields and valley. Can't do any proper archaeology, it's not allowed. I draw present-day maps, and check them against ancient maps." He indicated the maps and folders in his rucksack.

"He's harmless, he potters about, just a bit boring when he chats on about his research," Martin had told me. Martin went for his walk at the same time Cleo and I came out to the garden. Gerald usually timed his walk to greet us, and chat.

"What's up with Gerald this morning? No usual chat?" Martin had arrived at my gate. He stopped, and stared after Gerald.

"No, I only got a wave and a grunt," I replied frowning.

"He's limping. Why is he wearing a hat? He told me

he hates hats," Martin said.

Cleo's meows grew louder, and she wove in and out of my ankles.

"Madam wants her breakfast," Martin said, looking down at Cleo with a smile. He gave a last puzzled glance at the portly figure of Gerald across the fields, and strode off.

After feeding Cleo, I played with her until she got bored with my antics. She curled up in her basket. Cleo gazed at me through one half closed eye, watching as I got ready to go for my breakfast at the Priory. I knew it. She knew I knew it. The moment I closed the front door, she would make tracks for my bed! I should have closed the bedroom door, but I couldn't!

As I walked across the courtyard, I thought about exercise. Damp, moorland walks held no appeal. Should I try and go to a gym somewhere. Who was I kidding? Much too long a drive across the moor. That would be my excuse. I knew the real reason, my lumpy figure was never, ever going to be displayed in Lycra.

Sitting back in my chair, after breakfast, I sighed. My plate was absolutely clear. If it hadn't been bad manners, I think I'd have licked the plate. "This wonderful cooking, is putting weight on me. I need to exercise, urgently! I should eat muesli every single morning."

Martin, Jim, Sheila, all stared down at their empty plates. There were nods of agreement.

"There was a plan for a gym to be built," said Hugo. Despite eating far more than each one of us, he never put on any weight. "Funds are no longer available for that scheme. We could put some exercise equipment in the old back kitchen. Would that work?"

"That's a great idea," said Martin.

"I'd definitely use it," agreed Jim.

Perhaps I could cope with that. I didn't have to wear Lycra in the back kitchen, did I?

"We'll look out what basic stuff we need, and order it. The kitchen could do with a fresh coat of paint, but otherwise..." said Hugo.

"My Tom will help out there," said Demelza. "He's home for a while, waiting to start his next degree. He'll be glad of a little extra money." Her pride in her son was evident. No wonder, he was about to become a doctor in some exotic plant science. "He won't charge much," she added, staring at Hugo.

"He'll get paid the going rate. There are enough funds to get all the equipment we need, and to pay Tom," Hugo reassured Demelza.

"Well, what's your programme for today?" Hugo asked.

"It's the hairdressers for me, where Arabella worked." I said.

"Stonebridge for me. I'll pick up my library books that I ordered for my research. Then I'll meet Daisy in the village pub. Does anyone want anything from Stonebridge whilst I'm in there?" Jim asked.

"The Art shop has my Daniel Smith watercolour paints in for collection. Can you pick them up for me? They are already paid for?" I asked him.

Martin and Sheila smiled conspiratorially at each other. "We're going house hunting. You too have been already, but it's worth us going to see what we can find out." Sheila bounced excitedly on her chair, white fluffy curls jumping about her head, "I can't wait! The agents won't know that their Penny is dead. After all they didn't know it was a false name."

"I'm very grateful to you all. I should be doing

something to clear my name. But what can I do?" Hugo lifted both hands in a gesture of despair, and slumped back into his chair.

"Hugo, I've been thinking about that," began Jim. Leaning forward he gazed earnestly at the young man. "If it's not too painful, why don't you write a timeline out? Add any detail that may help build up a character profile of Arabella. Start from the moment you first met, and how you met."

Silence fell in the kitchen. All eyes were turned towards Hugo. Staring down at his hands, he gave a deep sigh, and then obviously came to a decision. "Yes, I can see that may well be of some value. I'll start immediately."

"Bring your papers into the kitchen, where either Demelza or Maggie can be with you." At our puzzled expressions, Jim continued. "I think it best Hugo has an alibi at all times. I'm worried that this murder business is not finished with. If he has someone with him...." His voice trailed away.

Colour drained from Maggie's face as she took in the full importance of Jim's words. "I'll make certain he's with me, even if he has to follow me, and the vacuum cleaner." The determination in her voice made us all laugh. Hugo gave her a grateful smile.

As I drove to the village, I passed Wishing Well Cottage. What would Sheila and Martin find out, I wondered. Poor Jasper, he was having an exasperating few days.

I realised that it was the owner's day off at the hairdressers. There were only two other customers beside myself, and one left soon after my arrival. A middle-aged lady was having an improbably blonde hairstyle refreshed in tin foil. A young girl shampooed my hair, whilst two other stylists gossiped with each other. After my shampoo, I waited for my stylist. As I sat drinking the lukewarm coffee, I listened to their chatter. Then Cindy joined me, "I've looked over the cottage for sale across the road," I said, waiting for some reaction. Silence. One woman looked at the other, and then both shrugged. The woman with a head full of tin foil, opened her mouth and forgot to close it. "It's not for me, it's for my niece who is thinking of moving here. She asked me to look over that one, and Willow cottage up the road."

"Best get Willow cottage for her," said tin foil lady.

"Yes, tell her to buy that one," the stylist agreed.

"Why?" I asked. The plain bold question startled them. Again, meaningful glances were exchanged. Cindy, her badge on the icky pink nylon overall, proclaiming her as the head stylist, paused thoughtfully as she combed through my hair.

"The owner of Wishing Well cottage, Penny, worked here," she said.

"Did she? Why did she leave such a lovely cottage and her job in here?" I asked.

"Well, to be truthful…" Cindy began.

"Might as well be, everyone else in the village will tell her if we don't." Tin foil lady turned in a chair towards me. "She was a cow. A selfish, arrogant cow and I'm glad she moved away. David, from outside Bodmin town, won £100,000 on the lottery or premium bonds, something like that. She got her claws into him, and using that and his life savings bought Wishing Well cottage. He disappeared, and she put the cottage up for sale. Said she was going to live in France."

"Strange though, his twin sister came here. Created a great row, stormed through the village asking everyone if they'd seen her brother," said the other stylist, turning back towards her customer.

Leaning closer to me, Cindy lowered her voice. "The sister, accused Penny of taking her brothers money and killing him. She asked if we'd heard gunshots or shouting. She even got the police down here, and asked them to investigate his sudden disappearance. His credit cards hadn't been used, nor his phone, there was no sign of him at all."

"Did they find him?" I was breathless, holding my breath in excitement at this tale. A sudden whoosh as I finally let it out, startled us all.

"No, said he could have gone off anywhere with his cash. Stupid fat policeman said he'd have gone off like a shot if he'd won it."

"Has anyone ever seen or heard from him again?" I asked.

"No, not a sign anywhere. That's sister of his swore she'd get even with Penny. Said she was certain Penny had murdered her brother, and that she'd murder her!"

Gossip about other villagers swirled about me. I didn't hear one word of it. Looking at my watch, I realised it was only thirty minutes before Sheila and Martin viewed Wishing Well cottage. On an impulse I reached for my phone. I texted Sheila. 'Last wealthy boyfriend of A. vanished. Check out the strange new rockery in the middle of the garden when you view!'

Cindy had taken considerable care and the style looked great. Just a few purple streaks. "Thank you, I'll be back in a few weeks. I love it."

I walked along the tiny High Street towards the pub. The village stores carried everyday basics and looked well patronised. A small shop, held vintage and unusual bric-a-brac items. A city refugee, I thought, seeking a new life in the country. Staring in the window, I realised this must have been where Arabella shopped. There was even an identical bread bin. I wondered if they distressed them all deliberately. As I walked on towards the pub, a taxi drew up outside. A man got out, and turned to pay his fare. His hair was dishevelled, his trousers were muddy at the knees, and he was flushed with anger. He raised a hand towards me in recognition.

"Jim! What the hell has happened to you?" I gasped.

CHAPTER FIFTEEN

"Not here, let's get inside Daisy." Jim gestured to the pub. I walked into the lounge bar, my mind whirling. "Over there, it's quiet in the corner," Jim said. He walked over to a table in a small alcove. It was early, and we were the only ones in the pub. At this table, we had our backs to the wall, and could see every entrance into the room. I thought, Jim is ready... for what? "I'll get drinks, and the menu," Jim said. He went up to the bar, interrupting the landlord's study of his newspaper. Jim came back, put down a double whisky on the table, and a mineral water in front of me. Hands in my lap, I waited for him to finally feel able to talk. Suddenly, that wonderful rarely seen smile flashed over his craggy face. He pushed back the white hair from his brow. "Thanks Daisy," he said.

"What for?" I asked, puzzled.

"Not badgering me with endless questions. For waiting, until I was able to talk. You are a rare woman indeed, Daisy Dunwoody."

At this unexpected praise, I flushed. For goodness sake Daisy, I chided myself. This is ridiculous! Blushing like a teenager at a kind remark. At your advanced age!

Reaching into the shopping basket he had put on a vacant chair, Jim fished out a small parcel. "Your paints."

"Thanks," I said, putting them unopened on the table beside me. Hurry up and tell me what's happened, I wanted to shout at him. But wonderful woman that I was, I remained silent.

He took a large gulp, and swallowed the whisky. It was unusual for Jim to drink whisky in the morning. It was especially early for double whisky. It wasn't yet midday. Again, he pushed back his hair. Taking a deep breath, he looked up at me and began his story. "My library books had gone. I went to the desk. They had come in, and been wrapped in white paper. My name was written on them. The librarian put them on the bookcase with the other reserved books. They'd gone, they'd been stolen!" At my surprise and exclamations, he nodded, and picked up his glass. He took a sip, then another huge gulp. "I got to the car park, and discovered I had two flat tyres. Each tyre had a nail driven into them. That's when I got the muddy knees. The garage towed my car away, and I got a taxi here."

"It was deliberate, the attack on your tyres?" I asked him.

"The mechanic from the garage, said that it was no accident. Both nails had been deliberately driven into the tyres."

"The attack on your tyres, your books being stolen, all point to our burglar friend," I suggested. "Should you tell the police?"

"I doubt they'd bother, or want to hear it. We'll keep a log of all these incidents. Then we'll have it ready if we need to tell the police," Jim replied.

"What's he after? Does he want you to stop your research? Or is he a demented Knights Templar fanatic?" I said.

Jim shook his head, "I don't know, it beats me."

The pub was filling up. The food looked good. I stared around at the other tables, trying to decide what I'd eat.

"Thought we'd join you!" the voice came from the entrance door. Sheila and Martin came in. They were both as muddy as Jim.

"What have you two been up to?" Jim asked. His eyes rested suspiciously on Sheila's gleeful face, and muddy trousers.

I wasn't muddy. I sat with my new hairdo, smart

clothes, and felt decidedly out of it!

We'd ordered the home-made Cornish pasties, with salad of course. Somehow, we'd all forgotten they came with chips. That's what we all said. But we knew we were lying.

"Jasper took us round Wishing Well Cottage," Sheila began, waving a chip around in her excitement. "I'd just got your text about the rockery. We looked from the upstairs window, and saw exactly what you meant. Looked like an ancient burial mound in the middle of the lawn. Jasper said there had been a pond there when he sold it to Arabella."

Sheila took a large swallow of her artisan vodka. It was her latest craze. She loved keeping up with the latest trends. Her eyes crossed, and she choked. "When I went out there, I thought I'd have a closer look at it," she finally got out between splutters.

Martin took over the tale. "Sheila pretended to trip beside the rockery, and dislodged some stones. Quite a few stones. We made a mess digging further holes, to see what was underneath the rocks," Martin shuddered. Poor Martin, his fastidious personality was being thrust out of its comfort zone with our investigations.

"Did you find anything?" I asked, leaning forward in my eagerness.

"Well," Sheila said, and looked at Martin. Martin nodded at her, and both seemed unwilling to continue. "When we looked at the biggest stone, I dug further down. I made a bigger hole and I..." For once, Sheila had come to a speechless halt.

"I knelt down to help her. We both smelt something foul coming up from under that loose earth," Martin said.

My fork stopped midway to my mouth, chip dangling. I slumped back in my chair, and stared at them.

"You both smelt it?" Jim asked. "Did Jasper?"

91

"No," said Martin. "He was the other side of the garden, answering his phone. That's when we took the opportunity to dig under all those rocks."

"He was taken aback when we asked to wash our hands. He obviously thought we were two daft oldies," laughed Sheila.

Jim drained his whisky. He set the glass down on the table with a thump. "I'm going to dig up that rockery tonight. Luckily, we're having a mild spell of weather, and there will be no frost. Anyone else want to come?" He raised his hand, to stop us all speaking at once. "I don't know what law we'll be breaking. We'd definitely would be in trouble if we get caught. So, no worries, if you don't fancy it."

"Count me in!" I cried.

"And me!" cried Sheila, jumping up and down in her chair in excitement.

We were ready for action. The grandfather clock in the Priory Hall struck midnight. It was time to go. I tried not to think how ominous it sounded. Earlier, we had met in the Priory kitchen for a light supper. Maggie had produced an omelette and salad, with fresh fruit to finish. "Last thing we need, is a heavy meal," she said as we sat at the huge oak table.

I ate sparingly. Naturally law-abiding, and conscientious, I was nervous. I looked across the table towards Martin. His meal was not being eaten either. The omelette was in bits, and being pushed around the plate.

"There is no law involved, except perhaps trespass," said Jim. "Don't worry, we'll be in and out of that garden in no time," Jim pushed his plate away from him. I noticed he had no bother in clearing his plate.

"Martin will keep watch. Crouch down in the car and keep your balaclava on. Then your face won't shine white

92

in the moonlight," said Jim. Earlier that day he had produced four balaclavas. Not one of us had commented. I don't think we knew what to ask, or what to say. Martin nodded. I thought his relief at not having to enter the garden, was blatantly obvious.

Jim spoke again, "Maggie and Daisy are with me. Spades, a large heavy-duty polythene sheet, and gardening gloves. We'll wrap everything up in a blanket. Don't want insomniac nosy neighbours hearing clattering tools. Any questions?"

"What do we do if we find…" Maggie paused, unable or unwilling to put into words, what we were all thinking.

"If we find something, a body perhaps," Jim paused, and looked around the table. Leaning forward he said solemnly. "We get the hell out of there! We want no further involvement with Inspector Tenby!"

Nods around the table in agreement, greeted this pronouncement.

Chairs were pushed back, and we made our way out to the courtyard. Gloves, flashlights, blanket wrapped spades, and a waterproof sheet were placed in the boot. All dressed in black, we were ready for the adventure ahead. Jim, stared at my sweatshirt in horror. "My wardrobe for grave robbing is limited!" I snapped at him. My new brighter jazzy image meant that I had no longer anything sombre. "It's black! All the sequins are black!" Jim sighed and shook his head. I stomped over to the car door, pointedly ignoring Maggie's grin.

Sheila's knees were playing up. Her rock shifting whilst cottage viewing, had caused them to swell. "I wish I was going with you," she muttered.

"So, do I," said Hugo, standing beside her. "I don't think you should be doing this, any of you." He looked anxiously at us all. Then he gave a great big sigh, "I'm worried. I don't like the idea of you getting into trouble because of me."

"We're going," Maggie glared at Hugo. Her arms were on her hips, and she took up a defiant stance as she turned and faced him. Her vehemence caused him to stare at her, as if seeing her for the first time.

That long solemn face of his, cracked into an extra wide grin. "Thank you, thank you all."

"All phones on vibrate only," said Jim. "Okay, let's go."

Sheila rushed, or hobbled speedily, up to the SUV, Jim wound the window down. "Hot soup and bacon rolls when you get back," she promised.

The journey to Wishing Well Cottage, seemed long and tortuous. Darkness gave the lanes, trees, and stone banks a menacing quality. Cheerful cottages in daylight, now loomed menacingly at the roadside. Nervous, excited, and unused to criminal activity, we were all deep in our own thoughts.

"Drop us off with the gear outside the cottage, Martin. Then, you turn and park up the hill. Text us, if you see or hear anything suspicious. We'll text you when we need picking up."

Martin sighed in relief. Being so nervous, we all knew he'd have been of little use in the garden. This way he played a vital role, but out of the action.

The side gate was unlocked. Careless Jasper, I thought. Jim had no need for his little wallet of tools. It was a cold night, but thankfully no frost. The moon shone in fitful bursts, through the cloud cover. We trod carefully, trying to be quiet. It was late, but there could be some restless sleeper awake in the village. The lawn was damp. Our footprints left tracks across the grass. I shrugged. Nothing could be done about it. Perhaps the early morning sun would burn them off. The mound sat halfway down the lawn. Rocks and shrubby plants, sat on and around it. Two ugly frog ornaments, large and incongruous, sat on top of it. I'll swear they glared at us as if they knew what we had come for. They were daring us to disturb them.

"Okay," Jim put down the blanketed tools, and handed them out. "Sheila said she disturbed the soil at the back of the mound, near to the neighbour's fence." Jim walked around the rockery. His pencil light flickered over it. "Here it is, we'll start to dig here."

Maggie spread out the large polythene sheet, ready for the rocks and soil we'd clear from the mound. "I only hope we can replace it, so that it looks undisturbed," she said.

Jim began digging out soil onto the sheet. Maggie and I moved the rocks Sheila had pulled out earlier, and placed them on the sheet. As we disturbed the soil, a foul stench seemed to waft into the air. "That's the smell Sheila and Martin told us about," Maggie whispered.

Jim moved beside her, and sniffed. "It's that old-fashioned fertiliser of blood and bone. It's still used in some country gardens. That's no dead body smell," he said.

I stared at him. He knows about decomposing bodies; I'll think about that later. That 'later' list was getting longer.

We lifted more rocks, and dug out more soil. A grating sound came from beneath Jim's spade. "That's solid," he bent forward and scraped away some more soil. "It's the old concrete liner from the pond. There's no chance that anybody could be buried here."

It had been an utter waste of time. How stupid of us, thinking that we would be so clever, and find the missing

David. As if we could beat the police, and at our age. Those dreadful words came unbidden to my mind, and I began to help clear up the mess we'd made.

A sudden thump on top of the fence startled me. A squeak escaped me. I swallowed hard, closing my mouth shut before I made any more noise. I dropped my spade. A scratchy thing hit my head, knocking my hat over one eye. The furry body jumped down at my feet, and then strolled up to the top of a frog. The cat sat on it, and stared at us, before washing its face. Frantically, I tried to keep my balance. I was standing half in and half out of a hole, left by the removal of a rock. I flailed my arms about and took a step back, arms still waving in the air, and tripped over my spade. I crashed onto some plants, squashing them flat as they cushioned my fall. I flung out my hand, and felt it crash through ancient wood. Then came a loud splintering sound.

A light illuminated next door's garden. "Pussycat? Is that you making that noise? Come on in now. It's getting cold. Come on pussycat, bedtime."

The voice came nearer to the fence. I froze. I was still lying amongst the shrubby plants. My hand was stuck into some wooden thing. Any movement I made, could alert the neighbour to my presence. I didn't dare move a muscle. I was scared even to breathe. The moon came from behind a cloud. We were motionless silhouettes. Maggie was hunched over the soil, a rock still in one hand. Jim stood, his spade poised in the air. In the midst of this tableau, the cat sat, licking his paws. He was completely unconcerned at the consternation he'd caused. Jim moved. In a flash, he'd scooped up the cat, thrust it onto the fence, and gave it a slight push.

"There you are pussycat! Come here. Time for your night-time treat." Relief in the neighbour's voice was evident. We heard her carry the cat into the house, close the door, and lock it. She then turned off the light.

Her relief was nothing compared to ours.

"Please, I'm stuck. Can you help me out? I'm frightened to move. My hand has gone through some splintering thing," I whispered.

Jim rushed to my side. Putting his hands under my shoulders, he hauled me to my feet. I staggered back, clutching my hand and arm. Jim knelt down. He pushed the plants aside. "It's wood. I think it's the old well cover. It's almost rotten, and your hand went through the edge of it. Daisy, have you got any splinters?"

"No, thank goodness. I'd put on my heavy-duty gardening gloves. They've protected my hand," I replied.

Maggie joined us. We both looked down, as Jim continued to clear away the plants. "Is it the wishing well? Is this what the cottage is named after? Why so near the fence?" Maggie whispered.

"The cat lives in a brand-new bungalow. It's been built on the garden, previously owned by the cottage," Jim replied absentmindedly. He pushed aside everything with the spade.

Maggie and I directed our flashlights upon the broken wood. Jim used the spade as a lever. There came a loud splintering sound. The wooden cover broke, and jerked upwards. Then came the overpowering stench!

CHAPTER SIXTEEN

The wooden cover had split apart. The part which had trapped my hand, fell at my feet. The other part, slid across the squashed plants. It came to rest against the fence. I stood shaking, rubbing my hand and arm. Jim stepped forward. Maggie and I, about to follow him, halted. Immediately our hands went to our noses. We hurriedly retraced our steps. The smell was appalling. It took a tremendous effort not to cough and gag. Maggie, rushed to the other side of the garden. Now, I understood Jim's casual dismissal of the fertiliser smell. This was a hundred times worse, and this stench could never, ever, be forgotten. With a glance back towards me, Jim walked to the edge of the well. He played his flashlight round it. "Can you point your light down there?" Putting a handkerchief over my nose, I walked over and stood beside him. My torch also played round the broken splinters of the cover, and brick ledge around the well. "Stay there, keep pointing your flashlight down the well," Jim said. I stayed where I was. I didn't want to see what was down there. I knew it was awful, horrific, and that was all I needed to know! Jim knelt and placed one hand on the bricks. Holding it high, he played his torch around the bottom of the well. I saw him stiffen. After a moment he rose to his feet, shaking his head.

"Yes, someone down there. I'd hoped it was a fox or similar animal, but it's definitely human. We've got to get out of here. Let's pack everything up ASAP! Check, and double check that we've left nothing that could link us with this crime."

"What about the soil and rocks? Do we try and get it all back in place?" Maggie asked, coming across the garden to join us.

"No, get the tools, and that sheet. There's no sense in hiding the fact that someone's been here," Jim said.

Horror and fear of discovery, all helped to speed our exit from that garden. Jim walked around again and again, checking we'd left nothing. We reached the gate. Maggie had texted Martin to come and pick us up. It was a solemn group that climbed into the car. Maggie whispered the news to Martin, as Jim and I piled our gear into the boot.

"We'll make an anonymous phone call to tell them about the body. We can't be involved with this murder as well as Arabella's!" Jim said.

We found a phone box. Jim made the call, with gloved hands. Maggie and I sat saying nothing. I think we were in shock. It had all sounded fun, somehow unreal, looking for a body. Finding it, had been unexpected and horrifying. Martin, stared from one of us to the other, muttering under his breath, and shaking his head.

Jim got in the car. We'd decided to tell the others when we got back to the Priory. It was too difficult to explain over a phone.

Jim was about to drive. Suddenly, all our phones sounded an incoming text.

"Tenby is here! You've been stargazing, and investigating druid rituals near Minions." That was the same message we all received.

"Oh hell! That's all we need!" Jim said.

We turned into the lane that led up to the Priory. Jim stopped the car. Grabbing our digging gear, we passed it down to Jim. He stuffed it into a culvert in the ditch. Carefully, he pushed back the foliage hiding the culvert. "We'll retrieve it later," he said.

The drive up the lane was at a deliberately slow speed.

Maggie, jolted by the rutted surface, still managed to reel off facts from her phone. "The village wasn't called Minions before the eighteenth century. It was known as Cheesewring village. Rich in prehistoric remains, the surrounding area has an ancient stone cross nearby, the Longstone," Maggie said, scrolling through the information on her phone. "We'll say we went up to Rillaton Barrow. It's a Bronze Age burial mound. A gold cup was discovered there in an archaeological dig. They rebuilt the chamber where it was found in the early 1900s. Phosphorescent moss can be seen growing on the walls."

"Would we see that in the dark?" asked Martin.

Ignoring his remark, Maggie persevered with our factual tuition. "An old druid spirit is said to haunt the area holding the gold cup out to strangers passing by. When they drink from it, it refills itself automatically. Someone actually saw the ghostly monk last month!"

Jim groaned. "This is the last type of romantic twaddle I want my name linked with."

"If you drink from the cup, it refills itself magically!" Maggie continued.

"That's what I need," the two men chorused together.

"A cup that fills itself with wine, again and again. That would be fantastic!" said Martin.

Despite the horrific find at the cottage, and the dread of what Tenby might have in store for us, we all laughed. We strolled into the library still smiling. Nervously maybe, shocked even, but we didn't appear to be. Jim's eyes gleamed with satisfaction as he glanced approvingly at us. Hugo and Sheila sat beside each other on the sofa. They looked nervous and very worried. The large bulk of Inspector Tenby had been squeezed into an armchair. He stared at us under bushy eyebrows. A large man, fleshy and big boned, as my mum would have said. The eyebrows, and a cheerful jowly face gave the impression of an off-duty Father Christmas. I wasn't fooled by his jolly exterior. The eyes that regarded us were hard and cold. They had all the warmth of a shark, and that same intensity of focus. When they lit upon me, I fought hard not to feel guilty or frightened. I stared back, willing my features into a polite disinterested look. I hoped my colour remained unchanged.

"Stargazing, on such a gloomy night?" was his opening remark.

"We thought it might clear up, my weather app said it would," Maggie waved her phone at him.

Maggie was good. That had been a great reply, off the top of her head.

"Tonight, Gerald Stubbs was attacked by an intruder in his cottage. Did any of you go near his cottage tonight?" Tenby looked from one to the other with a piercing intense stare.

"Gerald?" I queried, looking at the others.

"That funny man, who walks past the cottages each morning," Maggie replied.

"I don't know where he lives," I said.

"Nor do I," said Sheila and Martin together.

"I know he lives up St. Breward way, but I don't know where. I wouldn't want to. He's a peculiar, boring little man," added Jim.

"He thinks you were one of the intruders. Mr Stubbs says that you are trying to steal his research," Inspector Tenby told Jim. "You and Mr Stubbs research the same Knights Templars stuff, I believe." Those eyes, now sharper than ever seemed to bore into the older man.

Jim stiffened. Anger suffused his face, and his voice crackled with it. "We do not! No way, does my research include rubbishy pseudo-archaeological clap trap. My academic research, is based on facts, primary source material…"

Tenby raised a hand to cut Jim off in indignant mid-flow. "Yet, you venture out on a cold winter's night to put in some research into…"

I interrupted. Jim was getting angrier by the moment. This was the time for Ditsy Daisy to step in. "Tonight, was my idea. I heard that the monk with the gold cup had been seen haunting up at Rillaton. My hairdresser told me that I must go and see Minions, and the Cheesewring at night. Spooky, eerie and sooo very exciting. Maggie wanted to come with me."

"Yes, I thought it would be fun. The guys, Jim and Martin came with us. They came to check we didn't get carried off by the ghostly monk, or fall down a mine shaft," Maggie chipped in.

Jim sank back in his chair, flickers of amusement in his eyes. The anger seeped out from his body. I felt relief.

"Why did you, an inspector, follow-up a routine burglary? Why did you come to seek us out?" Hugo asked.

We all jumped. He'd been sitting silent on the sofa beside Sheila.

"Yes, it is unusual for an inspector to bother with such an insignificant matter," Jim added. There was an unusual sharpness in his tone of voice.

Inspector Tenby, settled further into his armchair. Then he looked down at his hands. They were broad with spatulate fingers. It was obvious that he was coming to some decision.

"Mrs Dunwoody, you had a burglar last night attempt entry to your cottage. Is that correct?" he asked me.

"Yes, I phoned the station this morning to report it," I answered him.

"Hmm, there have been other incidents, including a

fire." At our nods of agreement, Tenby continued. "I do not like coincidences, or random incidents. There was the one murder here in the Priory. Now we have this intruder business, and the fire. This burglary, at Gerald Stubbs place, I don't like it. Have we a murderer? A burglar? Or are they one and the same person?" He looked round at us all again. "That's why I'm here. You say you did not burgle Stubbs place tonight." Raising a hand, he quelled our indignant comments. "If you didn't burgle him, who did and why?"

Silence fell in the room. I think we were all surprised at this show of frankness. This was contrived, I thought. This man did nothing without a reason. What was he up to?

"I'd like a detailed account of your previous break-ins. Mrs Dunwoody, … and….

Inspector Tenby's phone rang. I saw Jim give a start, and he glanced at me and raised an eyebrow. I swallowed a grin at the inspector's ring tone. A complex man was our inspector. I'd had no doubt before, but now I was certain. What modern day inspector and policeman, had Dixon of Dock Green theme tune for his ring tone? My Gran, had loved the programme, and had watched all the videos again and again. Was this ring tone meant to be funny? "Yes, yes. On my way!" For such a large bulky man he rose to his feet with sudden lithe purpose. He strode to the door. "Gerald Stubbs was assaulted tonight in his own cottage, and an attempt made to steal his research!" He turned, and pointed his finger at Jim. "You are the only rival in this area, working in his field. I'll be back, to check out this Stubbs thing, and your alibis later!" He reached for the door handle and went out, closing it behind him with a sharp click.

"Who does he think he is? I'll be back! Thinks he's that tough guy from the film. I'll be back!" Sheila mimicked him. Rising shakily to her feet, she leant hard on the arm rests of her chair. "Come on! Soup and bacon rolls in the kitchen! Hugo and I are desperate to know what happened."

We all rose and followed her. Jim and I walked behind the others. Leaning towards me, he whispered, "this gets crazier by the minute. We need to talk. Okay by you if we chat later?"

I glanced at him and nodded.

The soup was piping hot, and home-made. Chicken and vegetable, it was delicious. After the chill of that garden, we needed the warmth and comfort it gave. Sheila, had a knack with bacon sandwiches. They were crispy on the outside, and absolutely scrummy inside with bacon and butter. We told the story of our discovery, over the bowls of soup. No one spoke whilst we ate the bacon sarnies! The cloistered kitchen, the shadows dark in pools behind the stone pillars gave an added eerie feel to our story.

"If only we knew what was happening at Wishing Well Cottage. Tenby's call must have been about the body," Martin said, as he reached for a glass of wine. "Certainly, he rushed off in a hurry, couldn't wait to get out the door."

"Let's go to the village pub for lunch tomorrow, we'll hear all the gossip then," Sheila said.

"That's a good idea. I can come as well." said Maggie.

"Great, if we hear nothing before midday, we meet up for a pub lunch!" Sheila clapped her hands, almost bouncing in delight on her chair.

The soup and the sandwiches were finished. We were all yawning. It was very late. Dishes were put in the dishwasher and the table was cleared. The kitchen was left in darkness.

The courtyard that evening, seemed menacing. Martin went into his cottage with a sleepy good night. I was glad of Jim's company to my door, and his abrupt, "I'll check all over your cottage."

I wasn't normally nervous. But in such a short time living at the Priory, I'd found two murdered dead bodies. I didn't want to be the third! I opened the kitchen cupboard door, took out two glasses and reached for the whisky bottle. Handing it and a glass to Jim, I poured sparkling water in the other and cut a slice of lemon. Dropping the slice into the fizzy water, I followed Jim into my lounge. He'd thrown another log on the burner.

"Do you think Gerald lied? To cover up his injuries from last night?" I asked Jim. I sat in my chair the other side of the log burner and watched him.

"Yes, I do. That tin opener that you threw must have left quite a mark. It'll be interesting to see if he chats tomorrow," replied Jim.

"What if it's not a fabrication? What if he was really attacked? We have to take that possibility into account." I said, watching my lemon slice bob up and down in the fizz.

Cleo had made herself comfortable on Jim's lap. Her anger at my staying out this late, had been made plain by her pointedly ignoring me.

"I wonder how we could find out for certain. We need to know," I said.

"Yes, there is an urgent need for clarification," Jim said. His long, elegant fingers were stroking Cleo, to her obvious delight. She was purring loudly.

The refreshing tang of the lemon slice was sharp after the greasy bacon sandwiches. Could I put my thoughts into words? Seeing Jim's questioning look, I knew that I had to try.

"If it's Gerald, I don't see him as a threat. He's more

of an irritation. Someone else investigating Templar research, or even the Templar treasure legend could be dangerous, possibly unbalanced."

"I've been thinking on those lines myself Daisy. There are fanatics out there. Some are fanatical about UFOs. And there are the others who've swallowed the da Vinci code whole."

Weariness seemed to sweep over us both. An overwhelming feeling of helplessness and impending... What? Saying doom, even to myself, was fanciful and melodramatic. However much I tried to rationalise it, and shake it off, that feeling crept into my very being. For a long moment, we both sat, in silence.

Then, Jim put down his empty glass and rose to his feet. "Good night Daisy. Perhaps everything will be clearer tomorrow. That was possibly David's body we found. We've had a successful start to our investigation."

I smiled weakly, and said good night to Jim. I locked my door. Turning, I leant back against the door. What was Jim going to talk to me about? He'd said very little. Whatever he was going to say, he'd changed his mind. Why? What had been so important? Successful start to our investigation he'd said.

"The start of what I wonder?" I said to Cleo. Once again, I was in favour. It was bedtime treat time. As I fed her, I stopped. I rushed back to the front door. Yes! I had locked it. I finally admitted it to myself. I was afraid. Afraid of someone out there. Someone, who wished us harm. This person, was able to murder at will, with impunity. Could he or she kill again? If so, who would be the next victim?

CHAPTER SEVENTEEN

Next morning when I walked into the Priory kitchen, Demelza was cooking breakfast. Jim and Martin who were always early risers were already in the kitchen. Sheila much preferred breakfast alone in her apartment, especially if she'd had a bad night.

Maggie joined us, swallowing a yawn. As she took her seat, her phone rang. "It's my cousin," she said. "She lives around the corner from Wishing Well Cottage, next door to the cat lady." The phone gave animated squawks and Maggie listened intently. She gave a nod, a murmured assent, laughed and then closed the phone. "An anonymous phone call told the police about a body in the well. My cousin says the lady heard the police arrive, and crept out into the garden to listen behind the fence.

"That's our cat lady!" whispered Jim to me.

"She must be exhausted; our cat lady had a busy night!" I said.

"There was a man with a big booming voice," Maggie said.

"Tenby!" Martin and Sheila cried out in unison.

Maggie continued, "she heard him say that the man had obviously been stabbed before being thrown down the well." Maggie's voice had dropped to the merest whisper, but it fell into the quiet and echoed around the room. That sudden silence in the room crackled with menace. Not fear, not yet, but there was no mistaking the uneasiness that gripped us all

I crunched my last piece of toast. "Are you all certain that Arabella killed this guy, possibly David? If she did it, how did she get him down the well? Was she strong enough? Could she have killed him?" I asked.

Maggie gave a hard, brittle laugh. "Oh yes, Arabella could have killed him. I always thought she was cruel. She even offered to ring a chicken's neck for me when it became too old to lay!" At Sheila's shriek of horror, Maggie laughed. "Don't worry Sheila. That's the old moth-eaten hen having a happy retirement in the kitchen garden. Arabella was surprisingly strong, she'd lift heavy pieces of furniture for me when I was cleaning."

We sat, absorbing these remarks.

"Why did she stay around here? Why didn't she move away?" I asked.

"She needed the money from the sale of the cottage. That, added to the remains of our bank account would give her a great start to her new life in France." Hugo said. His normally quiet speech held a harsh bitterness.

"Oh Hugo! The dagger she gave you! I'll bet she was going to kill you. You would be next after that poor David," Maggie's voice rose in a shriek.

Hugo's eyes widened, and he lost some colour. Indrawn breaths and gasps came from us all. It was a grim thought that she may have intended Hugo to be the next victim.

"I wonder if the police have checked out other wealthy male stab victims?" I said.

"Oh Daisy! You mean how many more victims has Arabella killed?" Sheila said.

An uneasy silence fell yet again. No one knew what to say. The enormity of the various, horrific possibilities filled our minds. I knew there was nothing to get hold of. Nothing tangible seemed apparent.

"Are we still on for the pub lunch?" Sheila asked.

Jim put down his coffee cup, and shook his head. "No, the whole village will be full of police. How can we explain to Tenby our presence there? Sorry Sheila, its simple normal type activities today. We don't want to draw suspicion or attention to ourselves."

"Shame, but I see your point. I was looking forward to that lunch and doing a bit of spying," Sheila said. "But there's no reason why we can't investigate on the Internet is there?"

"No, that's the best way for the moment," Jim replied.

"And I have to set up my other computer. That will take several hours," said Martin. His face was alight with excited anticipation. Martin looked both happy and relieved to be at home messing about with his computers.

Jim stood up. He put his chair in carefully under the table. Standing with his hands upon it he turned and glanced round at everyone. "We have to carry on as normal. There's less chance then of arousing Tenby's suspicions. This morning I'm going to Temple Church. Artefacts linked with the Templars are there and I'll record and photograph them."

Hugo also stood up. Looking at Jim he gave a nod of approval. "Jim is correct. We should also keep in contact with each other at all times. Sheila, take your iPad and knitting, and sit in with Martin in his cottage. Okay by you Martin?" Hugo then turned to Maggie. "I'm going to start clearing out the back kitchen, ready for the gym equipment. Can you help me Maggie?"

I hid a smile at her obvious delight at his request. All eyes turned towards me. "I haven't any plans. What should I do?"

Hugo said, "Daisy, you can go with Jim. Take your sketchbook, and play the artistic tourist. Okay?"

"Good thinking Hugo. Makes good sense. In the meantime, Maggie you keep in touch with that cousin of yours in the village. She's a valuable link to David's murder, and the police activity there," said Jim.

"Okay. Let's get going. I think today is going to be so dull and boring after all the excitement and drama of the last few days," Sheila sighed and limped out of the door.

"Let's hope you're right Sheila. A dull boring day would be a treat." I laughed as I followed her into the corridor.

How, oh how I wished for a dull, boring day for a change. My smile faded. I knew that wasn't going to happen. Somehow, I knew there was evil hovering around us. I glanced towards Jim. His face was also set in rigid lines, of apprehension.

Hugo spoke softly to Jim. "I hope Sheila's right. I doubt it. Whoever's behind this, hasn't finished with us yet."

"I don't like it," Jim said. I put my art materials in the back seat and stared at him. He stood one hand on the car door, looking back at the Priory.

"Don't like what?" I asked.

"Arabella's murder and now this dead body and the..."

"Templar Creeper," I interrupted him as he seemed uncertain as to how to phrase it.

"What did you say?" his head jerked round at me.

"It's Sheila's idea. The prowler, burglar, or whatever he is, needed a name. So, he's now the Templar Creeper." I answered as I got in the car, and fastened my seatbelt.

"That Sheila is something else," Jim muttered as we drove out of the Priory Lane.

"She certainly is," I replied. I smiled as I thought of her. Sheila had a zest for life and was forever young.

We headed for Temple village. Traces of frost lingered in the hedgerow. Spiders webs traced a delicate tracery. The sun broke through the wisps of mist that hung over the valley. Cornwall was bathed in a magical early morning light, which was all its own. Jim had books, maps, and a brand-new camera in his bag. I had my phone for photos, and a sketchbook with ink pens for drawing. My painting was enjoyed preferably in the comfort of a warm room. I loved painting from my photos. I had never dared admit this to my fellow art club members. That was akin to artistic heresy! A true artist painted 'en plein air', in hailstones, gales and rain etc. Not this lady! After all, I never professed to be a true artist.

The wrought iron gate stood sentinel at the top of the downward path. I placed my hand on it, and looked down at the tiny stone church. It was a simple structure nestling in the valley, serene and peaceful. Silence, thick and blanket like lay over that valley. The slight breeze wafted away the last of the morning mist. "Hard to imagine how noisy it would have been years ago," I remarked. At Jim's surprised look at me, I gave an irritated snort. "Once I decided to come here, I researched the whole area. Temple Church, was an original holding of the Knights Templars. A lawless place for much of its existence. It also became like Gretna Green performing runaway marriages."

Jim raised his hands in mock surrender, "Okay, okay. First thing I'm doing is to check out the original Templar artefacts that are set in that wall. After that, I'll go inside the church."

As we walked down the path to the church, neither of us spoke. But it was a companionable silence. I enjoyed Jim's company. There seemed to be a growing bond between us. I didn't like it, it worried me. I didn't want to get involved again.

"I'll take photos outside, then I'll go inside," I said.

Jim strode away, his camera ready, and notebook in hand. If he'd heard me, he didn't acknowledge it. His thoughts were already in the long distant past.

I took my photographs outside. A few sketches were made of the church and valley. Hitching my bag over my shoulder, I looked round for Jim. A rapt expression was on his face as he studied the last of the Templar artefacts on the wall. I smiled to myself, as he did fancy stuff with the zoom lens on his camera.

The church door swung open at my push. The perfume of flowers mingled with that indefinable smell of an ancient building. I knew this church was a restoration. Yet somehow, the essence of that original church was still present. Did the thoughts and prayers of those supplicants of ages past, cling to the very ground and hover in the air? Sunlit beams of light played upon the floor, dust motes dancing within them. Birdsong was a loud choral melody. I knew of its violent past. Underlying all, was a spirituality that lay deep within this ancient holy ground. Where had this spirituality come from? Ancient pagan rites had been overlaid by Christian practices. Was it a pagan or Christian spirituality that imbued the valley with the magical serenity? I didn't know, and I didn't care. Turmoil had engulfed me before my arrival in Cornwall. That accumulation of stress, my hasty removal, and now two murders had left me with jangling nerves. A sense of the many changing aspects in my life swept over me. Not that impending doom, the horror novels are so fond of. Just a knowledge that the change already in motion, was becoming fast paced and dramatic. That change had been inevitable after the breakup of my marriage. Selling the family home had been foreseeable. But the most dramatic and ongoing changes had been my hasty decision to move to the Priory. I could have gone to Bournemouth with Elsie, instead of dashing headlong to Cornwall.

The zipped inside pocket of my Kipling bag held the

paper. I loved my Kipling bags. Everything had its place, and my keys were always attached in my bag. So many trips and activities with Elsie had been delayed because she could never find her keys. Kipling bags were fashionable, and helped that failing short-term memory! I smoothed out the creased folded paper on my lap. Even after many, many readings, it still had the power to shock me. There had been conversations cut short at my entry into a room. Whispers that drifted towards me, with the urgent, "hush, she's here!" I was only a child. As that child, I'd learnt to expect the hurried evasions. The avoidance of a direct answer to my questions. That old favourite, "haven't you got homework?" echoed down the years. I grew older, and the questions faded into the background. Teenage life, student days, marriage and a career took precedence over everything.

I'd been packing. I'd known I was moving. The decision still hadn't been made as to exactly where. The arrival of Cleo put paid to some of my plans. So, all I knew at that moment was that I was going. The watercolour in its antique frame had always hung on the wall. I was taking the watercolour down when my phone rang. It startled me, and I'd placed the frame hurriedly on a low table. Cleo jumped up on the table, and brushed against the frame. It shattered on the tiled floor. First, I checked Cleo. She was fine. She'd jumped away as the frame fell onto the floor. I picked up the glass shards, and broken wooden frame. The watercolour in its mount fell apart onto the floor as I lifted it up. Two women were standing with a baby outside a wisteria covered cottage. A folded letter slid out. I'd sat on the floor beside the debris. I read the letter. I must've sat there for some considerable time because my knees became locked together. I'd had to struggle to my feet. That letter decided me. The startling revelations within it spurred me on to investigate further into my past. The letter had shown that my past and my origins were in Cornwall. It had also shown that they were on Bodmin Moor. The Priory advert on the Internet seemed heaven sent. Maggie's friendliness on the phone had decided me.

Now, I began to wonder if the devil himself had a hand in it! I'd read it many times since then. Rereading it again, I sighed. Folding it back into its original creases, I placed it into my bag.

Peace and tranquillity crept slowly through my body. Tension knots at my neck and shoulders slowly unravelled. The tumultuous thoughts whizzing around my brain slowed down, and faded away. I felt myself beginning to relax for the first time since coming to Cornwall. Bathed in the colourful sunlight from a tiny stained-glass window I slumped back. The hard wooden chair seemed almost as comfortable as a recliner. Moments passed, and still I sat. I was lulled into an almost trancelike state.

Then, two shots rang out. There was a dull thud and a groan.

CHAPTER EIGHTEEN

I sat very still. Surely, I'd imagined the noise. I'd been so deep in my meditative thought. Okay, I was dozing! A groan came from outside. That sound was unmistakable. and certainly no figment of my imagination!

I ran to the church doorway. The bright glare of the sun blinded me. I stood still waiting. My new cataract free eyes finally adjusted to the bright glare.

"Stay there, Daisy. Don't come out."

The urgent whisper stopped my head long dash out of the door. Jim lay sprawled a little way up the path. Blood seeped slowly into a pool around his shoulder. His arm lay at an awkward angle. The usual smart pale blue polo shirt was dirty and red with blood. Seconds passed as I tried to assess the scene before me. I stood in the doorway and looked round. The grassy area in the vicinity of the church, and up the hills seemed devoid of life. Looking further around me, I saw nothing. No movement anywhere. Where was he? Where was the gunman?

"Stay back Daisy. He may shoot you as well. I'm not badly hurt. I'll try to move slowly back to the church door," Jim said.

That initial shock and panic was leaving me now. On all fours I crept through the open doorway. If only I could reach Jim. Imperceptibly, Jim had dragged himself nearer the church. The birds no longer sang. The leaves and branches of the trees hung motionless. An ominous stillness gathered in the valley. My fingertips touched Jim's one good hand. He stretched it out further towards me. His other arm hung loosely at his side, covered in blood. A groan escaped his lips. Come on Daisy, I thought. Get him inside the church. He'll be safe there. A quick grab, that's all that's needed. One further stretch, and I grabbed his wrist. He half rose to meet me. All my strength went into that last tug as he leant forward. We tumbled back through the doorway. Too late! We'd almost made it. Another shot rang out. Jim gasped, and gave a sudden jerk. I heard the sound of the bullet hitting flesh. His whole weight slumped onto me. I rolled him over, heedless of his wounds. Flinging myself at the door I pushed it shut. I sank down, my back against the huge wooden door. Great gasping sobs shook me. I felt so helpless. I reached into my bag for my phone. Frantically I pressed buttons, and waved it around above my head. No signal! A smothered groan came from Jim. He lay still and unmoving in an untidy heap. I was galvanised into action. I dragged a heavy wooden praying chair towards the door. Useless I realised, but it would have to do. It gave me some feeling of security, as I wedged it best as I could.

"Where are you hurt?" I knelt down beside Jim. "Let's get you back against the wall, and I can check you over." We managed it. Blood oozed sluggishly from the wound in his shoulder. Another bright red had begun to stain his trouser leg.

"It's okay, nothing too serious." He murmured this, and even tried to smile at me.

"Just the traditional flesh wound?" I said. I tried to smile at him, but I knew it was a grimace.

Settling him back against the wall, I peeled the shirt from his shoulder. Reaching for my bag, I took out a packet of tissues. "You hold these in place to stop the blood at your shoulder. I'll look at your leg."

Jim gave me a nod. His good hand shook as he held the makeshift pad. His face was ashen, more from shock I thought, rather than loss of blood. His anxious glances towards the door made me nervous. I knew he was worried that the gunman would come in and finish the job. He wasn't the only worried one! I was on the alert for any sound from outside. I took some more tissues, and placed them on the welling blood on his leg. Then I took off my scarf and wound it tight around the wound. My hands shook, and I had to swallow hard. I'm squeamish! I have white coat syndrome! It's even written on my medical notes. Any hospital drama comes on TV, I've got the remote to the off switch before the title music ends. Yet here I was knee deep in blood. I was almost a Florence Nightingale! Not really knee deep, to be honest. But my legs, jeans and hands were covered in blood already.

"It's only in a fleshy part, no artery. The bullet is still in there," I said.

"I thought so," he said.

"Sorry, I'm not digging it out. I've only got a nail file!" I tried a feeble attempt at humour. A weak grin was his reply. That was us. Trying to keep calm in the true heroic spirit.

"That bloody bastard! What the hell is he doing this for? Why in heavens name is he shooting us?" I muttered.

Jim stiffened, and put a finger to his lips. He didn't need to. I'd already heard the slow deliberate footsteps approaching the door. Jim tried to move. He tried to reach his foot, but he sank back with a groan of pain. A weapon! That's what I needed. My eyes frantically roamed the ancient church. But churches do not have a ready supply of artillery or blunt instruments.

A vase with a bunch of wildflowers sat on a window ledge. White china, it was plain and simple. It would have to do. My bag, had I anything in it? Hairspray! I grabbed it and rushed behind the door.

Jim watched my preparations with horror and disbelief. "Throw the flowers out. Hold the jug high like a club," he whispered.

I shook my head. I'd never hold it high for long. Or have the force to hit him. Arthritis limited my shoulder mobility. The footsteps stopped. He was outside the door now. Jim struggled to move, closer to help me I thought. Again, he stretched out to reach his foot.

I swallowed hard. Jug of flowers was in one hand, and the aerosol was ready in my pocket. My breathing came in short panting gasps. Slow it down Daisy. Keep quiet, keep calm, I told myself, and my hand tightened on the jug handle. I felt rather than heard movement outside the door. I readied my arm with the jug of wildflowers. I'd noticed them on my way into the church. A fresh simple display that had shone against the sombre stone walls. It was with deep regret that I held them in readiness.

"Throw the flowers away, use the jug as a weapon," Jim whispered urgently again.

I shook my head. The little strength I had in my hands might not even break the jug on his head. Surely the surprise of a face full of flowers and a china jug, followed by my hairspray attack would deter him? There was a shuffle of feet outside the door. Then it was pushed very, very hard. The chair slid back and fell on one side with a crash. The door was opening, and it slammed back against the wall. A masked figure dressed all in black stepped over the threshold. The gun in his hand swung round and pointed at Jim.

"Take that you bastard!" I yelled. The woolly hatted figure, and the eyes behind the slit holes turned towards me. Stepping forward from the shadow behind the door, I stared into those glittering eyes. I swung the jug of flowers straight at his face. The satisfying clunk and crash of breaking china, was followed by a screech from the man. A horrible stench from the stale flower water soaked into the woolly hat. Flowers rained down everywhere, catching onto his hat, scarf, and coat. Shaking water and flowers from his head and shoulders, he staggered back. I took the aerosol from my pocket. Holding the aerosol high in both hands, I squirted wildly into his face. Gasping breaths, and strangled swear words followed my squirts. Words that should never have been uttered in a church! Disorientated and obviously stunned at this bizarre attack he stepped back. Another shake of his head, a wipe of his eyes and he regained his balance. His hand tightened on the gun. My aerosol was empty, and I stood helpless. I looked at Jim. No help there. He lay, sprawled unconscious on the floor.

"You bitch!" The words were hissed at me. The venom and anger within the man came in waves towards me.

I stepped back. With slow deliberate footsteps he came towards me. There was nothing I could do. This was it. I saw his finger tighten on the trigger. My foot knocked against my handbag. The aerosol of my favourite perfume rolled across the uneven floor towards me. A metal canister in its vivid blue and black stripes lay at my feet. It only took a second or two. In a flash, I bent down, knocked the top off, and shot perfume spray at the man's face. He dropped the gun. His hands flew to his eyes. A scream broke from his lips, and echoed round the church. Turning he rushed out of the church door, and I could hear his feet pounding up the path. The clang of the iron gate signalled his progress out of the churchyard.

Jim's breath was regular, but he was ashen faced. Had he hit his head when he fell? Was he in shock? I was no nurse and I was beginning to panic. Frantically I tried Jim's mobile. No signal at all. Jim always left a spare old phone charged up in the car. He said no one would ever steal it, and that it may come in useful sometime. Maybe that would have a signal. Or perhaps my phone would get a signal higher up the hill. I got the keys from Jim's pocket. I picked up the fallen gun. Gingerly, I held the gun in my other hand. I left the church.

Slipping through the still open door, I stood for a moment. I cast anxious glances around me. Could the masked man be hiding nearby? The tension I felt made my neck and back tighten into hard knots. The churchyard was quiet. An eerie silence. Hairs prickled on the back of my neck in fear. Clutching the gun tightly, I ran up the path. My thoughts were chaotic. What if the man came back? I'd never used a gun. Could I? What if I shot and killed him? I didn't want to go to jail for killing a man. But I didn't want to let him kill Jim. I certainly didn't want to be killed by him either. My hand shook as I opened the driver's door. I crouched down on the seat with a cautious look round me. I opened the glove box. "Got it," I muttered. Still hunched down I opened his phone. Two bars! A few moments later, I sank back, weak with relief. The police and ambulance were on their way. Another anxious look round, and I rang Maggie.

"Maggie, Jim has been shot, we are at Temple. The gunman…"

"Daisy! Daisy hurry back. He's coming! I'm fading… I can't any longer." Jim's voice wavered up towards me, and finally fizzled out.

Sticking the phone into my jeans pocket, I took the gun into my hand. I held it as I'd seen in so many TV shows and films. I stepped out of the car and began running. The man was creeping back towards the church doorway.

I slipped through the iron gate, keeping it as quiet as possible. He'd not realised I'd reached the car, and was now above him. I tiptoed down the path. His crouched figure was about to enter the church. He held a large branch in his hand. He had it raised like a weapon. I had nearly reached the church door. The man was about to step forward to enter the church. "Don't go any further!" I shouted. He whirled round. The branch was still raised, and he made as if to run towards me and hit me.

"Don't come any further! I'll shoot." I held the gun with both of my hands. It was shaking. Even with both hands, the gun was certainly not steady. But it was pointed in his direction.

The man stopped. The branch fell down a little bit as he stared at me. Then he laughed "You stupid old bat. You don't know how to shoot a gun. You're too doddery to hit me."

I agreed wholeheartedly with him. But no one called me an old bat and got away with it. And I wasn't doddery. Pointing the gun again at him I took a deep breath.

"I think you just point the gun and shoot." I said very quietly and calmly. I began to squeeze the trigger.

The birds took fright. They wheeled around in circles, squawking, and shrieking in fright. Again, the valley resounded with the sound of gunshots. And again, blood slowly trickled from a wound.

CHAPTER NINETEEN

Blood dripped down the gunman's arm. He dropped the branch, and clutched the now useless arm. "You old bitch! You shot me," he shouted.

My finger was still poised on the trigger, and I stared down at the gun in my hand puzzled.

"I shot you! For God's sake Daisy, lower that gun before you shoot me," Jim shouted.

"Oh! Sorry," I said. I dropped my arm quickly. Jim stood leaning against the doorway. A small gun was in his hand. Pale, and obviously in pain, he looked as if he had complete control of the situation.

The man stood motionless. Looking from one of us to the other he just stared.

"Put your hands up and kneel down," Jim said waving the gun towards him again.

Sirens broke the silence. They were drawing nearer to us. Jim, began to pale and sway slightly. He slid gracefully down the door frame onto the floor.

"Stand still, don't move." I raised the gunman's gun, and pointed it at him.

The gunman laughed at me. He turned on his heels, and fled round the back of the church. He'd known I wouldn't fire at him. He'd known I'd be unlikely to hit him. And he'd known my priority was to tend to Jim.

I ran towards Jim and knelt down beside him. The tiny gun, almost like a toy lay on the floor where he had dropped it. His trouser leg was pulled up. A neat gun holster ran around his ankle. "That's what you were reaching for every time you passed out," I muttered. Now I understood the strange contortions he'd been doing after he'd been shot. The sounds of the sirens grew louder as they got nearer and nearer to us. Jim had a gun holster.

Why? Who was he? What the hell did it mean? Kneeling beside Jim, thoughts ran through my mind. Cop shows, and murder mysteries all seemed to merge in a mad whirling kaleidoscope. An urgent panic seemed to possess me as the sirens grew ever nearer. On an instant, my mind was made up. I took the ankle holster from his leg, and shoved it down deep into my bag. The tiny gun was pushed down beside it. Then I looked at the gun I held. It was the gunman's and it had only fired two shots. I held the gun tight in both hands. I pointed it at a tree, closed my eyes and pulled the trigger. "Sorry tree, but I'm certain I missed you." Now hysteria was setting in. I was apologising to trees! I put the gun in Jim's hand, pressed hard, and placed his finger on the trigger. Jim had kept his true identity secret since his arrival at Barton Priory. I didn't know what that secret was. But I reasoned that I should keep that secret for him. I took off my jacket and put it beneath his head, trying to make him more comfortable. I walked to the open door of the church and waited.

Footsteps running down the path, and loud voices told me that help had arrived. Jim was still unconscious. He lay against the door. The tell-tale sock and trouser leg were neatly arranged. No hint of what had originally lay beneath was in evidence. The voices were all around me. Faces swirled around me.

"Sit her down. She's going to faint!" an arm came around me. I too, sat slumped against the doorway.

"Daisy! We're here. Have you been shot as well? Daisy, it's Maggie and Hugo." There was a gentle hug from Maggie. I grabbed her hand so tight. I was afraid if I let go the nightmare would continue.

"This guy is okay. No vital organs damaged. Looks like he bumped his head when he fell," one of the paramedics called over to us.

"There's a pool of blood over here. Was that from the old guy as well?" said the young policeman. He looked down at it, and then gazed at Jim.

Shaking my head, I took a deep breath. "No, it's the gunman's blood." As I spoke, I saw Jim's eyes open. As he focused upon me, I saw his memory return. He gave an anxious look down at his trouser leg. "The gunman dropped his gun when I hit him with a vase of flowers. Then I attacked him with hairspray, and perfume. Jim picked up his gun and shot him." Looks of disbelief and horror passed between the group. "Jim picked up the gun and shot the gunman with his own gun." I said the words loudly and clearly, looking straight at Jim. Our stories had to be the same. I only hoped that he understood my meaning. Jim gave another quick glance down at his trouser leg. He took a surreptitious feel for the holster which had been on his ankle. Then his hands stretched out to the gun beside him, and gripped it tightly. Jim's mouth twitched in a tiny smile. He looked at me and gave a nod. He realised what I'd done. I knew the bullets wouldn't match if they caught the gunman. Never mind, I'd make up another story when that happened. I was getting good at this! Would we ever find that gunman? Would we ever know why he took aim at Jim?

"I'll go to the hospital with Jim. Maggie, you take Daisy home. Here are the car keys. I'll follow the ambulance in Jim's car." Hugo handed over his keys to Maggie.

I walked up the path. I touched the iron gate as I passed through. Somehow, I felt superstitious about it. Stopping for a moment I glanced back down towards the tiny church nestling in the valley. It was a crime scene now. That early serenity that had bathed the church, on our arrival had gone. Violence had visited Temple Church once more. I stood shakily at the car, and opened the passenger door.

"Can you get in, okay? You're not too badly shaken up?" Maggie's concerned voice broke through my muddled thoughts.

"Yes, I'm okay." I climbed into the passenger seat. A deep sigh escaped my lips, and I sank back.

"Just a minute! I need a word with you. I want a complete statement from you. What exactly has been going on here? Wait!" The voice came from the car just drawing up behind us. Out of the driver's window Inspector Tenby's voice echoed round the hills.

Maggie stared at me. Then, she threw back her head and laughed. The car shot forward as she drove down the lane, towards the main A 30. A glance in the side mirror, showed him standing in the lane staring after us. He was practically jumping up and down in fury. "He can wait for his wretched statement. Let's get you home!" said Maggie.

Maggie rushed us back to my cottage. She practically frogmarched me into my bedroom. I stripped off my blood stained and dirty clothes. The shower helped. Some of the horror and fear washed down the plughole. Only a small amount. Bouts of uncontrollable shaking periodically overwhelmed me. It took some time throwing on sloppy trousers, and an oversized sweatshirt. A quick blow-dry of my hair, fingers scrunching it into shape. I didn't bother with lipstick. My ashen face would have resembled a clown's mask with a bright red gash across it.

The mug of hot tea cupped in my hands was soothing and warming. I'd still been cold after my hot shower. The coldness was deep within me, a combination of fear, horror, and bewilderment. Cleo was purring on my lap. Maggie sat down on the sofa, tutting, and shaking her head. The tension began to dissolve. I was beginning to slowly relax and unwind. The angry roar of the car shattered the peace of the courtyard. Car doors slammed one after the other. Voices raised in anger and argument echoed, bouncing around the courtyard walls.

"You go and check out the whereabouts of those other oldies. See what they have to say for themselves." Hugo's voice could be heard in protest. "I don't care what you have to say. I have my job to do," was the angry reply from Tenby.

Maggie looked out of the window. "Hugo and the other policeman have gone into the Priory. But Tenby is beating a path to our door!" She turned from the window and went to the door.

Before she reached it, the knocker banged again and again. Maggie opened the door. His fist raised ready to bang again, Tenby stood and glared at her. His face was red with fury.

"You drove off without stopping. I know you saw and heard me!" He stomped in, his eyes bulging, large fists clenched tight with rage.

"Prove it!" Maggie said in a flat voice that brooked no argument. She ushered him in, her face a mask of disapproval. "Take it easy Inspector. Daisy's been through a lot. She won't see a doctor. I think she's still in shock."

"Harumph," said the inspector. His large feet stomped across to me. He looked down at me with his angry eyes.

"Hello inspector. Do sit down. Maggie, please could you get the inspector a cup of coffee? Or would you prefer tea?" I pushed a plate towards him. "These are Maggie's fantastic chocolate chip cookies. You simply must have one of them."

They both stared at me. My unexpectedly pleasant hostess manner flummoxed them both.

"Oh yes, we were both enjoying a cuppa. Can I get you one inspector?" Maggie said.

The inspector stood still. His angry fists relaxed a little. He looked first at me then at Maggie. It was the biscuits that did for him. No one got that weighty without a sweet tooth. And the inspector was exceedingly plump around the middle. One mouthful was all it took. With a sigh he sank back onto the sofa, and gratefully drank the mug of strong tea. Another deep sigh, the mug was drained and placed on the table. The keen look beneath those beetling brows was now directed towards me. "You've stopped shaking now. Ready to answer my questions?"

"Yes inspector."

"What took you to Temple Church? Who knew you were going?"

"That's just what we've been puzzling over," Maggie said, before I could reply. Her head shake showed the futility of our thoughts.

My story was soon told. No one knew, only the group at the Priory. We didn't know why Jim was attacked. It was easy at first. The truth poured out of me in a steady stream. Desperately, I tried to keep that effortless stream going. I had to omit the business of Jim's gun holster. I felt my colour rise as I fudged that last shot at the gunman.

Tenby's mobile rang. "Great, I'm on my way. I'll interview him myself."

Closing his phone, he turned to us both. "Your friend Jim is fine. He's being kept in, for a few more hours for observation. He'll be home tonight. I have to interview him now." He strode to the door. "Daisy, we'll take your statement at the station tomorrow, and then you can sign it." Opening the door, he stood with his hand on the doorknob. "Thanks for the tea and biscuits. You are one plucky lady Daisy, pleased to hear you're okay. Those biscuits! Never tasted any so good in my life!" He closed the door. We heard him mutter under his breath as he crossed the courtyard. "Fantastic biscuits, absolutely fantastic."

Maggie wiped her eyes. The laughter from both of us swept away the terror of the morning.

"Who'd have thought it? The way to the inspector's heart was a mug of strong tea, and chocolate chip cookies." I said.

We were still laughing when Hugo, Sheila and Martin came in. It took time, more tea, and definitely more chocolate chip cookies before we were all up-to-date with each other's news.

CHAPTER TWENTY

We gathered together that evening in the kitchen. Demelza had left a chicken casserole in the oven, and Maggie was about to dish up. I felt so restless, and needed to take my mind off the day's events. Reaching for a large alcoholic glass full was not in my best interest. A book! That was what I needed. An escape route from the drama of the last few days could be found in an entertaining book. I'd been in the library, but I'd never explored it thoroughly. It was time I did so. I'd find myself an amusing cheerful book to read. "I'm going to the library to get a book to read," I said to the others.

The door opened onto the booklined room, and I walked into it, surprised to see all the lights on.

"Hi, I've always loved looking around this old room. Absolutely enchanting, the history and learning in all these bookshelves. I wonder if anyone actually reads them." I jumped, startled at the unexpected voice of Sarah. She was standing in the centre of the room beside one of the desks. The well-manicured hand with scarlet nails fondled the books on the desk. A sneering smile, the lipstick echoing the red of the nails was directed towards me. The agate eyes were hard and their hostility was obvious. That smile is as false as those nails, I thought.

"You've come to see…" I stammered. She smiled at my surprise and confusion.

"I've always had the run of the place. Both Daniel and I were frequent and welcome visitors to the Priory. Arabella always told us to make ourselves at home. We have a key, one of the genuine old iron ones." She swung the heavy metal key, and stared insolently at me.

"Arabella is dead. You no longer have the run of the

place. Can I have your key please?"

The voice startled us both. It was Hugo. He rose, from the depths of a huge armchair. Unnoticed by both of us, he'd been sitting there all the time.

Sarah flushed red at first. Gleefully, I realised her face matched the red of her lipstick and nail polish. Reaching into her bag, Sarah thrust a flyer towards Hugo. "I've come with a personal invitation. Both Daniel and I hope you can make our Italian night." White now with anger, she flashed another false smile towards Hugo. Then she turned to me, "Do come, we'd love to see you all." The paper, headed with the Red Lion logo, was advertising a themed Italian night. Sarah placed it on the desk. Then, she turned and walked towards the door.

"One minute, Sarah. The key please?" Hugo's voice was polite but firm. "After Arabella's death, the police have told us to collect all keys." The words were spat out with an unexpected venom from Hugo. So unusual coming from such a mild-mannered man.

Both gave each other equally insincere smiles. As I was nearest to her, she tossed the key to me. Then, she minced out of the door.

"She had a key! This changes everything!" Hugo exclaimed. "I'm phoning Tenby right away. This changes everything." As he strode towards the phone on the desk, he smiled at me. "Jim is back already. He discharged himself about four o'clock and got a taxi back. He is fine, a real gallant hero. All the nurses were impressed by his bravery."

"I'll bet they were!" I said dryly. "Just getting a book to read." I turned towards the end of the library. Not only could I get my books, but I could also listen in to Hugo's phone call to Tenby. At the far end of the library, I searched for the modern books. I was in no mood for heavy tomes of intellectual learning and thought. I was delighted to find a couple of shelves of paperbacks. As I browsed through the books, I listened avidly to Hugo's call to Tenby.

"Yes inspector. Sarah had one of the old keys. There were a number of them, but on looking into the drawer I've discovered some are missing. Arabella obviously gave some to her friends and acquaintances. There is no way I can change the lock, that door is listed. I've decided to lock it and bolt it permanently. The locks on the side door will be changed tonight, and a few, very few will be handed those keys. They will have to be signed for in a book."

I couldn't stay any longer. It would look so obvious that I was listening. So, I picked my books, and went towards the kitchen. I'd picked an old P.G. Wodehouse because they always make me laugh. I'd also picked out Dan Brown's *Da Vinci Code*. I'd never actually read it. I was puzzled by Jim's scathing comments about it. I'd put the film on to watch one night. But I'd fallen asleep halfway through. Tonight, I'd read it and do some research on Holy Grail groups and societies. I walked past Hugo standing beside his desk. He thrust the flyer at me, and continued sorting keys.

Holding the key I took it into the kitchen, and placed it on the table. "I've been to the library for something to read. I found Sarah there. She had a key!"

Maggie and Sheila stared at me. "Sarah had a key!" Maggie repeated my words.

"She was waving around this iron key. Sarah said Arabella had given it to her and Daniel. Hugo was sitting in one of those big armchairs, neither she nor I had seen him. He jumped up and was absolutely furious. He took the key from her and sent her packing. He's now phoning Tenby!"

I took my place at the huge kitchen table. My place. Such a short time had passed since my arrival. Now I had my own seat at the kitchen table. I had my own mug, and my own armchair in the lounge. In such a short time! Was it a good idea? Did it make me one of the gang? Should we all be so set in our ways to have special places? Should I be settling in so well when I was only on a temporary lease?

An aroma of lavender and rose swirled around me. The perfume was so intense, that when I inhaled my senses swam. This was yet another time that I was conscious of it. Previously, I'd asked the others if they smelt anything, but I always got a negative reply.

Yesterday, Demelza and I were alone in the kitchen. "Daisy, I sense that The Lady is seeking you out. That's her perfume you smell. Lavender and rose, she made it herself in this very kitchen. She knows you belong here. She's curious about you that's all. Soon you'll be able to speak with her. She's only shy." Demelza smiled at me and left the kitchen. Questions bubbled up in my mind. But Demelza had gone, there was no one to ask. Cautiously I swivelled around on my chair, looking intently around the room. Looking for what? Looking for whom? Demelza is telling me stories to wind me up, I reassured myself. The perfume grew stronger and then vanished. Only the smell of home-made cookies lingered in the kitchen.

My coming to Cornwall had been to begin my search. I hadn't even started. When was I going to begin that search? I knew I was scared. I was scared as to what I would find. I also realised that the results of my search could influence my decision to stay.

Hugo stormed in. The usually calm man was almost incandescent with rage. "Have you told them?" he demanded of me.

"Yes, I told them that Arabella just walked in…" I began.

He interrupted me, "Yes, she and Daniel often popped in to look up stuff in the library! And I discovered that Arabella allowed them to use our main computer! It was before they got the Internet at the Red Lion pub. They were actually using our computer!"

Maggie poured a glass of wine and gave it to him. Taking it, Hugo looked down at the glass.

"No thanks Maggie," he handed the glass of wine back to her. "I need something much stronger." He strode over to the cupboard, opened the door, and brought out the whisky bottle. "Who wants one?" He turned to us all, raising the bottle high. "It's been such a shock. When I told Tenby, he called me an idiot. He said I should have realised what was going on. And he was right." The whisky glass was drained in a single swallow. His shaking hands poured out a refill. Hugo sat down on a chair at the kitchen table. He cradled the glass of whisky in his hands. "I've never been so angry," his voice cracked with emotion. The long white fingers of the academic ran through his blonde hair, which then stood up in wild peaks.

"Completely understandable," Sheila patted his hand. She leant towards him and grimaced. "Anyone would feel angry. It's as if Arabella allowed the privacy of your house, and your computer to be invaded and violated."

"That's it exactly Sheila! You understand what I'm feeling."

"We all do," said Jim. He had joined us, bandaged and white faced. In time to hear Hugo's angry words, he looked round at us.

"Yes, of course we do," the chorus arose from each and every one of us.

"Right, let's go," Martin stood up. His chair crashed

back against the stone walls.

"Go? Where?" said Hugo.

"To that computer of yours in your library," said Martin. "I can check. If someone has been using it, I can track their footprints. I can see where they've been and what they've left behind them." He pushed his long hair back, and raced towards the computer.

"I'll go back to my cottage. I have a gadget I've been hoping to use," Jim rose from his chair and bent over the table towards us all. "I'll check for bugs!" he whispered.

Maggie and I glanced at each other. Her eyebrows rose in silent query. I shrugged my shoulders, and shook my head.

Hugo swallowed the last of his whisky and stood up. "What talents you all have between you. Let's make use of them!" The door closed behind him as he followed the other two men.

"This is so exciting!" Sheila clapped her hands, and rushed as fast as her stick would allow after the two men to the library.

"What do you think they'll discover? What does all this mean?" Maggie whispered to me.

Again, I shrugged my shoulders. I didn't know what to say. What had Daniel and Sarah been up to? What else would Martin find on the computer? And would Jim find any bugs with his listening device tracker thingy? And why would a gentleman of his years have a gun holster on his ankle, and carry a bug detector device around with him?

"Come on," said Maggie. She rushed towards the door. "Come on Daisy, let's see what they find out."

I didn't need telling. Already on my feet, I followed Maggie down the corridor towards the library. What would we find out? Would it help? Each further advance in our knowledge seemed to bring us into more danger.

Martin sat at the desk. His fingers flew over the computer keyboard. "Can I search everywhere Hugo? Have you anything you'd rather keep private?" he said.

Hugo slumped into an armchair. "There's only one thing. I kept it from everyone. Tomorrow, I was going to lay all the facts before you. I'll tell you now, and that will leave Martin free to search everywhere on the computer."

No longer angry, Hugo looked exhausted, miserable, and worried. Another whisky would be needed, I thought. "A large amount of money is missing from the bank account. Arabella had obviously cleaned it out. It was a final payment for the cottage renovations. I'm on the verge of going bankrupt." A huge sigh escaped him, and he ran his fingers through his dishevelled hair yet again. "I'm an academic, an archaeologist. I don't understand figures. Arabella said she did. Foolishly I left all the money transactions to her."

Jim who'd come in and heard the last part of this speech walked over to Hugo. He placed a finger on Hugo's lips. On entering the library after us, he'd being walking up and down with his gadget.

"Nonsense!" Jim said. "Look, you've missed that amount there." We all stared at him open mouthed. He signalled to us all to be quiet. Then he wrote on a piece of paper and held it up to us. 'Keep talking rubbish, the library is bugged!'

CHAPTER TWENTY-ONE

Silence. There was a complete silence. When you're told to talk rubbish, nothing ever comes to mind! Martin glanced at the gadget, and looked around the room. He was the first person to understand. "Sorry Hugo, my mistake. I can't see anything unusual in your computer. I'm just a guy who knows the basics. No computer nerd here." We realised there was a problem when we saw the expression on Martin's face.

"Oh. Well, that's fine. Let us all go to the kitchen. The meal is nearly ready," Maggie said in stilted tones and walked out the door.

'I'll carry on here in silence.' Martin wrote on another piece of paper.

Jim grabbed it, and wrote 'so will I.' Then he wrote, 'go to the kitchen but do not discuss anything other than the weather.' He waved it at us. "I'll come into the kitchen in a little while," said Jim.

Sheila limped back to the kitchen. Her eyes were shining with excitement, and she was grinning broadly. Maggie and I were not so excited. We were horrified and appalled. I was becoming frightened. Our enemy seemed to have unlimited eyes and ears everywhere. Their surveillance of us seemed limitless and unhindered.

"Will the dinner keep until the guys come in?" I asked Maggie.

"Yes, this casserole will be fine. Just what we need on a cold evening."

"I'll bet those guys are playing computer games. That's what they'll be doing, you mark my words," Sheila said.

The three of us sat. We stared at each other, fiddled

with the cutlery, and moved our glasses around the table. We didn't know what to say. The men walked in. Their faces were grave. Hugo's hair looked as if he'd been in a gale. He'll soon be bald if he continues that habit, I thought.

Martin put his finger to his lips.

"I told them you'd be playing computer games. Who won?" asked Sheila.

Martin smiled at her. Sheila made this quiet nerdy guy laugh. It was obvious that he felt at ease with her, "I won the game of course."

Jim smiled down at Sheila, and nodded to Martin, "it was only because Martin was cheating."

Surely, this laughing animated conversation, false as it was, would put any listener off the scent?

Jim walked round the kitchen. His eyes intent on his gadget, he pointed twice. Once, up high at a stone ledge. He circled the room and pointed to an ornamental urn on the dresser. Taking a pad of paper, he wrote on it. 'There are two bugs in here. Two bugs in the library and one in the lounge. I'll check the cottages next.'

Maggie took the paper off him, 'What should we do? Call the police? Remove them?'

Jim grabbed the paper back from her. 'How about setting a trap? Our plan to go to Temple was obviously overheard. I think we ought to think out a plan. The gunman knew all about us coming, and lay in wait. Why don't we set a trap for him?'

This is so hard to get my mind round I thought. We are having one paper conversation going on, and another innocuous false one in speech.

"Ice cream and apple crumble? After we've had the casserole, how would that be?" asked Maggie. Her voice was unnaturally stilted.

"Yes please, that would be great," I answered,

knowing that my voice would be just the same.

Hugo turned to Martin and pushed the pad towards him. 'Everything okay on the computer?'

Martin wrote furiously. And then pushed the pad back towards Hugo. We all looked over Hugo's shoulder to see the writing. 'No. Someone's been messing with the lease and deeds, and your bank account. Tomorrow ASAP, you must go to your solicitor and to your bank. I think perhaps the police, and a fraud expert need to check it thoroughly.'

Hugo groaned, and put his head in his hands.

"Let's have our dinner, and then we'll all have a nightcap in Daisy's cottage," said Jim.

Startled at this invitation on my behalf by Jim, I glared at him. What the hell was he up to now? Why my cottage?

"Just another five minutes and I dish up," said Maggie.

"Okay, Daisy and I will get the cottage ready. We won't be a minute," Jim slowly limped out the door. The bullet had grazed his bad leg. Both Maggie and Sheila watched him leave. No one asked how he was, we all knew how much he would have hated any fuss. Hugo shrugged, and stared down into his now empty glass. I stomped after Jim. I was furious, and I was puzzled. Maybe it was the medication he was on. How he managed to wander around with those wounds I couldn't imagine. I'll hold my tongue, and wait and see what he has to say. It was just as well I did so.

When we got out to the courtyard, Jim leant against the wall. The pain was etched on his face. "No one knew you were coming into the cottage. I think it may be clean, but we better just check." Slowly he limped towards my cottage. I knew better than to offer my arm for support. "Bloody bug mania! Who would have thought in such an isolated place as this? Such an oddball crowd are here. Who would have thought it had been bugged to this extent? Why bug any of us?" He stood at my front door and turned to stare at me. "Why? What was so vital that somebody had to hear our every word? Who the hell is going to so much trouble?" He thumped my front door in anger. With his good hand of course. "What's he after? What the hell does he want? He's even willing to kill for it! Why?"

Jim limped into my kitchen. He had been lucky. His bullet wounds were not serious. The leg, although it had bled profusely at the time, had only been a graze. The shoulder had also been nicked. He had been fortunate or the gunman was a terrible shot. The shock and pain, however, were not so easily shrugged off in an older person. Now Jim was ashen faced. He needed rest and painkillers. Even he had to admit that he was in no state to climb any stairs. Jim explained the gadget to me, and I checked upstairs. He had been correct. My cottage was clean.

"Martin and I will do his and Sheila's apartment. What about Maggie's flat?" I suggested, proud at my new found proficiency as a bug hunter.

"No need. Doubtful they would bug Maggie's flat."

After our meal, Jim and I returned to my cottage with Maggie and Sheila. Martin arrived, and we went off on our bug sweep.

We completed the task and returned. I pushed open the cottage door. Chocolate chip cookies still sat on the plate. Thank goodness, there were some actually left for us.

"Coffee or tea?" Maggie jumped up, and served our drinks. She stood watching and listening, as Martin and I told of our findings.

"Sheila's apartment is clear. No bugs there," said

Martin.

"Oh no! That's not fair. I so wanted to be bugged!" Sheila's face fell, and crumpled in disappointment.

Swallowing a grin, I said, "Martin has one in his lounge. Jim has one in his study upstairs, one in the kitchen, and another in his lounge."

"Jim is obviously special," sighed Sheila enviously. "I wish I'd been special."

Maggie put my mug of tea down in front of me. She handed Martin his coffee. For a moment she stood, perfectly still, thinking aloud. "Who did it? That's obviously the most important question. What I can't get my head round though, is when did they do it? Hugo, Demelza, and I are usually about. I can't remember anybody suspicious coming around."

"Perhaps it's when we had the refurbishment. The cottages and the Priory house were all replumbed and rewired..." began Hugo.

Maggie swung round towards Hugo. "Yes, you're right Hugo. But you've got the timing wrong. It's Sam the electrician! Don't you remember Hugo? He came here a couple of weeks ago. It was the week before Arabella died."

"Yes, he called and said it was a follow-up inspection," Hugo said. "Unusual I thought. But I was impressed at the care and consideration he was showing. To think that I was delighted to see him, and gave him the keys for all the cottages."

"Who's Sam?" I asked.

"He's a huge burly tattooed guy. He let me look at some of his tattoos. I didn't ask to see the hidden ones!" Sheila shuddered. Then Sheila brightened and looked at me thoughtfully. "How about it, Daisy? Shall we have some tattoos done?"

"No!" I was horrified at the mere idea. The appalled

looks on the other faces, echoed my thoughts.

"Never mind about his tattoos! You've all missed the point," Maggie was almost jumping up and down in her excitement. "Listen to me. What you don't know is that Sam is Gerald's new lodger! He lives in his annexe."

A stunned silence greeted this news.

"Gerald's lodger. That would explain how Gerald knew so much about my research," said Jim.

I reached for the last chocolate chip cookie. I had a sneaking suspicion that they were from my emergency tin in the cupboard. I suppose, as the hostess I should have offered that last one around. But I didn't. Well, it was my cottage after all! "Could Sam have been our gunman? Could he be the Templar creeper?" I mumbled, with my mouth full of cookie.

"What about Arabella's killer. Could he…?" Jim's voice trailed away. His exhaustion was increasingly obvious. His pallor was noticeably whiter. The lines around his mouth, showed the effort he was making to ignore the pain.

Maggie got up, walked over, and stood over him. She put her hands on her hips. She means business I thought, hiding a smile. Maggie exchanged glances with me. I nodded at her. "You should still be in hospital! If not hospital, you need your bed. Martin, you go with Jim. Help get him ready for his bed. Tomorrow, we'll discuss what to do about the bugs, murderers, gunmen, and everything else. Tonight Jim, you need some sleep and rest. We all do!" Turning, she looked round the room. Everyone got up, mumbled good night, and left.

Silence. Cleo, had been sitting beside Jim as usual. Now, she wandered towards me. I sat still in my chair. Should I let Cleo out for her evening tiddle? No. I got up and double checked my back door was locked. I pushed

Cleo's toilet box into a more prominent position. I went back, and checked the back door again. I walked towards the front door.

The gentle knock on it startled me.

"Daisy, it's Maggie here."

Relieved, I opened it and smiled my relief as Maggie walked in.

"I'm staying the night with you. I brought fixings for breakfast. We are all going to have a power breakfast here in the morning. Sheila can't wait!"

We both laughed. Bustling about, Maggie soon made up the spare bed. I got ready for my bed. I was so relieved to have her presence in my cottage. "Thanks Maggie, I'll sleep better knowing you're here."

"I'm certain that we'll all have a good night's sleep," said Maggie.

We did. At breakfast, everyone said they had slept well. There had been no alarms. There had been no fires. No burglars, and no gunshots. Jim, despite his injuries, looked better.

Bacon sandwiches or sausage baps were dished up by Martin and Maggie.

"I don't do cooking. But I do know how to make a good bacon sandwich," said Martin.

"Wow! This is great," I mumbled through a mouthful of bacon sandwich. "Lots of oozy butter as well."

"No butter on mine! Never, ever have butter on a bacon sandwich!" said Jim. His horrified gaze lingered on my plate. He actually shuddered.

Hugo was leaning against the kitchen counter. He'd opted for a sausage bap. He'd finished it, and was licking his fingers. "Before this argument continues endlessly, let's work on a plan of action. Do we tell the police about the bugs? Do we work out a plan to catch the culprit? Or...."

Then, the screaming began.

CHAPTER TWENTY-TWO

We raced out of my cottage. Jim and Sheila brought up the rear. Sheila as usual, was slower than the rest of us. Jim's leg wound had stiffened in the night. He was clumsy getting out of his chair, and limped painfully. Hugo and Maggie led the way. They ran through the Priory kitchen, into the corridor towards the sound. No longer, startled screams, it was a retching, sobbing sound.

"What the hell?" Hugo stopped abruptly. We others, bringing up the rear, cannoned into him.

Demelza, an arm around the crying Sally, the daily helper, just pointed. The front door was wide open. On the doorstep, a cloth, and brass polish lay abandoned in haste. Light flooded down the oak panelled, stone flagged floor of the dark hall. We all stood, aghast, staring into the now lighted doorway. It was like a macabre film set, staged in brilliant sunshine to maximum effect. Hanging from the door frame were two dead rabbits. The notice in block letters, was large and to the point. "**IT WONT BE RABBITS NEXT TIME!**"

"Oh no. Will it never end? Will I ever get any peace in this bloody place?" Hugo moaned.

I glanced at Maggie. I was startled by the expression on her face. She cared for him, that was obvious. It was not as a lover might. Her expression was that of an exasperated mother for her spoilt child. I had got it so wrong. Maggie cared for Hugo, but she certainly was not in love with him. Was there even a flicker of contempt in her eyes?

Jim got out his phone "I'll ring Tenby. Close that front door, and all go into the kitchen."

Tenby came back again. He looked at the 'crime scene' and called the forensic guys. Then he left, leaving a young constable behind.

"He didn't stay long," said Martin, as he watched the inspector's car disappear through the archway.

"Burglary in a toff's posh stately home, missing teenager, and an oil tanker in the ditch. Inspector's got his hands full this morning," said the constable.

We stood around in the kitchen.

"We can't talk here," said Martin, and pointed around the room miming listening ears.

"Okay then, a discussion in Daisy's cottage," said Jim.

At my look of consternation Maggie leant towards me. "I've got two tins of chocolate chip cookies for now. I'll make some more later with some apple cake, and flapjacks." Maggie laughed at the expression of gratitude on my face.

Everyone settled down in my cottage, Cleo loved company. She flirted with the men, and was fussed over by Sheila and Maggie.

"What about the bugs? Do we tell the police about them?" Sheila looked around at us.

"Or should we set a trap? Hands up for the trap?" said Jim.

All hands went up, except for mine. I was willing, in theory. But I was the only one who had seen the fanatical venom in the man's eyes. I was scared of him. I was the only one who understood the evil in him, and his strength and determination. Should I warn them? Would they even listen to me? That message, those rabbits, and his single-minded violence terrified me. We were getting into something best left to the police. I must warn the others. The chatter ebbed and flowed around the kitchen. I opened my mouth. I closed it again. No way would any cautious words of mine make headway. The excitement and purpose fuelling this conversation was mounting. It was useless. They were all determined to wreak vengeance on the guy. Catching him was important to them, but vengeance on him was creeping into the conversation. I remembered Tenby's words, "vicious bastard, he's not letting up, is he?" Tenby had warned us to stay together, avoid open fields and take care. I only hoped the others would act on it.

Jim had to go to the surgery for his wound to be dressed. I offered to drive him. He got in my BURT'S BANGERS van without a word. But I knew there had been a raised eyebrow and a shake of the head. He'd hidden it as he got in. But I knew!

"This is quite a comfortable seat," the surprise was evident in his voice.

"My last car died on me. This was ridiculously cheap, and was an excellent bargain in so many ways."

"Yes, I think I know why it was so cheap," Jim said.

"Removing the logo wouldn't be easy. I can't afford to do it," I stated firmly.

"I wasn't, oh well, I was thinking of it," Jim admitted with a grin.

We drove along the high banked winding lanes in silence. Not a comfortable companionable silence. It was a brooding silence.

"What do you think about trying to set a trap?" Jim asked me.

"I'm not sure about it. This guy is evil. He is determined, and could be more violent next time."

We drew up outside the village surgery. We were early. Jim waited for a few minutes, then looked over at me. "You don't like the idea? Do you?"

I stared out over the car park and the hills beyond. I saw nothing. I only seemed to feel the terror of that moment at Temple Church. I seemed to relive the moment when I thought Jim had died, and it was to be my turn next. "No. I don't like it. We don't even know whether Arabella's murderer and the Templar creeper are the same person. Are there two murderers? Have they got different motives?"

Jim began to get out of the car. He paused, and looked back at me. "Tenby is getting nowhere. We must act. We must go after him, or them. We can't just sit and be picked off one after the other. We are sitting ducks. Or perhaps rabbits?" The grim smile didn't touch his eyes. They were hard, and so very, very angry.

I thought of those poor rabbits strung up at the front door. Needless killing. Just to make a point. Just to frighten us. Jim was right. We couldn't just wait until he picked us off one by one. Jim had a plan, that I could tell. His planned excursion to Temple Church hadn't gone too well. Would this new plan fare any better? I sighed. Leave it to Tenby? Or be proactive and try to lure the gunman into a trap? Our plan might work. Or it could go wrong with catastrophic results. Which one would it be? I sat looking out of the window. An incoming alert had me reaching for my phone. Mind whirling, I pushed all thoughts of the Priory, Templar creeper and murders from my mind. I smiled as I saw Jake's name in my inbox. Two beaming faces holding out hands full of tiny gold nuggets was the first thing I saw.

'Hi Mum, we struck gold! Only a few tiny ones, but next time it might be a ripper!! Your place sounds fantastic. We were so worried you'd end up in a horrid boring bungalow beside Elsie. Murders, fires, and burglaries sound so much more fun. Good on you. Mum! We'll be staying another month. Both of us are loving this lifestyle. We are trying to figure out a way of earning a living here permanently. Keep those exciting emails

147

coming! Lots of love Jake and Lisa.'

I closed my phone. I wondered what they would think if I told them I was sitting outside a doctor's surgery. My friend was inside having a bullet wound dressed. They had worried I would be bored! They were pleased that I was having some excitement. I'd had enough excitement! I was hoping everything would calm down. Perhaps boredom might have been preferable. My friend. Was Jim my friend? Or was he becoming something more? I liked his company. I know he liked mine. We were at ease with each other. That was where it had to stop. Only a friend! That was all Jim could be! My own quest to Cornwall was just as important to me, as his Templar's research was to him. His was a hobby and an interest. My quest could possibly be life changing, both for myself and Jake. Up until a few days ago I'd have said Jim's research into the Templars could only be dull and boring. And I'd have been so wrong! My research had taken a backseat. Put a man with a gun in your face, and family history no longer seems important! I reopened my phone. I'd reread Jake's message again later. Better see what else was in my inbox. I scrolled down. The usual sales for clothes, shoes, and other stuff filled my inbox. Then my eye jumped to an unusual email address.

It was Elsie's daughter. "Hi Daisy, I found a bungalow two doors away from us. Newly refurbished, with a small garden. I'm certain you'd love it, and the dear little pussycat of course. Mum and I have already viewed it. We think it's got your name on it. We can book a viewing for you on Saturday. Do come and spend the weekend with us and see what you think. xx."

Damn! I didn't want to go to Bournemouth. I didn't want to look after Elsie. Her daughter wanted me as a carer and companion for her mother. I'd known Elsie for years, and loved her. Maybe it was selfish of me. But I didn't want to sacrifice the last few years of my life for her and her daughter. They knew I had only a temporary let on my cottage. Hugo was going to finalise all that legally. How was I going to get out of this bungalow business without hurting their feelings.? What was I going to say?

I jumped as a text came in. It was from Sheila. "Meet Maggie, Martin and me at Polzeath. We'll bring picnic supplies. Urgent conference meeting!"

I texted back, "Jim still in surgery, will come when he's out." It could only have been a few moments when Jim emerged from the surgery. He sat down in the passenger seat, easing his leg in with great care. I heard the muffled groan as he closed the door. Deliberately I refused to ask how he was. Instead, I passed him my phone with Sheila's text.

"Any idea what it's about?" he asked.

"Not a clue. But this idea of a picnic sounds great."

"Maybe," said Jim, as he stared out of the window. The clouds were scudding overhead, the forerunners of the snow in today's forecast.

I shrugged. "What's a little snow?"

I drove towards Polzeath. There was a silence in the car only broken when Jim turned to look at me, "Thanks Daisy."

"What for?" I asked.

"For not asking how I was after I'd seen the nurse. You understand I can't stand fussing."

"You'd have only snapped at me," was my reply.

He laughed appreciatively.

The large Priory SUV was already parked when I drove up beside it. There were plenty of parking spaces overlooking the beach. No one else had ventured out in this weather.

"Come on in here! Jim can take the front passenger seat with Martin. We girls will squeeze in the back," yelled Sheila. Her grin was wide, and her curls bouncing as usual.

Maggie handed out hot Cornish pasties fresh from the bakers. I was given my cheese and onion one. We washed them down with hot coffee, also fresh from the bakers. That was finished off by flapjacks. We all sat stuffed, almost comatose in a carbohydrate haze.

"Salad and fruit for supper," Maggie said in a hopeful healthy tone.

The wind had risen and waves swept into the bay. It buffeted the car with sudden gusts. Sprinkles of snow danced across the windscreen. Too small and fine to stick, they were the promise of the heavier snow to come. A couple of windsurfers were blown about in wild jerks and swirls across the bay. I could see Jim in front of me, he was trying hard to be patient. His flicking fingers were the only outward sign. Maggie pointed to them and grinned at me. I watched, waiting for the inevitable outburst.

"Okay. What's this meeting for? Why isn't Hugo here?" Jim demanded.

Martin twisted round from the driver's seat in which he was sitting and looked at Maggie for help.

"No. It's your discovery. Go on Martin," she shook her head at him. Then she settled back into her seat, finishing off her flapjack.

With a large gulp, Martin began speaking. "As you all know, I was instructed by Hugo to go through the Priory accounts." His gaze swept across us, and a nervous tick at his eye became even more pronounced. Swallowing hard, Martin continued. "Financially, Hugo is ruined. There was very little actual money in his inheritance. The

150

restoration work took all of his cash. Behind his back, Arabella had taken out loans, to continue with the project."

"So, the restoration and renovations were all done with borrowed money. What happens now?" asked Jim.

"Now the loans are due, and the bank requires heavy interest payments, at the end of the month," Martin said.

"What does Hugo say about it all?" said Sheila.

"He never wanted the Priory. He never liked it as a child when he visited it. Since the murder, and all the bad stuff going on, he hates the place. Says the only solution is to sell it. Hugo's just received an offer from an American university. They want him as a professor, and he's got the chance of going on an archaeological dig for a year. It's what he's always wanted. He's desperate to go," Martin said.

"He'll sell the Priory. What about us? We've made our homes there. What will happen to us?" wailed Sheila.

I thought of the email I'd just received. Elsie and I had been at school together. We'd been friends before and through marriage, and our children had played together since babies. Elsie had known about the 'floozy,' and kept quiet. Not wanting to hurt my feelings she said! After all, he'd had affairs in the past, and I hadn't bothered. Why did this one matter? This one mattered because idiot that I was, it was the only one I'd found out about! I felt betrayed by her, and we had quite an argument. She felt I should stay with Nigel, and didn't understand my need for a new life, and a complete change. The day before I travelled down to Cornwall, Elsie rang. "Daisy, we've not seen much of each other lately," Elsie began. No apology, which made me fume. What did she want from me? She was the one who had ghosted me! "My daughter wants me to move to

Bournemouth. The quiet life there would suit you. We're worried about your odd style of clothes and hairstyle. There's a nice flat near to us, and we found a sweet little runabout of a car for you. You can replace that nasty van you've got, and settle into a nice, retired life next to us." Elsie rambled on, talking about how we could go for walks, go out for tea together, play bingo and go to tea dances. No apologies, and... suddenly it clicked! Elsie was lonely! She'd given up driving, and her daughter worked all day. I could move there and be her chauffeur and companion. I swallowed my anger; I knew this was Elsie's daughter's scheme. And now they had found yet another property, this time a bungalow!

"Lovely idea Elsie, but I have a cat now. She'd hate being stuck in a flat and I signed a lease on a cottage on Bodmin Moor. I'm packing now, I move in tomorrow." I had answered her that time. There had been a snort, cough, and a huffy Elsie had rung off.

Now Elsie's daughter had emailed me. There was a wonderful bungalow for sale near them. This bungalow was mine for the taking. Close to Elsie and her daughter. It had short walks to the seafront, shops, and the many cafés and restaurants. I remembered a conversation I had with Elsie before my move.

"Of course, you have to get rid of that silly van. The neighbours would not take kindly to that! I do hope that you have got over that silly notion of colouring your hair, and having it in that nasty style. My daughter and I both preferred your old look. You looked your best in twinsets, and those comfortable polyester trousers with the elastic waist." Elsie had waffled on in a similar vein. I'd put the phone down feeling depressed. The email I had just received from Elsie's daughter had a link, and I'd looked at the bungalow online. It looked quite nice from the front. Inside, it needed completely gutting. I was not going to sit in an old-fashioned chocolate brown bath! Outside, the patio garden was tiny and was overlooked by a block of prison like flats! What if I stayed at the Priory? If I could? Would I prefer to be in Cornwall? Were these new friends more important to me now, than Elsie my old friend of many years?

Martin's voice broke into my thoughts. "Do we all want to stay at the Priory if it were possible? Would you all be happy staying in your present accommodation? I know we were all given a temporary lease. Then we had to decide. Who wants to go? And who wants to stay?" his face was solemn. He stared from one to the other of us, as if trying to read our thoughts.

"I'll stay. My home and my job are both at the Priory. I've been here now for four years, I love it. I'd hate to leave. I'm certain that Demelza would also stay," said Maggie.

"All my research is connected with the Priory. It's ideal for that. I too love the Priory, and would definitely opt for staying," said Jim.

Was it my imagination or was Jim staring intently at me?

"Got my vote! My family live nearby. My grandson and I love the Priory. And, best of all, it's got a great broadband signal! Count me in," said Sheila. "I love this group. We've become the Priory Five, and we should stay together. We've yet to get to the bottom of Arabella's murder, and sort out the Templar Creeper. Do say you'll stay Daisy. You will stay, won't you?" Sheila pleaded with me. She put her hand on mine and gave my arm a little shake. "Stay Daisy, you must stay!"

"Do stay with us Daisy," Maggie said. "We've all loved getting to know you, and having you here."

Martin nodded at me, took a large gulp, and said, "I'd

like you to stay Daisy," he reached forward and patted my hand. That was a demonstration of affection so unlike the reserved Martin, that I was very touched.

Jim looked at me. That intent look was back in his eyes. "Daisy has to make this important decision after such a short time of living here. We've all been here far longer than Daisy. Don't pressure her. Give her a chance to think it through."

"Stay Daisy! Stay Daisy! Stay Daisy!" Sheila bobbed up and down, those curls bouncing madly on her head. Her childish chant made me smile. It was so incongruous coming from a woman in her eighties.

"Don't pressure her Sheila!" snapped Jim. "It's a huge decision she has to make."

"I know your friend Elsie wants you to go to Bournemouth. If you prefer to go there, we'd understand," said Maggie.

I thought of Jake's email. I thought of Elsie, and her horror and disgust at my new look, and my van. Elsie had seen a nice little second-hand car that would be ideal for me and for her to run around in. She'd seen a couple of properties for me. They were both overlooked and gloomy. Thoughts of Bodmin Moor stretching out from my garden at the Priory came into my mind. That open space stretching out towards the rocks still took my breath away. Opening the curtains each morning was a joy. The splendour of the wild moor helped make my decision. Jake's email warning me not to get stuck looking after Elsie, not when she had her own daughter, ran again through my mind. I looked round at my new friends. Were these new friends more important to me now than Elsie? The old Daisy would not hesitate. She'd go to Bournemouth, with the safe sensible option. Was I the old Daisy? I knew Elsie had changed, she'd withdrawn from life and was living in the past. Had I changed? Who was I? I didn't know any more. All I knew, was that I was no longer that Daisy who'd had driven down to Bodmin Moor. Could such a life changing decision be made so quickly? Should I decide in an instant?

"I'll stay," I said. My tummy did a wobble, and I shook a little. I loved it here. I loved these new friends of mine. There was also the letter. I had to investigate. Staying here was the ideal place to find out the truth. And it was past time that the truth was unearthed.

There was an immediate cheer from Sheila. Maggie hugged me tight, and Martin grinned at me. A smile actually reached Jim's eyes, and his satisfied nod was his reaction. It was enough for me. I felt a warm feeling inside me at his obvious delight. Why did I feel such a warm feeling? I squashed it immediately!

"Toast! To the Priory Five!" Sheila raised her coffee cup. We all thrust plastic cups together in a toast. "The Priory Five," was solemnly intoned.

Jim gave a shake of his head, that eyebrow went up. But his smile was warm and genuine as it rested upon Sheila, and then me. I looked quickly away.

Warmth from him unnerved me. It unsettled me.

"Oh no! How will we manage to stay there? If Hugo leaves and sells the Priory, what will happen to us? It's all very well toasting each other," Sheila's face crumpled into disappointment. She looked like a small child who had been denied a longed-for treat. "Who's going to buy the Priory? And will they let us stay on in the Priory?"

CHAPTER TWENTY-THREE

All eyes turned towards Martin. He reddened. He cleared his throat. A handkerchief was produced from his inner pocket. Martin liked neatly ironed hankies, which he washed and ironed by himself daily. Beautifully! Martin gave his nose a good blow. Crushing the hanky into a tight ball he stuffed it back into his pocket. He looked at each of us in turn before he spoke. "I played about with Bit coins when they came out some years ago. I was fortunate, and made some money."

Sheila opened her mouth to speak, but Jim waved a hand to quieten her.

"The Priory was valued after Arabella's murder. Hugo thought even then of selling the place. He has spoken to me several times about it. So, yesterday we completed the purchase. I now own the Priory. However, I will only live there myself if you all stay. I don't want to live there if none of you are there."

Silence. Sheila was finally struck dumb, but her eyes were wide with astonishment.

It was Jim who spoke first. "That's great, that you have bought it. What are the terms and conditions that we... How will you...?" Jim stammered, seemingly unable to phrase it properly.

Martin drew in a deep breath, "I bought the Priory, ruins and land from Hugo. The complete package. I didn't want it sold piecemeal. The estate should be kept in its entirety. I don't want to break it up. I don't want to go down that road, so I won't be selling you your properties. I will however give you all a 99-year lease, on payment of a peppercorn rent."

"There will have to be safeguards on both sides written into the lease," murmured Jim. His gaze was thoughtful, and approving as it rested upon Martin.

"I'm staying," said Sheila. "We all are. Aren't we?" Jim nodded, and Maggie and I said yes.

"Sounds good to me, the Priory Five forever!" Sheila clapped her hands. I don't think her grin could have got wider without causing damage to her face. "But what's a peppercorn rent?"

"An old saying for a token rent. Sometimes it was paid with one peppercorn, or a pound coin, or even a red rose each year," Jim replied.

"I like that. But I'm not going to give Martin a peppercorn. He can have a red rose from me!" Sheila grinned at the blush that rose up into Martin's face.

"A lot of legal stuff to sort out with you all, but it should proceed smoothly as I have a great solicitor," Martin said.

Jake and Lisa would be delighted I thought. I would enjoy writing this email to them. But oh, how I dreaded composing an email to Elsie and her daughter! The wind freshened, and the snow began to fall around us in earnest. Inside the people carrier there was a warm fug full of excitement, and fresh possibilities for the future.

"Hugo wouldn't let us search for the Templar treasure in the ruins. He wasn't keen on us exploring, but it will be different now. Won't it, Martin?" Sheila asked.

"There can't be any treasure belonging to the Templars at the Priory. Surely that's impossible," said Martin.

"The Templars had immense wealth and religious artefacts of gold and precious stones. At the height of their power, they were free from laws and taxes. There was an enormous build-up of wealth. It was never discovered. Some said it was buried in France, others said it went to Scotland," explained Jim.

"Didn't they have the holy Grail, and the Turin

Shroud?" asked Maggie.

"Some people said it was a bloodline. The direct descendant from Jesus and Mary Magdalen was the real holy Grail," I added. My new knowledge from the *Da Vinci Code* by Dan Brown coming in handy.

"Yes, yes," Jim said. He was staring intently at the waves crashing against the rocks. Other waves dashed across the flat expanse of sand. Exhausted, they finally ended in a bubbling swirl.

He turned towards us. "There is no reason that the wealth of the Templar's didn't come to Cornwall. There is a story of the Black Madonna. There is one in Blisland church. Far-fetched that story may be, but those pictures and statues of the Black Madonna have always been linked to the treasure. They were painted or made with a reason. Expensive materials were used to produce them. Could they be a link?"

"So those secret symbols and strange signs that Dan Brown mentions could really be true?" I asked.

"There is fact mixed in with the fiction. Masonic symbols are ongoing and do come from archaic ones. The history of Temple Church and the...."

"A black Madonna! I know where there is one! In the Priory kitchen there is a black Madonna!" Maggie interrupted Jim. Her voice rose in increasing excitement. "Let's go home! I'll show you a black Madonna, Jim. I'll show you!"

The journey back was made with increasing anticipation. Jim's feverish excitement could be seen in the restless fingers on his knee.

"So, you are a bitcoin millionaire," said Sheila. "You don't act like one. You never flash your money around."

"It's a good job Arabella never knew. She would have eaten you alive," Maggie remarked. "A millionaire you may be, but she'd have had you bankrupt in no time, just like Hugo." A harsh quality had crept into Maggie's voice at the mention of Arabella. She had never liked the woman. For her deceit and bankrupting of Hugo, Maggie would never forgive her.

So many lives would have been disrupted but for Martin. His wealth meant that homes and jobs were saved.

We tumbled out of the SUV. Jim's pain was forgotten. He almost ran towards the kitchen door. We followed behind, all eager to see the Black Madonna.

Jim suddenly stopped at the door. "Wait! The bugs are still in place! We haven't decided whether to tell Tenby or set a trap," Jim said.

"We'll discuss that later," Maggie said impatiently.

"Yes, let's see it, let's see it," Sheila pushed Jim towards the door.

"Talk about it in code. No using correct names," Martin said.

"The poster! That would be good, we can discuss the poster," Sheila clapped her hands and grinned.

Jim shrugged his shoulders. Maggie pushed him to one side and unlocked the door. "It may be a false alarm. I might have made a mistake."

"Remember, all discussion on the artefact in mime, about the poster, or written down," Jim said with authority.

We all nodded, and rushed in after Maggie. This was the door we now used, after the listed oak kitchen door had been permanently locked and bolted. This other entrance to the kitchen was down a long corridor. The light in the corridor was dim. An old-fashioned flickering light bulb gave very little illumination. Maggie fairly flew down the corridor. I don't know who was more excited, Jim or Sheila. I grinned at Martin, we were both keen, but not to the fever pitch of the other two.

Maggie stopped still. She gave a stifled yelp, then pointed with a shaking finger. We all cannoned into each other, as we came to a sudden halt.

"What's up Maggie? Hurry up into the kitchen. I can't wait to see it," Jim said.

"Look, look down there," Maggie pointed again at the door with greater emphasis. "Is that blood?"

The door was slightly ajar. Beneath it oozed a dark red spreading tide.

I edged closer to Jim, peering around him. "Is it? Is that blood?"

"Yes, it's blood," he said, staring down at the ever-widening pool.

CHAPTER TWENTY-FOUR

Stepping to one side of the puddle of blood, Jim pushed the door gently. "It won't budge. There is something heavy behind it, perhaps it's... Martin, come here and give me a hand. We have to push the door to get into the kitchen. But gently!" The two men pushed. Slowly the door moved back little by little. Sheila had grabbed my hand. Maggie's hands were clasped tightly over her mouth. Silence hung around us. Fanciful thoughts of ominous auras from the past flitted through my head. The stone walls, some dating back to the Domesday book surrounded us. Jim thought some stones could be Roman, and used to build this part of the Priory. Evil and violence witnessed over the ages past, pressed against us. This overwhelming antiquity, seemed far worse in the flickering lights of the corridor. Did past evil enjoy watching present-day violence?

"I can slip through that gap," Maggie said. The door was now slightly ajar.

"If you could Maggie. I don't want to hurt anyone if they're lying behind the door," Jim's words ended in a whisper. "Are you sure Maggie?" Jim gave her a doubtful look.

Jim would have gone himself, but his injured leg made it difficult for him to manoeuvre through the door way.

"I'll go," Martin slid through the gap. His hand went to the kitchen light switch. Light flooded the kitchen, spilling out of the doorway into the corridor. No longer an eerie scene, we were now bathed in normality. Well, as normal as it could be, with blood seeping around our feet!

"Hugo! It's Hugo! I'll pull him away from the door and you can all get in," Martin disappeared from view.

There was the sound of a heavy object being dragged, and Martin grunted.

The door swung wide open. We all stepped over the pool of blood and stared down at Hugo. He lay sprawled upon his back. An ugly wound oozed blood from his forehead. Most of the blood came from the slashes upon his arm, which had obviously been against the door, the blood seeping beneath. Some of the slashes seemed superficial, but one deeper than the other was still bleeding. As Maggie bent over him, I grabbed clean towels from the drawer and knelt beside her. Sheila, meanwhile, rang for an ambulance, and of course the police. Martin did what he could to make Hugo comfortable, bringing cushions, and a blanket from the lounge. It was Jim who told us how to bandage him. Maggie and I both knew rudimentary first-aid. But it was Jim, who seemed to have an in-depth knowledge of how to treat knife wounds. He told us which way to bandage, and make Hugo comfortable.

"Hugo must've been attacked in the kitchen. Hugo is a well-built man, he must've been taken unawares," said Jim.

"Why attack Hugo? Arabella had all the motives imaginable. Why Hugo? He's the one who's suffered most. He's hoping to leave tomorrow. He'd no interest in Jim's research and no interest in the Priory. So why attempt to kill him?" Maggie turned to us all, her voice rising in exasperation.

"Yes, why now? They offered him the position if he could start immediately. He's even got a flight booked," echoed Sheila.

"Could that be why? Could the killer have heard that he is leaving tomorrow? Could this botched attempt be a desperate last chance to kill Hugo before he leaves the

Priory for good?" muttered Martin.

"The injuries are not life-threatening. The only problem may be the severity of his head injury," Jim whispered, looking down at the inert body of Hugo. "Hugo couldn't have been the intended victim. He would have been dead at once if he'd been the target. But he's here, he's been attacked, and he's lying here in a pool of his own blood. I think he was here in the wrong place at the wrong time. Somehow the intruder thought the coast was clear. He thought no one was here. That's why he walked in to the kitchen. It must have been a shock for him to find Hugo, and why he picked up the kitchen knife to attack Hugo."

"There's been quite a struggle." I pointed at the upturned chairs, and broken crockery. "That milk jug is still dripping milk down off the table. This attack has only been recent otherwise the milk...."

"You're right," Jim said. His voice rose. Was it in excitement? "I think we've interrupted the murderer. He must've heard us driving into the courtyard."

"Then where is he now?" asked Sheila.

I grabbed her arm and put my finger to her lips. Turning to the others, I motioned them all to be quiet. I rushed over to the kitchen notepad. It was always kept by the kitchen door, on the countertop beside the phone. Shopping essentials, proposed meal absences, and of course phone messages were written down here. The others watched as I began writing. They clustered about me peering over my shoulder. My face must've shown how important my thoughts were. I had realised why Hugo had been attacked. Jim had been right; Hugo hadn't been the intended victim. Hugo had been making a coffee. The spilled milk, coffee granules across the worktop were the evidence for that. I was exasperated at their obvious ignorance of what I was trying to say. So, I wrote quickly. 'Hugo was in the kitchen, making a coffee. The intruder thought the place was empty, that we were all out. How did he know we were out? What had he come into the kitchen looking for? How did he know how to look for it? It's obvious, the SUV is also bugged!'

Silence. Jim reached for the pad. He held it up and read it again. The others also read it in a stunned silence.

The sound of breaking glass from the library made us jump.

"The killer! He's still here!" Sheila yelled. "Let's get him!"

Martin and I were first out of the door. A large window in the library had been shattered. The darkly clad figure glanced back at us. He began scrambling through the broken window.

"Too late! He's getting away," Martin shouted, as he rushed into the library.

I was behind him. I picked up the nearest thing at my hand and flung it at the intruder. All right, it wasn't a sensible missile. I was in a library for goodness sake! Handy, sensible missiles for throwing at burglars do not lie about on desks. The huge dictionary of some ancient language was the only thing I could grab. It flew through the air in a jerky, haphazard fashion. But it reached my target! There was a satisfying thunk as it landed on the back of the intruder. A gasping scream came from the figure. It lurched forward, his hands were outstretched trying to protect his face from the jagged glass.

"Gotcha!" I yelled. But he recovered and raced off.

Martin reached the window first. "We'll never get him now."

I was out of breath as I stood beside Martin. He was right. The figure had reached the safety of the trees, and was soon lost to view.

"That was a great shot Daisy," Martin said as he picked up the book. "But the book is now damaged. Hope Hugo doesn't need it on his trip."

"Let's hope Hugo is fit enough to go on his trip," I replied.

Martin's face grew solemn, and his fingers smoothed the bent pages of the book. He tried to straighten the cover. "Yes, let's hope so." Then he grabbed my arm and shook it. "Daisy! Look at the glass in the window." Martin was staring intently at the glass shards still attached to the window frame. "It's blood! Your book missile made him cut himself on the glass. Must have been from his hand as he reached out to steady himself."

"And his face. I'm sure he caught the side of his face," I said.

"Maybe the police can get DNA or some forensic stuff from it. Is it possible? Can they do it?" Martin said.

"That would be great if they could," I said.

We both turned as sirens blared out across the valley.

A few moments later an ambulance and police cars drove into the courtyard. By this time, Martin and I had reached the kitchen and told the others about the burglar. And more importantly about the blood!

"What do we tell Tenby? He will be here any minute," I asked the others. Reaching again for the pad, I wrote, 'the bugs?'

Jim took the pen from me. 'After Hugo goes to hospital, we all go to Daisy's cottage. Tenby can join us there. I think we may have to tell him about the bugs. It's getting far too dangerous for us to go it alone.' He showed the pad round to us. We all nodded silently. All at once, the kitchen was crowded. Paramedics tended to Hugo, and two policemen rushed in. Hugo was put on a stretcher, and taken out of the kitchen to the waiting ambulance. A policeman asked us to leave the kitchen. It was now a crime scene. Jim looked crestfallen. He glanced round the kitchen as if the Black Madonna herself would appear.

"I'm going with Hugo. I've known him longer and know his personal details," Maggie said. A significant look from her was directed at Jim. "Whatever decision you make, it's fine by me." Maggie left the kitchen.

I'd seen her obvious affection for the wounded man. But I could see now I'd been so wrong. Not love, Maggie had only friendship for Hugo. She was not in love with him. The voices in the corridor heralded Tenby's arrival. His deep voice could be heard, and then Maggie's softer tones. I was absolutely certain that I'd heard the words, "chocolate chip cookies" from Tenby.

Sheila and I went off to my cottage. But not until after Sheila had raided Maggie's cake tins. She had grabbed the chocolate cookie tin and thrust it into my arms. Then after looking in a couple of tins, she smiled at one. "It's Maggie's fruitcake. I adore it. We'll take that one as well."

Gingerly, we sidestepped round the puddle of blood on the floor.

Sheila stopped, and looked down at it. "Poor old Hugo! Let's hope we get this murdering bastard soon." The set angry expression as she looked down at the blood, transformed her face. No longer the cheerful bubbly person we knew. Another Sheila stood there. "This has got to stop. I won't rest until we catch this guy. I only hope Jim has to shoot him dead. He doesn't deserve to live!"

Angry eyes glared at me, "I agree, I agree!" I flung up my hand to show how serious I was. This was one scary Sheila. I wasn't about to argue with her.

We were the first to my cottage, and began sorting out coffee and cake. Martin, Jim, and Tenby came a few minutes later. They sat in solemn silence.

"DNA will be taken from the blood on the glass. If, and when we get a suspect it can be used," Tenby said. "But why have we to discuss things in your home Daisy? Why not in the Priory lounge or library? Any particular reason?"

Sheila and I had made the coffee, my tea, and cut the cake. Martin gave out the mugs to everybody. There was a pause as everyone sipped the hot coffee, and started on their cake.

"Did Maggie make this cake?" Tenby muttered through a huge mouthful.

"Yes, she's a fantastic cook," Martin said.

"Mm, Mm, her beef stew and dumplings are unbelievable," said Sheila.

"But her apple pie is her greatest triumph," Jim said. His eyes were misty, as he fondly remembered last night's apple pie and home-made custard.

"A great cook like this, and such a good-looking woman, why hasn't she been snapped up?" Tenby asked.

Sheila looked at me across the room and raised one eyebrow. I nodded, and grinned.

"Her husband died eight years ago. She's never met anyone else," Jim said.

Another mouthful of cake was munched with obvious delight by Tenby. "This is fantastic," was his appreciative comment.

Jim stood up and looked round at us. "Shall I?" At our murmurs of assent and nods of approval, he put the bug hunter and a sheet of paper on the coffee table.

"What the hell? That's top-grade military equipment. How the hell did you…?" Tenby barked the words out at Jim. First, he reached for the bug hunter turning it over and over in his hands. The normally bored expression was gone from his face. Instead, a sharp penetrating glance was directed upon Jim. He reached for the bug list. He read it, then read it again. "So that is why we are in Daisy's cottage. No bugs here. What made you think of looking for them?"

"It was the attack at Temple. No one knew Daisy and I were going there. We didn't know we were going! It was decided over breakfast. I began to wonder...," Jim's reply. Angrily, Jim slapped down the paper. "But we were not clever enough for this guy. Otherwise, Hugo wouldn't have been attacked!"

"What do you mean?" Tenby asked.

"It was Daisy who realised. We've all been out in the SUV. All of us, except for Hugo," said Sheila.

"Normally, Hugo is always with us," added Martin.

"But it was a conversation we needed to have without Hugo being present," Sheila glared at Martin, daring him to interrupt her. "During our conversation, Maggie told us about the Black Madonna relic in the Priory kitchen. We were coming back to find it."

"Hugo was in the wrong place at the wrong time. Our burglar hoped to find the Black Madonna before we got home," Jim summed up.

"I don't understand. Are they one and the same person? I thought there were two different people. I thought Arabella's murderer was a different person to the one attacking us over the Knights Templars research," I said.

There was a silence. Everyone looked at me. Had I said something absolutely stupid?

"Daisy is right. We don't know if there are one or two people involved," Jim said.

"First things first. Let's check the SUV for a bug. Then we find this Madonna thingy," Tenby rose to his feet. He brushed the crumbs from his jacket and strode to the door. Pausing at the coffee table he lifted up the bug hunter. "May I?" he asked Jim.

At Jim's nod of assent, Tenby flung open the door. "What the hell are you all sitting there for? We've got to find a bug and a Madonna!"

CHAPTER TWENTY-FIVE

The bug was under the passenger seat. In a rare show of anger and frustration, Jim threw it on the ground and stamped on it. He strode off, limping as fast as he could towards the kitchen. Tenby glanced down at the smashed bug. He stared meditatively after Jim. He's realising Jim is not a typical retiree, I thought. I wonder if he'll investigate Jim next. We all followed Jim into the kitchen.

"There! Behind that cupboard," said Maggie.

The cupboard was pulled open and dishes thrust aside. Jim stared at the blackened blobby shape on the wall. His shoulders drooped, and he visibly deflated. "No, it's not a Madonna and it isn't black." He turned to us, and saw Maggie's crestfallen face. "It's an unusual artefact, possibly a Roman or Norman God, or gargoyle type of face. The colour is only years of sooty cooking." He licked his finger and rubbed. It came away smeared with grime and grease.

None of us wished for company, or food, and we drifted off separately for an early night.

Next morning, we gathered together round the breakfast table.

"Any news from the hospital?" I asked Maggie.

"Hugo's fine. They stitched up his arm and put a plaster on his head. He came to in the ambulance, and was furious at wasting time in the hospital."

"I know exactly how he feels!" came from Jim as he helped himself to muesli.

"What's he going to do? Is he going to go on his trip to America?" Sheila asked. "Surely he's in too much of a shocked state to even think about going."

"I'm going. There's no way I'm spending another day or night in this godforsaken hole! I don't know why you all love the Priory. I'll have a quick cup of coffee before my taxi arrives, and then I'm out of here!" Hugo said as he strode in.

Wordlessly, Maggie poured a mug and pushed it towards him. She glanced at the patch over his head, and the raised bulge of bandaging under his sweater arm. But she said nothing. None of us did. Hugo was in a bad mood, and no one wanted to argue with him.

Jim pointed to the bug and put a finger to his lips. Hugo just shrugged and shook his head.

"The police are letting you go to America?" Jim asked. "I'm surprised that Tenby would agree to it."

Hugo shuffled his feet, took a large swig from his coffee mug, and looked round at everyone. "That's why I'm rushing off. If he knew I was going to America today, he'd stop me. I plan on being out of the country, and on American soil by the time he realises I've gone. You won't tell him until I've landed, will you? I don't care who else knows I'm going. It's only Tenby that doesn't need to know." His eyes rested on each of us in turn. What could we do? We knew Hugo wasn't the murderer. We knew Hugo wasn't the Templar Creeper. He'd been his victim after all.

"It will be better if we don't know you're going. I suggest that you quietly disappear without saying goodbye. That way none of us will know that you're leaving for America," Jim said in a quiet voice.

Hugo drank the last of his coffee. He put the mug down on the counter. He leant forward and kissed Maggie on the cheek. A quick wave, and he'd gone. A silence fell on the kitchen. I don't know what the others thought. All I could think of was that poor Hugo deserved a fresh start. Inheriting the Priory had been the beginning of a catalogue of misfortunes. I wished him well in America.

"Have you heard? Isn't it terrible?" Demelza rushed into the kitchen. "What in the world is happening around here? It used to be such a sleepy place."

"What's happened?" Maggie asked her.

"It's the Red Lion! Daniel and Sarah took a week's holiday in Italy. Italian night would be a great idea they thought. They could bring stuff back, and make it really authentic."

Maggie poured another cup of coffee and handed this cup to Demelza. "So, what's happened?"

"When they arrived back home, they discovered that they had been burgled! It must have been just after they left. Sarah is distraught. She had a carved chest that she always kept locked. It's gone. The burglars must have decided to break it open at their leisure."

"How do they know it was just after they left?" asked Jim.

"The post behind the front door. The first day's post was pushed back, all the other days had piled up beneath the letterbox. There wasn't much damage, just some valuables taken and this chest. Sarah always kept it on her dressing table. Always locked. Everyone is wondering what she kept in it!"

"This is dreadful. Hugo attacked in our very own kitchen, and stabbed with one of our kitchen knives. Now the Red Lion burgled. Whatever will happen next?" Sheila sighed, shaking her head. Breakfast became a silent sombre meal.

Jim wrote on a note. 'Meeting at ten thirty in Daisy's cottage.' There were nods of agreement and we all rose and left the kitchen. We had talked and tried to act as normal. But knowing those bugs were there, made us self-conscious. There was no way a natural normal conversation could take place.

"Have you got a plan?" I asked Sheila and Maggie when they came into my cottage kitchen. They both shook their heads and looked at me. I shrugged. My mind had gone blank. I couldn't think of anything. Jim and Martin came in, and we settled down in my lounge with our coffee. I had my usual mug of tea. I would have liked to drink coffee; it seems to be increasingly good for your heart and health. But it always gave me tummy ache, and I felt a bit weird on it. A cup of tea did not fit in with my trendy modern look. Perhaps it would become fashionable soon.

"Sorry about the Madonna," said Maggie.

"It certainly looked like a rough outline of the Madonna. The blackness was caused by years of kitchen smoke," sighed Jim. "There may be some ancient artefacts and carvings somewhere else in the Priory. Hugo would never agree to us searching the cellars or the ruins properly. What about it, Martin? It's your property now. Shall we begin a thorough search?"

"I understand why Hugo was so worried. Those old buildings and basement cellars have been left empty for decades. They could be very dangerous. What I suggest we do is examine all the old deeds. I've been sent a huge portfolio of them. I need someone like you, Jim, to go through them with me. That will give us a proper plan to investigate. I don't like the idea of us just going in blind. We need a surveyor or structural engineer type guy to check it out before we enter," replied Martin.

"That's sensible," said Maggie.

"But what about the plan! We have to work out a plan whilst the bugs are in place. Never mind chattering on about secret passages in the underground crypts, and what have you!" Sheila was exasperated with the two men, and it showed.

"Tenby found that bug in the SUV yesterday. Under

the driver's seat. We then found the Madonna in the kitchen with Tenby. It's obvious that our listener is interested in all our Templar doings. We need to have another Knights Templar artefact to entice him back again. After all, Tenby said to leave the bugs in place for now," I said. There were nods of approval.

"Could we lure him down into the crypt?" asked Sheila.

"Do we do this on our own or with Tenby's help?" asked Jim.

"With Tenby!" Maggie and I exclaimed immediately.

"Sheila, that's a great idea. I suggest Martin and I look through those deeds and the ancient plans of the crypt and Priory. We can discuss some of it in the library. That would be where we would look at them anyway. We just have to work out a plan where we can lie in wait for him," Jim said.

"There must be something to make it worth his while. What Templar artefact would be likely to be found in the crypt?" I asked Jim.

"Let's say that there are notes written on the side of the plan. They suggest a Knights Templars cross was carved in a room. A Round room, they are commonly used as places of worship by the Templars. An arch way leads into this room, and it's thought that beneath the flag stones in the room Templar treasure has been buried," Jim replied.

There was silence.

"Is there a Round room? Is there such a cross?" asked Sheila.

"No of course not. I made it up," said Jim and laughed.

"But, but Jim," Martin stuttered and stared at him. "I looked at the plans this morning before breakfast. There is a Round room with a Knights Templars cross carved on the wall."

No one spoke. We looked at Martin. As if we were in a synchronised team, all heads and eyes swivelled across the room towards Jim. He sat there, utterly transfixed. I'd never seen him at a loss for words. I'd never seen Jim unable to think logically. But Jim was gobsmacked, poleaxed, whatever word I came up with in my mind, nothing fitted the bill.

"This, I must see," the words came out in a breathy rush. He flung open the door and dashed towards the Priory. We jostled each other through the door and raced after him.

Jim drew up to a halt. We all cannoned into each other and turned to look at the entrance archway. A car and small van was entering the courtyard.

My key was still in my hand ready to lock my front door. I stood like the others staring open mouthed.

"It's Tenby!" said Sheila.

"But his car is piled high with stuff," said Maggie.

His car door opened, and a small fluffy dog charged out towards us. Frantically barking, it danced around, tail wagging furiously. "Fluffy, Fluffy, be quiet. Shut up Fluffy," said Tenby. This was not the usual Tenby who arrived with questions. A large man, he was dressed in denim jeans. The generous paunch hung over the straining belt. Instead of the usual collar and tie and smart suit, he wore a vivid purple, green and yellow check shirt. Not one of us greeted him. Stunned by this casual apparition of our policeman, we were unable to find the words.

"Where do you want this stuff to go? I've got another job after this. Can't stand around waiting for you to gossip." A wiry looking little man climbing out of the van shouted at Tenby.

"Where's Hugo? He said he'd meet me here with the key."

"I think he went out earlier. I'm not sure where he went to, or when he'll be back," answered Jim. He had been the first of us to gather his thoughts together. "Why do you want Hugo? What's this all about a key?"

Tenby turned towards Jim. "My landlord decided to sell my flat. He found a buyer in a week! Hugo heard me talk about it to one of the forensic guys. So, he offered me the spare cottage. Knew it would be difficult to let after the murder there. He thought you lot would like a policeman living on the premises. You get a copper 24/7!"

Utter silence greeted Tenby's announcement.

It was broken only by the grunts and sighs from the little wiry man unloading boxes from the van. "When you finish chattering, will someone tell me where this lot has got to go?"

"Hugo said he'd meet me here with the key," Tenby repeated.

I shuddered, and saw Sheila and Maggie look at each other and grimace. Not one of us would move into the cottage where Arabella was murdered. A policeman like Tenby must be made of unimaginative stuff.

Of course, it was Jim who collected his thoughts, and spoke first. "Hugo no longer owns the Priory. He sold it this week. You'll have to ask the new owner if he's willing to let the property to you."

"Sold it! Why the hell didn't he..." For once words failed our usually loquacious policeman.

"I'm sure he'll let you move in. You're here now with Hugo's approval. I'm certain he'll honour Hugo's agreement with you," Jim said, with a grin at Martin. "Was there any paperwork between you and Hugo?"

"No, we were going to sort that out this week. My

landlord had sprung this on me. Hugo said the cottage was empty. He already knew me, so told me just to move in."

"Okay, let's get you moved in. I've the key here. That's okay by you Martin?" said Maggie.

Tenby looked puzzled at the mention of Martin. He visibly relaxed though giving Maggie a beaming smile. "There's another problem! My daughter went off to Dubai this week. She got a wonderful new job, and promptly dropped off her dog. Hugo did say that the puppy wouldn't be a problem." Tenby shuffled his feet and looked at us. An embarrassed look played over his face. "My daughter called the wretched puppy, Fluffy." The tiny black and white dog, rushed up to him again barking enthusiastically. I could see why she was called Fluffy. She was a bouncing ball of fur. She paused in her headlong rush and sat back, and began scratching her ear. Fluffy glanced round at us, and then took off again. Scampering in wild circles from one to the other, her baby bark increased in volume. "Fluffy, come here, come here."

I tried to hide my smile. Well, not really. Sheila and Jim were openly grinning at the huge authoritative policeman bending down, and trying to catch the little puppy. Then I froze. Tenby's anxious calls, the barking of the puppy all seemed to fade away. Cutting right through the hubbub came an angry hissing and swearing. I'd left my front door ajar. Cleo had slipped through it. She was taking one deliberate step after another towards the puppy. Her tail was ramrod straight. Her back was beginning to arch and fur was rising along its ridge. Glittering feline eyes were fixed upon Fluffy. The puppy was scratching again. Her legs were splayed awkwardly. The approaching sound grew louder, and Fluffy turned towards it. We all made a frozen tableau. It was if we had all stopped breathing in that instant.

Whirling round I dashed towards Cleo. The van man swung round. The huge tower of boxes piled in his arms came directly into my path. My shoulder and elbow caught the tower. A huge arc of boxes flew into the air and fell, opening as they did so into a clattering heap upon the cobbles. Lego spilled out in a rainbow of multicoloured pieces. Struggling hard to regain my balance, I trod on some Lego. I grabbed the now empty arm of the van man. We swayed together as if in some exotic dance, and my ankle went over completely. Sheila and Maggie had also rushed towards Cleo. The boxes hit Maggie in the face.

She staggered back into Sheila, who then slid on the still damp cobblestones. "My leg, I've dislocated my knee!" Sheila cried out, clutching the knee in anguish.

Fluffy sat in the middle of it all, boxes all around her and Lego scattered everywhere. She leant forward and began chewing a box lid. Cleo had now reached the puppy. Fluffy turned and stared wide-eyed at the irate cat now facing her.

CHAPTER TWENTY-SIX

It was over in seconds. It was over before anyone could reach them. There was a quick flash of a paw, claws fully extended. A bead of blood appeared on the puppy's nose, and dribbled downwards. Fluffy whimpered, and awkwardly tried to pat her nose. Then she sat down and gazed adoringly at Cleo. The hissing and swearing stopped. Cleo directed a scornful look at the puppy. She sniffed at it in disgust, and walked back into the cottage. As soon as the delivery was over, the van drove out of the courtyard. The driver had been too busy to stop for a mug of tea. Martin and Jim had helped the flustered Tenby with his boxes.

Maggie put the kettle on. She had cake and biscuits at the ready, of course.

I sat in my recliner chair with a packet of peas in a tea towel around my ankle. Sheila had her foot up on a pouffe. "Why did I have to have the frozen carrots? I want peas as well! The carrots are bumpy and knobbly," she grumbled. Sheila shifted in her chair, casting envious glances at my frozen peas. The peas moulded to my ankle whereas the carrots kept falling off.

"Whoever knew Lego could be so dangerous. Fancy a grown man playing with Lego," I muttered as I drank my tea.

"There's a posh name for them. Lots of adult men do it. Encourages mindfulness and is supposed to be relaxing for them. And, some rare old Lego sets are worth a fortune," Sheila said, scattering biscuit crumbs as she did so.

"You're kidding," I stared at her in disbelief.

"It's true honestly," she replied.

Fancy pieces of Lego being worth a fortune I thought to myself. It seemed hard to believe.

Jim entered the cottage. He looked tired and the limp was more pronounced. Moving boxes should have been left to the others. Saying so would have only infuriated him. I, very wisely, had kept quiet. Again!

"What are we going to do about Hugo's departure? We need to decide before Tenby comes in. We've got to work out what to tell Tenby," I said.

"Tell me about what?" The voice boomed from the doorway. Tenby entered, carrying Fluffy. "Can I bring her in? She'll sleep on my knee, she's exhausted."

"I thought, wondered..." My voice faded away. I was now speechless, and unable to think of anything to say. A tide of red surged up my face. Ridiculous at my age. Caught out and blushing like a teenager. Damn Tenby! Having him so near could give us a lot of problems.

"Daisy was talking about Italian night. Everyone living in the Priory has been asked to go. That must include you now. That's if you want to go to the Red Lion with us all," said Maggie.

Sheila gave Maggie a nod of approval. I stared at her. That showed quick wit and was said in such a casual manner. Well done, Maggie! A new problem now faced us. How could we investigate behind this policeman's back? He lived next door to us. How could we keep everything secret now? Surely, I thought, once the creeper and murderer had been found, that would be it? There would be no further need for the Priory Five's investigations. Would there? We could retire the Priory Five. One look around my lounge at Sheila, Jim, Maggie and Martin and my heart sank. This lot would never retire gracefully. There would be other problems to investigate. I was certain that they would find injustices and wrongs to be righted. I should have felt a dread within me. I should have felt horrified at the thought. Why did I feel a tiny spark of excitement?

The large chubby fingers of the policeman, clasped the steaming cup of coffee. Tenby stretched his long legs out. He took care to avoid our Lego injured legs. "Why were you all rushing out of the cottage when I came in? And what's all this about a new landlord?" he asked.

Jim placed his mug on the table. He took a deep breath. "Hugo was on the verge of bankruptcy. Martin had discovered all the details on Hugo's computer. Arabella borrowed money, took out loans and cleared out their joint bank account."

"Where's all the money gone?" asked Sheila.

I smiled to myself. Trust Sheila, to get to the point, especially the money point.

Martin took up the story. "Arabella left a complicated trail; she knew her way around the computer. I can see much of it spent on renovations, especially the cottages, and the Priory kitchen. Everything was of the highest quality. But there is a considerable amount of cash missing."

"The murderer must have it. Find him or her, and you find the money," said Sheila.

"Maybe, maybe. No one knows where that cash went. Hugo had been left with two options. He could declare himself bankrupt, or sell the Priory and clear his debts," said Jim.

"Easier said than done these days. Huge properties like the Priory with acres of land are notoriously difficult to sell," Tenby murmured through a mouthful of cake.

"Hugo not only found a buyer but a cash one. The solicitors worked out a preliminary deal in a few days! Guess who owns the Priory now? Go on, guess?" Sheila bobbed up and down excitedly, as she gazed at Tenby. The carrot ice pack fell off her knee, and crashed onto the floor.

Both animals jumped. Eyes widened. But they soon fell fast asleep again. Fluffy lay sprawled exhausted across Tenby's knee. Cleo sat beside Jim, her usual place on the sofa. She had pointedly ignored Fluffy's entrance.

"Martin! It's Martin! He's your new landlord!" shrieked Sheila.

Tenby jerked upright, almost tipping the puppy onto the floor. "Martin? Martin? Well, I'll be damned. Martin eh? Didn't take you for a money guy. What did you do? Rob a bank or win the lottery?"

Martin squirmed and reddened under the intense scrutiny from the large policeman. Beneath those shaggy eyebrows, the eyes held poor Martin transfixed. If Tenby was a stoat, Martin was the rabbit. He looked guilty enough to have robbed a dozen banks.

I took pity on Martin. "He's a computer whiz. One of his early ventures into cyberspace was into Bitcoins. That's where all his money comes from. Your new landlord is a Bitcoin millionaire."

Tenby stared at Martin in surprise. "Hugo said I had to discuss rent and all that stuff with him when I moved in. We'll have to have that conversation sometime Martin."

Martin nodded, and gave the policeman a nervous smile, "yes, later."

"A Bitcoin millionaire! Good for you. You own all this lot now. Very nice too. You don't mind me living here then? And Fluffy of course?"

"No, that's okay by me. As long as the others agree." At our nods of approval, Martin continued. "First it was a boutique hotel, then a retirement living style of home. Now we seem to have sorted out a unique way of living that suits us all." He paused, taking in a shaky breath, obviously at a loss as to how to continue.

Maggie took pity on the flustered Martin. "Most of the

projected amenities; the pool, sauna, coffee bar, and restaurant have never materialised. However, we have muddled into a way of life that suits us. Demelza and I are housekeepers. We provide breakfast and an evening meal, and with outside help we keep the place clean. The cottages are your domain, and looked after by yourselves. But help is available if you need it. You each pay a maintenance charge."

"Wow, that sounds great," said Tenby.

"As you know Hugo inherited the Priory from a distant uncle. Occasional childhood visits gave him a distaste for the place. He no sooner had inherited it, and Arabella appeared. Her enthusiasm and plans swept him away. But her murder crystallised his dislike into hatred," said Jim. "Last week he was offered a wonderful job abroad. A university professorship at an American university, and an archaeological dig for part of the year. It's just what he always wanted."

"When Martin offered to buy the Priory, it seemed fate. It was meant to be," sighed Sheila.

"Where is he? Hope he hasn't left already!" Tenby guffawed at the mere idea. Then his face stiffened. His eyes grew hard as they looked from one to the other of us. "Where the hell is he?"

There was a shuffling of feet. Well, Sheila and I were in no fit state for that activity. So, we stared at the ceiling, then the floor, and cleared our throats. Each one of us was trying to look innocent. We failed. We failed dismally. We gave the game away.

"Hugo's gone, hasn't he?" Tenby sat up straight. Fluffy nearly tipped onto the floor again. The tiny whimper of complaint, had Tenby clutching her.

"You knew he was going! As the husband of the murder victim…" His shouting faded away and he glared at us.

I looked at Jim. His lips were twitching. He was trying not to laugh. The angry policeman did not come across as frightening when cuddling a fluff ball!

It was Maggie who answered. There was an unusually sharp edge to her voice. "We all knew Hugo intended to leave. Foolishly, we assumed he would check in with you first. If he has left for America, it's without our knowledge. Not one of us knows where he is at this precise moment."

"If Hugo is gone, he's gone!" Sheila waved an airy hand of dismissal. "We have far more important things to discuss. There is the Templar creeper, not to mention Arabella's murderer. And are you going to join us at Italian night at the Red Lion?"

An exasperated Jim jumped to his feet. It would have been more effective and much more dramatic if he hadn't winced, and gasped at the pain. "This can all wait. It's vital we catch the Creeper. The bugs are all in place, and we must take this opportunity. We now have the Round room to investigate. Let's use that to trap our Creeper."

"Jim is right. We have to catch the Creeper. We need a plan right now," said Sheila.

"Sit down, Jim. Take the weight off your injured leg! Now, explain this Round room stuff to me. Is it going to be another damp squib? That figure on the kitchen wall didn't amount to much," said Tenby.

The explanation including descriptions of plans, buildings, artefacts, and Templar signs poured out of Jim.

Finally, Tenby put up his hand to halt the flow. "Okay. Enough of the historical stuff. Do you really think this Templar Creeper guy would want to see it?" A large forefinger stroked his chin, as he gazed thoughtfully at Jim.

"Oh yes! I'm certain that he'll be over here, as soon as he hears about it," said Jim. We all nodded agreement.

Tenby reached for his phone in his jacket pocket. I noted that it was done with extreme care; so as not to disturb the sleeping Fluffy. "I'll get a couple of chaps to act as a backup. They can disguise themselves as workmen and hang around. I'm going to give them guns, so you lot take care, and keep out of the way!" He closed his phone. "Now let's fine tune this plan before we go into the library. Another cuppa would help if you don't mind. Maggie?" Tenby smiled hopefully across at her.

Maggie rose to her feet. She smiled down at the policeman. "I suppose you'd manage another slice of lemon drizzle cake?"

"Yes please, Maggie. That's the best cake I've ever tasted!"

"We go to the library and chat about the maps and our suppositions. Why don't we go straight into the crypt? Why would we wait?" I asked.

Maggie turned back from the teapot. Everyone had wanted coffee and tea refills. "We've never talked about Martin buying the Priory in front of the bugs, have we?"

"No, I don't think so," Martin said. "It was mentioned in the SUV, that it might be a possibility. We only talked in here about me finalising the deal. Why do you ask?"

"Couldn't we talk about the discovery of the Round room in the library. Then say that Hugo asked us to wait for him. That would be a reason why we weren't going to rush straight in. It would make sense, for us to wait for the owner." said Maggie.

"That would work. Well done, Maggie," said Tenby.

"Hugo has gone to the dentist into Stonebridge. That would be a normal routine thing to do. And he made us promise to wait for his return, before we explored," said Sheila.

"Good idea, Sheila. Let's say Hugo is due back at five thirty and we have to wait for him. It's mid-morning now.

That gives our Templar Creeper plenty of time to affect an entry," said Jim.

"Shouldn't we go in and see what is actually there before he comes?" I asked.

"There's bound to be cobwebs, dust and all sorts of detritus. If it's disturbed by us, he'll know that it's a trap," answered Jim.

"Oh goody! That's great!" Sheila clapped her hands. We all looked at her in astonishment. Why was that so exciting? "Don't you see? All the spiders, mice and bats will have been cleared out before we go in."

Maggie and I wholeheartedly agreed with that.

"We'd better go to the library. Bait the trap, and catch our Creeper. Remember, normal type chitchat as well. Tenby, don't you speak a word," warned Jim.

Sheila jumped to her feet, forgetting her bad knee, and rushed to the door. A grunt of pain escaped from her lips. She grabbed onto Martin's arm for support. I grinned at the old girl. No injury was keeping her from the action! Old girl, I thought. I'm nearly her age. I groaned inwardly. Then I perked up. I'm only a trainee old girl!

The maps were spread out on the huge desk. Hugo's desk, I'd always thought of it. No more, Martin's desk now. Several books were also opened with reverent care. Jim and Martin didn't use white gloves. However, immense care not to handle the pages too much was taken.

"Parts of the Priory date back to before the Domesday book. Some stone arches date back to 1156. There are details of it being passed to the Widow Matilda in the old documents. It was owned after that by a larger Cornish Abbey. The dissolution of the Monasteries saw it pass into private hands. Luckily it was left intact. It was too small to attract vandalising attention. This family kept it in their hands, but let it out to various people. It was sold in 1990, and bought by Hugo's elderly uncle," said Jim.

Jim then began writing. He passed the paper to Maggie. She nodded and then lifted the paper and began to speak. "When is Hugo coming back?"

The paper was passed to me. "He's gone to the dentist in Stonebridge. He said he'll be back about five thirty. After you phoned him about your discovery, he was excited. He said you've not to go in until he arrives home."

"It's an amazing discovery. That map clearly shows that there is a room like a Templar meeting place. And it's just down the corridor, a sort of crypt room. Hugo always kept it locked up. The notes in the margin suggest there are Templar carvings, and reliefs on the walls," said Jim.

"What if there's furniture and stuff in there? And signs to where the Templar's treasures are?" asked Sheila. "Come on, let's find it! Hugo won't mind if we go in before he gets home, will he?"

Jim gave her the thumbs up. Tenby patted her approvingly on the back.

"We can't. Not now. We have to wait for Hugo. After all, he's the archaeologist. We can't go finding Templar artefacts without Hugo. He should be with us when we explore. He'll be back by five thirty. Surely, we can all wait till then?" I said.

"While we wait for Hugo, I'll check out these old estate books. There may well be other snippets of information in them," said Jim.

"Okay, we'll wait," sighed Sheila.

"I've got kitchen stuff to do," said Maggie.

"Lots of emails to reply to, that'll keep me busy," said Sheila.

They all looked at me. "Er… my painting studio needs

sorting out. Everything is still in boxes," I said in a rush.

Before we sat down in the library, Jim had produced two small boxes. He fiddled with the computer on the desk, and then went out to the corridor. One camera was placed at the entry to the crypt, the other overlooking the back-corridor window. The computer showed a split screen, both cameras showing emptiness. Chairs were brought round the desk. Silent and waiting we watched the screen.

"Go and do something! They won't come immediately. You could be sitting here for hours. And they may never come!" Jim wrote on a paper, holding it up for us all to see. He then wrote quickly, 'where are the backup guys?' He thrust it towards Tenby.

Temby wrote on the paper, 'they should be here by now!'

Exasperated by our refusal to move, Jim picked up a book and began rifling through it. We sat. The split screens were empty. The Templar Creeper may not have heard us. He may well have been on holiday. Would he come? If so, when? Staring at an empty screen should have been boring. It wasn't. We were all transfixed, just watching. Jim, getting more irritated by our refusal to move, grabbed a pen and pad again. 'He may not come. It might be just before five. It could be hours you're sat waiting here.'

We all nodded. And still we sat in a circle round the computer screen. Not one of us moved. Then, the window in the corridor slowly slid upwards

CHAPTER TWENTY-SEVEN

There was a combined intake of breath. Jim's hand gripped my shoulder. Sheila leant forward towards the screen. Every one of us seemed to stiffen. We watched the window open ever wider. The masked figure hesitated for a moment. He stretched over the window frame, and looked up and down the corridor. Cautiously he climbed through the window. He turned and gestured to the figure waiting outside. This man clumsily straddled the window frame, and landed onto the corridor floor with a thump. The first figure turned and glared at him. Despite their ski masks, his anger at the ineptitude of his fellow conspirator could be seen. They were clad in black from head to foot, the masks giving them a frightening look. The clumsy one pointed down towards the crypt.

With furtive glances about them, they crept on down the corridor. The heavy oaken door was soon reached. This camera, picked up their figures as they approached it. We saw Clumsy shoved to one side, and directed to point his torch upon the lock. The click and squeak as the lock was picked could be heard clearly. The first figure pushed the door open slightly. Directing the torch through the opening he peered inside the room. Clumsy was almost jumping up and down in his excitement.

"Text my men. We need them here now!" whispered Tenby.

Maggie, Martin, and I texted again and again. Nothing, no reply.

"They've gone into the blind spot behind the wall in the garden. They can't get a signal," said Martin.

Tenby looked at Maggie "Go for them Maggie, please. Rush them back here!"

Jim had risen to his feet, "the camera only shows the crypt doorway. I've got to get in there. They could be damaging stuff or..." his voice tailed off and he began edging towards the door.

"Wait." Unbelievably, Tenby was actually hesitating. "Wait a moment Jim. I can't let a civilian go in there. Wait, till my men get here."

"They'll get away if we don't act now!" Jim said.

"Are they moving furniture?" asked Sheila. Still sitting at the screen, she'd not taken her eyes off the crypt doorway. "Listen, they are moving stuff around in there."

"I'm going in even if you're not," said Jim.

Tenby pushed past him. "I'll go in first. I'll tell them I'm police and hope they..."

"They'll run," said Jim. "We'll be behind you; in case they do make a bolt for it. Come on Martin."

"Where the hell are my men?" muttered Tenby, as he strode off down the corridor.

Jim followed the policeman. His hand was at the small of his back. I grinned to myself. I knew Jim had his gun stuck into his waistband. Martin looked at me, shrugged and followed the other two men. He was rather white faced, and shaking a little. But he followed them.

I limped over and stood behind Sheila, to look at the screen. Upraised voices and shouts had me rushing to the doorway. I stood there, staring down the corridor. Gradually my eyes accustomed themselves to the dim light. Tenby had marched into the Round room. No longer was he keeping quiet. He was being the authoritative policeman now. His voice boomed down the corridor. "Police. Stand still. I..." None of us ever knew what Tenby was going to say next. Least of all Tenby.

The door to the crypt was now wide open. I could see

the figures by the dim light from the corridor, and their own flashing torches. I saw the black clothed fit guy pick up a chair. It was an old-fashioned, heavily carved dining chair. He lifted it and swung it with great force at Tenby's legs. The chair leg broke with the strength of his blow. Tenby was felled like a tree. His gasp and fall made me wince. The chair, now minus one leg, was swung round again. What a great weapon a chair could make, my brain noted. I'll file that away for future reference. There are usually chairs dotted about, no matter where you are. This time the chair connected with Jim. On his bad leg! Not only did I wince, but I also think I must have shrieked. Jim clutched his bad leg, and fell to the floor beside Tenby. I couldn't be sure. Did Jim fall on top of Tenby, or beside him? Anyhow, both men were struggling to rise and extricate themselves, one from the other.

That left Martin. Poor Martin. He did stand his ground, which was very brave of him. The chair was now flung aside. The huge burly figure rushed towards Martin, and pushed him. Only a slight push. But it was enough. Martin toppled onto the other two men. And they'd only just separated themselves one from the other. Now, Martin landed on top of them. They all began flailing about again. And cursing! It only took a few seconds. Only seconds before they were all on the floor. Only seconds, and the great big fit guy, came barrelling down the corridor towards me.

I stood staring at him. He was getting closer and I had no weapon. I was standing beside the door and there was nothing to hit him with. It took only a split second. There was no conscious thought that passed through my brain. One minute I was standing in the doorway. The next minute I'd reached over into the kitchen. Then, I'd grabbed a large bowl of leftover Christmas nuts from the shelf, and flung them down the corridor floor. They made a lovely crashing noise as they rattled and banged all over the stone flags.

The fit guy lost his balance as he stepped on a large walnut. He kicked aside a couple of smaller hazelnuts. He grabbed the doorway where I stood to regain his balance. "Bitch!" the word was flung into my face. Those same glittering eyes that haunted my dreams, held mine for a moment. Terror, fear, and that sick feeling of dread swept over me. What would he do? Was he going to really attack me? And what could I do? It was only for a second but seemed hours. He muttered, "old bitch," again. Then he was gone.

Clumsy followed him. He lost his balance, staggering the length of the corridor towards me. He fell at my feet. Dragging himself up by the doorway, he leant towards me. "Let me go. Don't try to stop me," he whispered.

"I… But…" I stammered.

"Let me go. I'll give you the evidence to catch Arabella's killer." He finally pulled himself up to his feet. "I promise. A murderer in exchange for my freedom!"

Did I think about it? Did I really absorb what he was saying? What was I going to do? A killer for his freedom was what he said. Could I believe him? It was seconds. Dimly in the background of this intense scene being played out by Clumsy and myself, I heard shouts and noises.

The men in the crypt had finally righted themselves. Tenby was limping up towards us. Martin was following behind, helping a very lame Jim. Maggie's voice could be heard in the kitchen. She was urging the policemen to hurry.

"I promise, a killer for my freedom," he whispered in my ear.

What was I to do? I stood by as he scrambled out through the window.

"Watch out for the nuts!" I shrieked.

Tenby was staggering down the corridor towards me. He was trying not to limp, but I noticed he certainly favoured his left leg. Martin and Jim followed. Martin was helping Jim, who was ashen faced, and clutched his thigh where blood seeped through his trouser leg. In their path lay the assorted nuts from Christmas. Scattered over the corridor they were my attempt at a deterrent. Trouble was, that deterrent didn't work on the bad guys. But it was proving very successful with the good guys! Tenby had avoided the walnuts and Brazil nuts. Unfortunately, his foot had landed squarely upon a small hazelnut. The tiny awkward shape had thrown the big man completely off balance. Lurching against the wall he shouted. "Why are these bloody nuts all over the place?" as he slid down to the floor.

"I threw them down to stop the creeper escaping," I muttered. Frantically, I began pushing them aside with my foot towards the wall.

"What are you doing Daisy?" Maggie had come up behind me, followed by two men. The men stared at my shoe shuffling in puzzlement.

"Never mind her! Get out of the bloody window after those two men in masks. Move, dammit!" shouted Tenby.

As the two men rushed to the window they too stepped on some nuts. But they kept their balance, and were soon clambering over the windowsill.

Jim and Martin reached us. Both men were making their way carefully along the nut strewn corridor. Cleverly, they slid their feet along the stone flags, pushing the nuts aside. "Daisy's idea?" Jim said. That hateful eyebrow was up when he looked at me. But his lips were twitching. I glared at him. I didn't find it funny at all.

Maggie grinned at me, and shook her head. "Nice try, Daisy," she said, and began sweeping nuts into a dustpan. "Lost them! What a bloody fiasco this has been. All for nothing. All that planning, the cameras, and all for nothing," stormed Tenby.

"How badly are you guys hurt?" I asked.

"We saw two of you attacked by chairs. Do you need a doctor? You two are limping badly. And your wound has opened up again, Jim," said Maggie.

Before they could answer there was a noise at the window. The reappearance of the two policemen told its own sorry story. "No good boss, long gone. They legged it over some fields and then went up on the moor. We can't follow them in this poor light." Their faces expressed their true feelings. They didn't want to tackle the bad guys in the growing dark. Definitely not on Bodmin Moor.

"Okay, okay. Not your fault guys. They had too great a head start. Back to the station. I'll catch up with you later," said a gloomy Tenby.

The walking wounded limped into the kitchen. All medical help was refused. Jim relented and had a fresh bandage put on his leg. "Before I sit down, shall I remove all the bugs?" said Jim to Tenby.

"You might as well, they'll certainly guess this was planned. Yes, get rid of them all," muttered Tenby.

"Thank goodness, I couldn't think of what to say," said Sheila.

"Yes, it was surprisingly hard trying to think of natural chitchat," said Maggie. She held up a whisky bottle and glasses. "Who wants a glass of this? Or would prefer tea or coffee?"

Unanimously they voted for the whisky.

"A strong tea for me, a builder's one please, Maggie," I said. Then I remembered, "Fluffy and Cleo! We left them alone in the cottage in our rush to catch the Creeper."

Maggie and I raced to my cottage. Tenby plodded behind us. Sheila, Martin, and Jim just waved us on our way. They sat at the kitchen table with their large glasses of whisky.

Flinging open the door I rushed into the cottage. What if Cleo had attacked the puppy? Would the whole place have been trashed by the puppy? I was so scared of what I would find. I could tell that the others were just as nervous. But what we saw astounded us. I stepped onto the doormat. I stood stock still taken aback by the sight that met my eyes. Maggie cannoned into me. Tenby, stood and stared over my shoulder. "Well! I never expected to see that!" said Tenby.

"Nor did I," Maggie said. My heart was still pounding from the dash to the cottage. It was also with the relief that my wild imaginings had been needless.

Fluffy lay curled up in a tight sleepy ball on the sofa. Cleo sat beside her. She was licking the puppy's face and purring. Cleo stared at us for a moment, and then ignored us.

"I must get back to the station. Do you think Daisy...?" Tenby said, looking at me hopefully.

I looked at the two animals. "No, it's okay. Leave them there. They look so happy together," I said.

"If you give me Fluffy's lead, I'll take her for a walk later," said Maggie. "Daisy will join me, won't you?" I looked at her. I was tired and it had been an exhausting day.

"You will? I'd be so grateful," the big policeman

stared at us with such relief and thankfulness. It was surprising to see it in such a huge, hard-boiled guy. He really loved his daughter's puppy.

Two anxious faces turned towards me. I nodded and gave a weak smile.

Maggie had put a chicken casserole in the oven that morning. Sheila and Martin prepared the table. Jim had borrowed a stick from Sheila, and returned to look again at the Round room. That initial dash to the Round room after the nuts had been cleared, had been such an anticlimax. A strange, shaped room, it had nothing exciting about it. Plain stone walls and stone arches, no carvings, no niches, and no reliefs. A huge oak table still stood with three chairs set in place round it. Was the plan wrong? Or was there another Round room? The third chair lay splintered on the floor, a mute witness to the earlier struggle. It was a silent meal. We were all dispirited after the bug fiasco.

After the meal, Maggie and I got ready for our walk. We put on hats, jackets, scarves, and gloves. Then we began to get Fluffy ready for her walk. Or tried to. She ran round and round the cottage in excitement. Her lead and puppy harness were a great source of fun. Eventually, with Maggie crawling about on the floor, the harness was put on, and the lead snapped into place. Meanwhile, Cleo sat bolt upright on the sofa. Horror on her face was obvious. Why was her new friend behaving in this mad erratic fashion?

"Tenby told me when he gave me the lead, she's had little training. It was an old lady who had her, and had never walked her. She got her just as a companion. Why do people do that? There are loads of elderly cats and dogs needing new homes. Why didn't she get one of those? All they're looking for is company and a nice warm home. They need very little exercise, if any," said Maggie.

"Now Tenby's daughter has gone to Dubai. Tenby has very little time to give this puppy; I think we've been lumbered Maggie," I said.

We both laughed at Fluffy. She was bouncing up and down, running at bushes and breaking away from them. The lead got tangled around us both, around Fluffy and then around a tree.

"If we're going to take on some of the day-to-day care of Fluffy, we make a rota. Tenby has to do his share! And she gets training!" I stated firmly. This new forthright Daisy was going to look out for herself.

"Quite right! Tenby can feed her and do the early morning walk. I'm too busy with breakfast. Daisy, can you take her for the morning and lunchtime. I'll take over in the afternoon for a longish walk and possibly training classes. If you feed her and Cleo together, then pass her over to Tenby when he gets home. What do you think? Will that work?"

It was growing dark, and the air was crisp. The sky was clear with so many, many stars. In the silence, only snorts and scuffling noises from Fluffy were the only sounds. By unspoken consent, we walked through the courtyard arch and along the path at the back of the cottages. We had lapsed into a companionable silence. We were near enough to run home safely, and near enough to scream for help. It had been unspoken between us, but our lives had been touched by violence and death. An overwhelming instinct for preservation and security now coloured our daily lives.

On the return to the cottage, we fed the animals, in

separate rooms. When the door had been opened between them, each rushed to the others bowl. Both of them, turned and gave us accusing looks. Each animal was convinced that the other had been given the tastiest food!

I made a pot of strong tea for myself. I poured a glass of whisky for Maggie. Tired out from her walk and all the excitement, Fluffy fell asleep at once on the sofa. I'd intended to have her sleep in the basket. I felt that that was now going to be impossible. She had staked her claim to the sofa! Cleo, jumped up, sniffed the sleeping puppy, and settled down beside her.

" It was yet another fiasco today. Jim's face when he found that the Templar round room was only a plain storeroom. Thank goodness, it wasn't my fault this time. After my Black Madonna, he'd never have forgiven me." Maggie sipped her whisky, and looked questioningly at me. "I was nearest to you. Our guys, were busy crossing the Lego hazard. I heard the first guy call you a bitch. But what did the second guy say to you? He was asking you something, wasn't he?"

CHAPTER TWENTY-EIGHT

I drank my tea. It was warming and comforting. It gave me time to think. Maggie's words brought back that desperate scuffle in the corridor. The viciousness of the first guy had startled me anew. When he had grabbed hold of me, I felt an overwhelming fear. His eyes glittered through his mask and held a frightening threat. Even now, I shivered at the thought. Letting go of me, he had dashed through the window.

Then, the second guy had stumbled over the nuts towards me. Over and over again, his words ran through my brain. "Evidence to prove who murdered Arabella, if you let me go!"

Did I let him go? Had it been a conscious decision? Or had he just slipped through my hands? His voice sounded sincere, should I have trusted him? My thoughts were interrupted again by Maggie's voice.

"I heard the first guy shout bitch at you. But I couldn't hear what the other guy said, he seemed to whisper. But I did think," her voice tailed off, and she looked at me. "I thought I recognised his voice."

"Yes, I did too."

"Gerald?" Maggie asked.

"I think so," I answered her.

"I know he is Templar obsessed. I always thought he was harmless though. I even like the man. He's not a bad man, just mad about the Templars. That guy who's living with him is a wrong one. Everyone in his village says that Gerald was stupid letting that guy move in with him. The gossip is that he's violent and evil," said Maggie.

"Yes, I think it was Gerald," I repeated.

"What was he asking you?"

Calm clear eyes looked into mine. I was not going to

lie to Maggie. Our friendship was recent. Yet, it felt as if we'd been friends for ever. "He asked me to let him go. His exact words were, I'll give you evidence for Arabella's murderer, in exchange for my freedom."

"Evidence? What evidence? And where did he get that evidence from?" Maggie sat upright in her chair at my words. "How could he have found evidence for Arabella's murder? Why hasn't he brought it to Tenby's attention?"

"I don't know. Remember how fast everything happened, Maggie? Everything was…" I cradled my mug of tea in my hand. Going over and over the events, and his words in my mind, got everything in more of a muddle. "Did I let him go? Maggie, I just can't be certain. Could I have held on tighter to his jacket? But…"

Maggie drained her whisky, and set her glass down with a decided thump. "Whether you let him go on purpose or not, doesn't matter. Getting evidence for a murderer is far more important than catching a guy for breaking and entering. We can only hope he was in earnest. And that he honours his promise to give you the evidence." Yawning, she rose to her feet. "Those two animals look settled. I'll leave you to pass Fluffy over to Tenby. I'm away to my bed, I'm shattered."

I locked the door behind her. Turning away, I walked towards the kitchen. Then I went back and double checked the door to be certain. I tidied the kitchen and put the dishes in the dishwasher. Fluffy's food and bowl I put on one side to give to Tenby. I'd only settled down in front of the television when I got a text. "Urgent case, sorry won't be back till after midnight. Tenby." The two animals were sleeping hard. Fluffy was on her back, her paws in the air. Cleo curled in her usual ball, had snuggled alongside the puppy. I typed in a reply, 'both animals asleep, leave her until morning. Daisy.' The reply was immediate, 'that's great, thanks, Tenby.'

I stood up, and looked at them both. Then I went into the kitchen. Cleo had arrived with a large basket. Curled up, she'd only taken half of it. She'd always sneaked into my bedroom, and my bed, when I was asleep. Tonight, their first night together, perhaps I could start a new regime. The basket was set down beside the log burner. I spread a warm clean fleecy blanket in it. Then I stood over the sleeping animals. Cleo opened one eye, and stared at me. She snuggled closer to Fluffy. The decision had been made. And it had been decided by Cleo! How could I let the puppy have an erratic lifestyle with Tenby? He loved her, and would always try to do his best for her. But his lifestyle was impossible for the security and routine of a dog. Fluffy and Cleo both had difficult early starts in their life. They had only known each other for a matter of hours, but it was obvious they had bonded deeply. I sighed; I now had a puppy! But she was not going to be called Fluffy! I'd stick to the Fl.... Perhaps Flopsy? No, that was worse! Got it! I bent down and picked up the puppy. "Come on Flora, into your new basket." I put Cleo into the basket beside Flora. They sniffed the basket, then the blanket, then each other. Flora, fell fast asleep. Cleo, gave herself a perfunctory wash, then licked Flora's face and fell asleep. "Whew," my breath came out in a rush. I didn't realise I'd been holding it! Before I went to bed, I placed a pile of cushions on the sofa. They had their basket now; I didn't want them back on the sofa!

It was seven in the morning when I put the kettle on for my lifesaving first cup of tea. Both animals had stirred when I walked past them into the kitchen. I smiled down at them. They had obviously spent the first night content together. Now they followed me into the kitchen.

Cleo, began dabbing her paw at the back door. I opened it, and let her out. Flora followed her. I got out their food, and their bowls ready for breakfast.

Strange snuffling noises came from the garden, and then I heard a tiny bark. Only a small, strangled sort of noise, but it was definitely a puppy bark! I dropped the cat kibble packet onto the counter and rushed out of the kitchen door. I heard the packet fall over, and kibble clatter onto the kitchen floor. Again, there came the most insistent series of tiny barks. Something was definitely wrong. Flora was sounding an alarm! Cleo stood with her tail swishing; her back fur raised in alarm. Flora rushed towards me, her tail wagging furiously. She reached up and grabbed a corner of my dressing gown, and pulled me towards the back gate. Both animals were staring at a large box. As I approached it, I glanced down at them. "Well done! What clever girls you are." It was a brown non-descript box. The flaps had been taped shut. There was a bright yellow sticky label stuck on the top of it. The word EVIDENCE had been scrawled across it in huge black lettering.

It took me a few minutes before I could gather myself together. I bent down and picked up Flora. "Come on Cleo, back to the kitchen. Your breakfast kibble is out. All over the floor!" I muttered. My cat had selective hearing. I think most cats do. She'd ignore commands, requests, and pleadings from me. But the magic word kibble caused her to rush back to the cottage. I put both animals in the kitchen.

I walked out closing the door behind me. At the bottom of the garden, I stared at the box. I knew better than to touch it. I looked at my gate. Someone had unlocked it, coming into my garden, and placing the box inside. I didn't like the thought that someone could break into my garden so easily. However, I was delighted to find a box with evidence written on it. What on earth could be inside?

I reached into the pocket of my dressing gown and took out my phone. As I did so, a text came in for me. 'I can walk puppy in ten minutes. T.' I smiled to myself. He was giving the old lady time to make herself presentable before his arrival. Well, I was as presentable as I was going to be this morning! I had washed my face and combed my hair. I texted back, 'Urgent, my back gate now! D.'

It had only been seconds before Tenby arrived. "What the hell is this?" he asked, looking down at the box.

I took a deep breath. I had to explain all about the second Creeper guy, and what he'd said to me. Tenby stared down at the box. He didn't say a word. I explained, and tried to justify myself. Silence. It spread out around me like a cloak. How I wished he'd rant and roar. He usually did when angry. This was so unnerving. "I don't know if I let him go. I don't know whether I should have tried harder to hold him," I almost wailed.

"If this evidence does catch a murderer, it was worthwhile letting him go," said Tenby. He reached forward and gave me an awkward pat on the shoulder. "Everything happened so fast in that damn corridor. He was a big bloke. I doubt that you could have held onto him for long."

One last look at the box, and he opened my back gate. As he went through he called, "leave everything to my guys. I'll get on to them right away". Suddenly Tenby stopped, and turned back towards me. "The puppy…" his face was a picture, police guy warred with puppy dad.

"It's okay, I'll deal with the puppy. Catching Arabella's killer is your priority." I said and watched him walk back to his cottage.

"Tenby!" Turning around, he looked at me. "The puppy barked to alert me to the box!" I was laughing when I entered my kitchen. Tenby had walked off with a proud grin on his face. My smile faltered when I saw not only had all the fallen pieces of kibble been eaten. The kibble packet was on the floor and Flora had her face in it.

"Out of the kitchen!" I shooed them out and retrieved the packet.

"You still don't know what was in the box?" Sheila said later as we sat round the breakfast table in the Priory kitchen. Maggie had dished up an early breakfast for Tenby, who'd been eager to get to work. His men had come and taken the box, after checking round my gate, garden, and the back path. I'd told my story about the second guy's words, yet again. Speculation had been running riot amongst us. Jim was still depressed after yet another false Templar alarm. He'd cast scorn on all our theories. Finally, he pushed his chair back and stomped off to the library. He was going to search again amongst the piles of papers and books.

I was thankful he'd gone. Jim would have noticed my reaction to the letter. All our post was delivered in bulk to the Manor house. Maggie left them out beside our plates each morning, or else piled them on the dresser. My letter was a large white envelope. Inside it, was a short note, an address, and a photocopy of a birth certificate. I'd read and re-read it, before folding it away quickly into its envelope. I stuffed it hurriedly into my handbag. I knew I'd changed colour. My hands were shaking. I was grateful that Sheila had opened her post. No one had noticed my perturbation.

Sheila had received yet another letter, complete with glossy brochure. It was inviting her to visit yet another care home. Sheila got them on an almost daily basis. If it wasn't a care home, it was sheltered housing. "Why me? Why don't you lot get any? I'm certain that you lot are in as much need of a care home as I am!" The papers were torn across, and then into little bits in her fury. My envelope was safely stowed away in my bag. This evening, I'd take time to look at it. This evening, I'd plan my next course of action. On my own, this was my special quest.

The loud bell like noise of the house phone made us all jump. Maggie walked over to it. "Hugo! Where are you? How are you?" We all straightened up in our chairs, and listened to the one-sided conversation. "Yes, Tenby was angry. We made it clear to him that none of us knew about your departure. Yes, we're all free from suspicion. You're in trouble though!" We all chuckled at that. "You had a good flight? They've even got you an apartment and a hired car for your immediate use. That's great, sounds as if you've landed on your feet. We've had some excitement here. You are yawning! You go to bed and..."

"I'll email him the full story," interrupted Sheila. "Then he can read it when he's had a sleep, and has got time."

"You heard that? Sheila will send it to the same email address. That's still okay? Thanks for letting us know you've arrived safely. Enjoy your new life Hugo!"

I put my plate in the dishwasher. "I'll get back and take Flora for a walk. Tenby dropped in her puppy crate for me this morning. She's been in that while I've been out for breakfast. I'll check she's okay."

"Flora?" Sheila and Maggie said that in unison.

"Flora! No way am I shouting Fluffy for her. That's the nearest name I could get. I think it works for her, don't you?"

Sheila nodded, then looked at me. "Daisy, you already

have a cat. Are you sure you want to take on a puppy? Tenby's daughter was originally in Dubai for six months. He told me yesterday, that she's been offered a permanent position out there. Having Flora, may not be temporary. You may end up having her permanently."

"I promised to help out when I can," said Maggie.

"I like Flu.. Flora. I don't know much about animals. Mother didn't like them. She thought they were dirty. I'd like to walk her, and even dog sit for you Daisy," said Martin.

"Thank you so much. Last night they curled up together. I hadn't the heart to separate them. I'll be honest, I was worried about taking her on. If you will all help me though, it will be easier."

Coat, scarf, gloves, were all for me. Harness, lead, and poo bags all for Flora. We set off on our walk. I went across the courtyard and under the archway. I wandered through the overgrown kitchen garden. That was something we all wanted to get sorted. Home-grown produce would be economical, and very nutritious for us all. I was planning to go out of the garden and along the back of the cottages, and then home. Flora was on her extendable lead, which took some getting used to! Flora sniffed, pranced, and jumped around. Puppy training classes were going to be essential for her. They would be far too physical for me. I thought they would be ideal for Martin. The classes would socialise both of them! Martin would have to mix with other adults, Flora would have to mix with other dogs. Yes, the more I thought of it; the better I liked the idea. The garden seemed to slumber in the early morning shafts of sunlight. Neglected, the glasshouses were broken, shattered glass lying around them. The beds overgrown with weeds and shrubs were fighting for survival. It was going to take a lot of work to get it in pristine condition and productive again. Martin, seemed keen to get going with it. I thought of the wonderful kitchen garden at Heligan. Perhaps one day, ours could look nearly as good.

"Come on Flora, time to leave the garden." I walked towards the garden gate, the puppy dancing beside me. I pushed it open, with difficulty, as was lopsided and dragged on the ground. I was so intent on it and the puppy, that I was unaware of the figure beyond the gate.

"I've been waiting for you!" There was no mistaking the voice, the bulky air of menace, and those glittering eyes.

CHAPTER TWENTY-NINE

Flora gave her little puppy bark, looked up at the huge man, and promptly sat on my feet. My heart was pounding in my chest. I clutched her lead tightly, my palms now sweating. Perhaps I could get back through into the kitchen garden. I shuffled backwards.

"Don't move! Don't even think of screaming!" the harsh voice grated in my ears. He thrust an arm across to the wall behind me. My escape route was barred. My other arm was gripped tightly. I wondered if a fingerprint could be taken off a bruise. I was shaking now. I tried not to show my fear.

"That's it. Just stand there quietly. I only want to talk to you."

"That makes a change!" My retort escaped my lips before my brain could protest. I shouldn't antagonise this man, I thought belatedly.

To my astonishment he laughed. I'd expected anger, rage, even a blow. But through the ski mask those hateful eyes crinkled up in amusement. He wore the usual dark clothes and that frightening ski mask. Some people exude jollity or serenity. This man had the overpowering aura and stench of evil. I'd read about it in books. I never believed it, thinking it too fanciful. It came off him in sickening waves. This man would stop at nothing, and do anything to get his own way. The hand remained resting on the wall. Obviously, it was to block my path, just in case I made a run for it. He needn't have bothered. My legs had turned to jelly. Even I, knew better than to make a bolt for it with a tiny puppy.

"I put the box out for your tame policeman this morning. We knew that you recognised Gerald in that scuffle. You said nothing, and let him go. So, Gerald has honoured his part of the bargain."

At my start of surprise, he laughed, relishing my discomfort. "Gerald is a fool. His obsession with family links to the Knights Templars is ruining his life. I thought we'd find real treasure. That would have been worth all this aggro. But no, Gerald now admits it's doubtful if there's any treasure anywhere! No treasure after all this trouble!"

"Why are you telling me…"

"Shut up and listen. We knew you'd not told on Gerald. Tenby would have been banging on our doors yesterday if you had. I want you to promise me you'll never tell anyone that it was Gerald involved in all this nonsense."

He grabbed my throat. "Promise me, you'll never tell the cops. I want it to remain our secret." He began to squeeze my throat. My head began to spin, and I began to gasp for air.

"I won't tell anyone," I wheezed out the words.

"Promise me!" he insisted.

"I promise," I said.

He let go immediately. "I reckon your promise is good. Sort of thing you'd keep."

By now my back was hard against the brick wall. I needed it for support. I was seriously worried that I would faint. I stared at him, wondering what he was going to do next.

"Tonight I'll be gone. Tomorrow I'll be sitting in the sun, a drink in my hand. In another country, with another name on my passport. That's the life for me. That crackpot Gerald can fester on this dismal moor. No treasure here, so I'm off." The hand was taken from my throat. He traced a finger down my cheek and under my chin. He lifted my face up with that finger. Then he looked straight at me and began to laugh. Not the usual harsh sarcastic laugh. This was a low purring laugh that sent shivers down my spine. "Daisy. Yes, I know your name. Daisy, you are a real bitch. In the whole of my life, you are the only person that ever got the better of me. If only you were twenty years younger. You'd be coming with me and what a team we'd make! I'll raise a glass to you when I relax in the sunshine. Goodbye bitch!"

He was gone.

Flora had wound herself round and round my legs. Her eyes were wide and she stared up at me. She sensed the atmosphere, and realised that I had been frightened. I bent down, untangled and lifted her up. I was shaking uncontrollably now. Her warm puppy body was comforting, and I buried my face in her soft fur. I couldn't stop shaking. Yet those last words of his made me laugh. I placed the puppy back on the path, and sent a text.

Shaking and laughing hysterically. I walked back to my cottage. Jim was already at the cottage door. One look at my face, the key held in jittery fingers, and he took the key and opened the door. My coat, scarf and hat were flung on to a chair and I was pushed onto the sofa. The kettle was soon boiling, and he returned with a strong cup of tea. I poured out the story of my latest encounter with the Creeper. I still shaking, and couldn't stop my hiccupping laughter. Jim sat down beside me on the sofa and put his arm round my shoulder.

"Drink your tea Daisy. Are you sure I can't give you some brandy?"

I shook my head. The mug of tea in my hands was comforting. Cleo and Flora scrambled up on the other side of me. Their concerned faces as they nuzzled my arm made me smile. It was a watery smile.

"Do you think he means it? That he really is going

abroad?" asked Jim.

"Yes, he knows he's the one who did everything illegal and violent. Gerald wasn't even at Temple Church. This guy acted alone most of the time, without Gerald's knowledge."

"You're right. Before he came, Gerald was just spying on me. He was anxious to find out what knowledge I had. Gerald was only looking for his family links, and ancient stones and legends. This guy was out to find treasure."

I'd drunk my tea. The shaking had stopped and the fear was leaving me. Jim was silent as he stared into space. He'd left his arm across my shoulder. I didn't know what to make of that gesture. It was comforting and frightening at the same time. Surely, I told myself, it's the gesture you'd make to anyone in distress. That was it. Only a comforting kindly gesture. Don't read anything into it Daisy, I told myself.

" My research means I want to establish links with the Priory, and this area to the Knights Templars. No thought of treasure entered my mind. Was there ever any treasure? If there was, I reckon it's hidden somewhere in France, the Languedoc area. There is no evidence it ever came to Cornwall. Some said it went to Scotland." Where was this conversation leading to? Why was Jim thinking so hard about the Templars now? Jim continued, still staring into space. I realised that I was a sounding board for the thoughts and plans he was formulating. "My research is purely academic. Gerald's is almost a family history quest. Primary sources and early books and maps are what I use. Gerald specialises in legends and myths. Mind you, legends have a grain of truth, think of Schliemann and Troy. We are both researching the same period but coming at it from different angles. It makes sense, doesn't it Daisy? Especially with that vicious bastard out of the picture. It solves the problem.

Everything about the evil Creeper has been solved!"

"What are you asking me? I haven't a clue of what you mean. To be honest, Jim. I'm fast losing patience with the bloody Templars! I'm tired of burglars and creepers. My most immediate problem is this puppy! I have to think about the practicalities of taking on another animal."

Jim ignored what I said, his mind totally focused. "Daisy, the bad guy has gone." I nodded. He was being patronising, but I was tired and let it go. "If Gerald and I join forces, we could combine our research. Then we could explore our separate avenues and help each other at the same time."

"Oh, I see what you mean," I broke in, before he could expand again in depth. "I've got it. No need for Gerald to spy. And no need for him to be a Creeper. Both of you can become best mates now. Is that it? That's bloody ridiculous! After all we suffered through that man."

Jim smiled at me. "I don't think Gerald is such a bad bloke. Surely you can understand and forgive him."

Jim's face was close to mine now. He reached up with a finger and pushed back a lock of my streaky purple hair. "Daisy," he leant towards me. He had an unusually intent look on his face.

CHAPTER THIRTY

"Daisy, Daisy!" The banging on the front door made us both jump. Flora set up a twittering bark. Jim and I sprang apart. Flushing slightly, he went to open the door.

"Let me in! I need to tell you! Let me in," Sheila's voice grew louder as did the banging. Sheila barrelled in, stick flailing around wildly. "Martin has been online to some computer guys."

"Sit down, you'll need oxygen if you don't calm down," I said.

She sat down on the sofa beside me. The wheezing gasps for air lessened. Sheila opened her mouth to speak.

"Wait Sheila. Let your breathing return to normal. You shouldn't get so wound up at your age," said Jim.

Sheila glared at him. "My age! You're catching me up fast. So less of that patronising tone with me!"

My hand flew up to cover my mouth. I loved Sheila's sharp retorts. It was so good to see the normally unflappable Jim reduced to flustered mush by her.

"Okay Sheila, out with it now," I said, anxious to call a halt to the escalating quarrel.

"It's Martin, he was on the computer," she began.

"You told us that already, get on with it," said Jim.

"I will get on with it if you stop your stupid interruptions. Let me speak," she snapped back at him.

My doorbell rang. I opened it to find Maggie there.

"Well? What do you think about it? It sounds promising doesn't it Jim?"

"I wouldn't know what is promising or not. Sheila is unable to tell us," was his sarcastic retort.

"All your fault, you kept interrupting," said Sheila.

Shaking her head at them both, Maggie said, "Martin has found a chap over Altarnun way. He researches chapels and churches of Bodmin Moor. He's got journals from clergymen from way back. One has information on the Priory and the Knights Templars links with it. They even mention the Round room and its Templar signs."

"Thanks Maggie," Jim rushed past Maggie to reach Martin and his computer. Sheila followed him.

"Tenby texted me earlier. His daughter Debbie wants to chat with us on Skype about the puppy. That's if you want to take the puppy on?" said Maggie. We both turned and looked down at the basket beside the log burner. Cleo was curled up in a tight ball, one eye open. She was watching us. Cleo knew we were talking about her friend. "Look at Flora," Maggie laughed. Flat on her back, all four paws in the air, fast asleep, Flora had the biggest share of the basket. Cleo snuggled into her.

"Do I have any option?"

"None whatsoever," Maggie said. "We all love both animals. We'll all help out with them."

"What's happened to you? You look a mess and you are shaking!"

Again, I sat on the sofa. Again, I had my cup of tea. This time it was Maggie's arm around me. "I didn't tell Jim everything. It was just so strange and almost embarrassing." My voice tailed off. Then I told Maggie all that the guy had said to me.

"He said what? Daisy, he propositioned you! The most villainous man we know, wanted you to go with him and be a villain!"

"Not me! Not at this age! It's the first time I've ever been grateful for my advancing years!" I said.

"This is too good a story to keep to yourself. Daisy, you must tell the others, especially Sheila. She will love it."

"Well maybe," I replied, draining my mug of tea. I wasn't sure about it.

"And Tenby! He must hear it all, even the embarrassing bits."

Tenby's daughter was going to Skype us after four thirty. Tenby rushed in at four thirty prompt, ready for our conversation. We were going to use Maggie's iPad. It could be moved around and show Cleo and Flora together. I had taken a long time to tidy everything in my lounge. It took me even longer to shower and scrub myself. The evil aura of my attacker seemed to cling to me. I got out my cat grooming kit. Cleo wasn't impressed by this, but tolerated a quick brush. Flora, absolutely loved it. She attacked the brush, and ran around the room with it. She thought this was the best game ever. I wiped her eyes with a damp cotton pad. That caused problems! She wanted to eat it.

Maggie entered to see Flora running around with the brush in her mouth. "Can you watch them Maggie? I've got to dress now. I did the brushing in my dressing gown."

As I walked past Maggie to my room, I tried not to stare. Maggie looked stunning! She was dressed in her usual uniform of jeans and sweatshirt. These were new, and of a stylish cut. Her familiar ponytail was no longer held by a rubber band. She had brushed it so that it hung loose, and was held back by a matching scarf. She'd even put on makeup, it was low-key and well applied. But it was there! She looked self-conscious. I tried not to stare at her as I went to my bedroom. I said nothing, but grinned to myself as I changed into clean clothes.

Debbie was bright and bubbly and luckily for her, looked nothing like her father. I was aware of her intense scrutiny of Maggie. What exactly had Tenby told his daughter about Maggie? I was certain it was completely unconscious on his part. Debbie was shrewd, there would be little she'd miss in their email and telephone conversations. The iPad was carried around the room. The basket with the twosome asleep, elicited oohs and aahs from Debbie. The garden, with its stunning views was visible despite the deepening twilight. A general view of my cottage, and plans for Flora's routines were outlined.

"I'm so grateful to you all. At the time I knew I shouldn't have taken her on, but I felt so sorry for her. She was being loved and neglected at the same time. Then came my promotion. Dad doesn't have time for her, but that would have been better than leaving her where she was. I love the name Flora! That was clever getting that from Fluffy."

"We'll leave you and your Dad to chat alone," I said.

Maggie and I left them, and went to the Priory kitchen. We found Jim staring at a large card. "We are all mentioned by name in this invitation to Italian night at the Red Lion. It's huge, and full of Italian phrases and flags and things." Jim's voice tailed away as he looked down at the card with distaste.

"Why are all our names written down? To make sure we don't cop out of it. It's all a bit over-the-top isn't it? After all, it's only a pub meal with an Italian theme. Inspector, you are mentioned as well on the invite," said Sheila, turning to Tenby as he entered the kitchen.

Tenby looked down at the card in Jim's hand, and just nodded. "Daisy and Maggie, I have to tell you that Debbie is so grateful to you both. She loved that puppy, and really only wanted the best for it. To see how happy she is with Cleo, and with you all, has put her mind at rest."

Maggie and I nodded and smiled our thanks. We were actually quite embarrassed.

"And now Inspector. It's time Daisy told you of her latest escape with the Creeper," Jim said as he leant back against his chair, and sneered at me. Yes! I'm certain that was a supercilious sneer.

"Before I tell you, have you any news on that evidence box? What was in it?" I asked.

There was a sudden quiet attention from everyone in the room. Even Jim sat upright in his chair and stared at Tenby.

"Nothing yet. Still doing tests, fingerprints etc. It certainly looks promising. That's all I can tell you at the moment. It's promising."

Then that laser like policeman stare focused on me. "What's all this Creeper stuff about?"

I told him. I told him all that I thought he needed to know. Looks passed between my friends as I became quiet. Tenby didn't need to know what the Creeper's last words had been to me. Did he?

"Interesting. It does seem that Gerald was in the clear. All the vicious attacks were certainly done by one person. A large burly person, who was physically fit. Not the image of Gerald at all!" Tenby said.

"Aren't you going to finish your story Daisy?" Jim said that sneer making another appearance.

There were gasps from both Maggie and Sheila. They glared at Jim. What had got into the man?

I looked down at my hands, clenched them tightly together. I swore vengeance! So, he thought it amusing, did he? When I had told my story, so did Tenby. His loud chuckles and Jim's laughter infuriated me. I stood up and walked out of the kitchen in my most dignified manner. Their chuckles followed me down the corridor and even across the courtyard.

CHAPTER THIRTY-ONE

"Well? How do I look?" I twirled around for the benefit of my audience. They sat on the sofa side-by-side. My cushion deterrent hadn't lasted for long. The cushions were nudged, pulled, and dragged onto the floor. Then they made themselves at home on the sofa. They both stared at me, then one licked her paw and the other went to sleep. "Some help you two are!" I said.

Black trousers, a sequinned top in lime green and black, was finished off with a new sparkling scarf to match. The dangling green earrings added a final touch, as did the green streaks to my hair!

"Ready Daisy?" Maggie's voice came from my front door. A final once over from my lint brush (dog and cat hair!) and I was all set for Italian night.

"No Tenby?" I asked as I climbed into the SUV, to join the others.

"He phoned the house to say he was still tied up at the station. He'll try to join us later," answered Maggie.

"It's a fixed menu. The card says we have two choices per course," said Sheila, waving the Italian Night card.

"I fancy the minestrone soup for first course. That will be all right for you Daisy, won't it?" asked Martin.

"Yes, I'll have the soup, pasta and of course, the gelato."

"The Tuscan pork roast sounds great," said Jim.

"I looked the recipe up on the Internet. The pork is soaked in brine with rosemary and sage for about eight hours. A paste is made of rosemary, sage, garlic and placed inside the pork, and the rest spread over the outside. Then it's roasted," said Martin.

"It's the roast pork for all of us except for Daisy. The mushroom and lentil pappardelle Bolognese should be delicious and very different," said Maggie.

"Sounds good to me, better than the usual cheese omelette," I said. "I'm not keen on lentils, though."

"I looked it up on the Internet, it's like a Jamie Oliver recipe. I don't think it's authentic Italian at all," grumbled Sheila.

The Red Lion was decked out in Italian style. Flags, check napkins and tablecloths, with candles in Chianti bottles gave us the Italian theme.

"It smells fantastic in here," Jim said to Daniel as he welcomed us. His pride was obvious as he ushered us to a table. We were all being polite.

"You've got a good crowd in here tonight," Sheila said to him.

"Invitations and bookings only. The pub is closed tonight for casuals." Sarah's voice came from behind me. Her slim figure and dark-hair looked stunning in a traditional Italian costume. The tightly fitting waistcoat showed off her tiny waist. Sarah knew she looked good. She dazzled all the men, and flirted with them. Daniel was not amused. Her antics obviously annoyed him. Deeply engrossed in explaining the intricacies of his Tuscan pork roast to Maggie, his eyes still strayed to Sarah.

We had finished our starters. "That minestrone soup was superb," murmured Martin.

We all agreed. Every one of us had gone for the soup. The wine glasses were filled again and again. I was offered more mineral water. Cold iced mineral water on a cold winter's day is no pleasure. I spent every outing with my glass of water. All I craved, every time, was a hot cup of tea!

My pasta dish was placed in front of me. It looked a

bit brown to me. Dark lentils with mushrooms gave it a muddy look. I was served first before the great production. Dishes of roasted vegetables, Italian style, and large bowls of green salads were placed on each table. The Tuscan pork roast was brought out, and placed at a top table with a great flourish. Daniel beamed at us all in delight when we broke out into spontaneous applause.

He picked up an ornate carving fork and felt around for the knife. A horrified look crossed his face, "I've forgotten the carving knife, Sarah."

Sarah rushed back into the kitchen, reappearing a moment later waving a large knife. She was halfway across the room when the front door of the pub opened. A bitterly cold blast of air swept in. Candle lights dipped and spluttered, giving off smoky plumes. The Italian flags fluttered madly in the sudden draught.

Tenby stood there. He was definitely not dressed for casual dining. Tenby was wearing his usual work suit when he entered the pub. For a moment, he just stood in the doorway looking around. He was not alone, two police officers followed behind him. One was a woman, her face set in hard lines. This was going to be no social occasion. Out of the corner of my eye I saw Sarah stiffen. She was beside our table, beside me. As I watched, her hand tightened on the knife. Conversation ceased in the entire room. All eyes were turned to the inspector in the silence. He walked into the room, first nodding at the policeman, and then the policewoman. The policeman walked across the room behind us, and stood at the kitchen entrance with his arms folded. He planted his feet firmly, and an alert expression crept over his features. He is ready for trouble, I thought.

Jim was sitting at the table opposite me. He'd realised he'd gone too far earlier with his sneering remarks. He knew I was really miffed at him. Being a sensible guy, he had kept clear of me, first in the SUV and then in the Red Lion. My miffiness was now forgotten. His avoidance of me was likewise forgotten. Our eyes met across the table. I saw his hand reach for his pocket. I spread my hands flat on the table. There were plenty of weapons on that bright red check tablecloth. He nodded at me, and I smiled back. We were ready for action!

That took seconds. In that short time, Tenby had reached the centre of the room. In the silence that had fallen, he cleared his throat. "I'm sorry to interrupt this festive occasion."

"No, he's not," muttered Sheila, "any excuse to get out of it. He's not a sociable guy our Tenby."

"Shush," whispered Jim, glaring at her.

Sheila subsided in a heap beside me. But her lips kept moving. I'd have loved to hear what she was muttering. I guessed Jim would now be included in that silent monologue!

"Recently, vital evidence came into our possession. This evidence has brought us here tonight. It concerns the murder of Arabella..." said Tenby.

He never finished with Arabella's surname.

"I'm not going with you!" Sarah flung herself forward. She grabbed my sparkling lime green scarf, yanking me back into my chair.

"Let me go to my car, or she gets it!" Her voice rang out into the horrified hush that had gripped everyone. She pulled the scarf tighter, and held the carving knife at my throat. That knife was large and very, very, sharp, just the way a chef likes it. Funny, how you notice things in moments of crisis. My scarf was new. It was unusual, with a sparkling silver yarn woven through lime green and black. Perfectly matched to my top, expensive and fragile, it was being horribly mistreated. And I don't like knives at my throat. Now, I was seriously angry. I'd never liked Sarah. In that moment I knew I really, really disliked her.

"Sarah? What are you doing? Put down that knife," Daniel's voice was hoarse as he shouted across the room. Complete bewilderment was on his face.

"Let's be sensible Sarah, we only want to discuss…" Tenby's calm flat voice of reason only incensed the woman further. Tenby's hostage tactics were not going to work with this lady!

"You want to jail me for Arabella's murder. You should be giving me a medal! I told you time and time again, that she was the murderer. Would you believe me? No! So, I did my own detective work. I found out she'd been a hairdresser and lived with my brother. Then he disappeared. She changed her name, but I found her." Sarah's voice grew high-pitched. She was screaming, as she quivered with rage. Sarah tightened her grip on my scarf, and waved the knife again in my face. "Arabella or whatever her real name was, had begun her old tricks again, this time with Hugo! She would have killed him with the same dagger that killed my brother. You idiots couldn't find her. But I did! And killed her with that dagger, and enjoyed doing it! How many men do you think she killed before my brother? How many?" Sarah shouted this last question, her voice now hysterical. I could feel her shaking beside me. The knife was wavering at the side of my face.

Jim's face was a mask of horror. He was helpless. I could see that.

Tenby was like a statue. The situation was out of his control. It was unexpected, no one had anticipated Sarah's reaction. Now, it was Sarah in command of the situation. The policeman at the kitchen door behind me, made as if to come forward.

Sarah whirled round towards him, the knife pressing into my throat as she did so. "Don't try it. I've killed once. I don't mind killing again. Especially not Daisy, I've never liked the nosy, interfering old bag. She's got it coming to her."

That did it! Nosy and interfering were fine. I freely admitted that was certainly me. But no one, no one ever calls me an old bag and gets away with it!

CHAPTER THIRTY-TWO

My gaze travelled round the room. It was stalemate. That knife was getting closer to my throat, and was sharp! Tenby, Jim, and the police officers stood uncertain, and seemed unable to move. All eyes were on the wild woman at my side. I'd had enough. This might be my last foolish mistake. But I was going to take the chance, I was going to break this impasse. I placed one hand firmly on the table. The other I slid towards my rapidly cooling vegetarian pasta dish. I took in a deep breath. In one sudden movement I acted. I flung myself to the side, away from the knife. I pulled hard against the tightly held scarf. With my other hand, I lifted up the pasta plate flinging it towards her face. Her grip loosened immediately upon the scarf. She flung her hand up to ward off the flying plate of spaghetti. I fell sideways onto Martin's lap gasping for breath.

Who knew Tenby could move like that? He launched himself across the room, and grabbed the knife. The policeman behind us rushed towards her, hauling her hands behind her back. The woman police officer handcuffed her in seconds. Torrents of abuse poured from her lips. Sarah kept shaking her head, as spaghetti ran down her face. Strands caught on her ears, and her shoulders were covered with creamy mushrooms. I don't like lentils. I was delighted to see her decorated in them.

"Take her away," said Tenby. He sank on the spare chair beside me. I was upright now, and checking my scarf for damage. That sudden jerking movement I had made would cause me grief tomorrow. But the pain I'd feel, I'd be grateful for. Much better than a stab wound! That would have been much worse and wouldn't have been helped by a heat pad.

"Daisy," said Tenby, and looked at me, "Daisy, I'm sorry I laughed at you earlier." He looked down at his hands for a moment, then stared back up at me. "I'm pleased to have you on the side of law and order. That Creeper guy was right!"

It was a quiet group that climbed back into the SUV. Martin turned to look at us. He was driving. He had developed a love for the huge SUV, and drove it whenever possible. "I'm absolutely starving. Shall we get fish and chips on the way home."

Sheila grinned at me as I took my place beside her. "Pasta is not a good look on you!"

I'd wiped some of it off earlier. Some of the pasta sauce still clung to my hair, and had now congealed into hard peaks.

Sheila continued speaking. "We'll go to your cottage, Daisy, after we stop for fish and chips. Then we can see to the animals whilst you wash and change."

The SUV stank of the all-pervading chip shop aroma, as we drove into the courtyard. Not one of us complained!

"Never! Never again. That Red Lion pub has seen the last of me. Even if we don't get into a row, or attacked, we never get a decent meal," said Martin.

As we entered my cottage Jim made straight for the whisky bottle. He poured out a glass for everyone. Then, looking at me, he grinned, and filled the kettle with water. I showered. Each drama that had occurred lately, required a complete change and shower from me. I held my new glittery scarf in my hand. It was a disaster. It had become a piece of string, edged with pasta sauce, with tiny bits of pasta caught in the glittering thread. I'd worn it tonight for the first time. The label said hand wash only. Another long look at it, and my decision was made.

No, I couldn't bear to wear it again. I couldn't even bear to look at it. It went in the waste bin.

That evening was spent going over and over the events leading up to tonight's arrest in the Red Lion pub. Maggie's phone rang. "It's Demelza." Maggie listened for a while, and then said, "thank you, that's interesting. Thanks for telling us." Maggie put down the phone and looked at us. "Demelza's cousin lives opposite the Red Lion pub. Yes, another one of her many cousins! Her husband met Daniel coming out with a couple of suitcases, and all his chef's knives and equipment. Daniel said he'd spoken to Tenby. He's given Tenby the address of his brother in London, and was leaving for good."

"Don't blame him! He had a rotten time at the Red Lion. A fresh start is exactly what he needs," Sheila said.

"Poor Daniel," sighed Maggie. "He was shattered by Sarah's outburst. But I'm beginning to wonder if he knew something wasn't quite right with her. Their wedding date was constantly being postponed by him. There was a weird catty side to her. I wonder if it had been caused by her brother's disappearance, or whether she'd always been like that. I'm sure Daniel must have seen it. Maybe that's why he was in no hurry to get married to her."

We were all exhausted. We talked over fish and chips. But it didn't take long for us to call it a night.

"But the dishes, we can't leave those for Daisy," said Maggie, as she rose to her feet.

"You go home Maggie, you've an early start tomorrow. Martin and Sheila can go with you. I'll clear up here with Daisy," said Jim.

"I can stay and help," said Martin.

Jim took his head, "no, you take Sheila home."

For once Sheila didn't complain. The excitement had exhausted her, and she leant on Martin's proffered arm with gratitude.

The dishes were stacked in the dishwasher, and Flora taken out for one last time.

"A nightcap?" I gestured to the whisky bottle, as Jim locked my back door. He nodded gratefully and reached for the glass I held out to him. After the kettle boiled, I concentrated on making another mug of tea. I was shattered, but still unable to relax.

"It's the adrenaline Daisy," Jim's voice came from behind me.

"What?"

"In a crisis the adrenaline surges through the body. Afterwards it leaves you drained, shaking, and somehow restless."

"You would know," I snapped.

"Yes, I would," he agreed. At my look of astonishment at this admission, he sighed, and walked towards the log burner. He threw another log on, and then sat on the sofa. "Yes, I would," he repeated." And that's all I'm telling you." His face had a pleading look, as if my acceptance of him as he was, meant so much to him. "It's a secret, and it has to stay that way."

"Okay," I said and drank my tea. I'd known, or guessed that he'd been something when younger. Something secret, something military or suchlike. I'd also thought it very unlikely that he would be able to talk about it.

"That's it, just okay?" He looked at me as if trying to read my face.

"Yes, that's it, okay."

He raised his glass to me, and I clinked my mug with it.

Jim's phone rang, "it's Tenby." He listened for a while and then closed his phone. "He phoned to bring us up-to-date. Sarah has been talking non-stop. Arabella always wore a pendant. David must have given it to Arabella.

227

Sarah said it was her grandmother's, and she took it back. The chest that was stolen from the Red Lion had a wallet with cash, travellers' cheques, and a plane ticket for France, all in Arabella's name. It was all pretty conclusive and damning."

"So that's Arabella's murderer in jail," I said.

"And the Creeper on the run," Jim said. He paused for a moment, "Daisy, would you object if I worked with Gerald on research? Tenby says he was ignorant of most that went on with the Creeper. When he found the Creeper had burgled the Red Lion, and what was in the chest, he insisted it should be given to the police. He can't be recognised as the burglar in the Round room, so Tenby is letting him go."

I stared at the log burner, as a log shifted throwing out a sudden shower of sparks. "No, I don't mind. He was just a foolish lonely guy, who got obsessed with his research. He was manipulated by the Creeper."

"Thanks Daisy, I'll contact him and we can pool our research, it will give us both different views to explore." The enthusiasm in his voice was unmistakable. Here was another lonely guy obsessed with his research!

I yawned, and yawned again.

Jim rose to his feet. "Good night Daisy lock-up after me." He bent over, ran a finger down my cheek, and kissed my forehead. He was gone.

I locked the door after him. Then I sank down on the sofa beside the animals. It was over. Arabella's murderer had been found. The Creeper had vanished to foreign parts unknown. Hugo had gone to America. We were now all living here, with Martin, our new landlord. I reached for my phone on the coffee table. Sometimes Jake's emails came in late at night. No, there was only one from Elsie. "Daisy, you'd have loved tonight! I went to a bingo session, followed by old-time music hall